Astoria : 1853

JANICE RICE

For Kaity, Lauren, David and Jonathan.

I am so proud to be your mom.

CHAPTER ONE

*"I have forsaken my house. I have left my heritage.
I have given the dearly beloved of my soul into the hand of her
enemies."*
Jeremiah 12:7

Liminka, Finland - October 1849
"Emilia! Stop!" Johan cried as he ran after her. "Wait
for me."

Emilia raced across the wetland near the Liminganlahti
Bay. Grebes and cormorants took off in every direction as she
sprinted past their nests. Her chestnut curls bounced under
the red handkerchief tied around them. She glanced over her
shoulder at Johan and giggled uncontrollably. She tripped and
fell headlong into the mud, spraying it in all directions.

"Emilia!" Johan gasped and caught up to her. His
fiancé was covered from head to foot in soupy muck. "You are
going to have to learn to listen to me, woman."

She pushed herself up slowly from the mire and started
laughing. "You would never have caught up with me if I
didn't give you a chance," she choked out.

"You did this on purpose? I don't think so!" Johan's
hands were on his hips in protest. His thick, wool flannel
came untucked from his dungarees and mud covered his
leather boots. He raked his fingers through his blond hair and
scruff of a beard.

"Yes, of course, I did this on purpose! This was a...a
test," said Emilia, rolling over onto her back side. Her wool
jacket and skirt hung heavy with the muck. She sighed and
placed her filthy hands in her lap.

"A test?" Johan circled the mud hole with folded arms.
"What kind of test?"

"A test to see how much you love me," Emilia said,
narrowing her eyes.

"You know I love you, Emilia," Johan said, softening. "You don't need to test me."

"Oh yes, I do," Emilia giggled. "Ouch!" She inspected her hands and pulled a thorn from her palm. Then she looked up at him, wiping her hands on her skirt. "I need to know *for sure* that you will love me no matter what state I'm in. 'For richer, for poorer'…for cleaner, for muddier…"

She grinned and Johan had to give in. Her smile was too tempting.

He fell to his knees in the mud in front of her and took her hands in his. "Emilia Kepola, I will love you, for cleaner or for muddier, until the day I die…" He leaned over and kissed her lips softly then leaned back on his heels.

Her eyes were dreamy and sparkled as she looked back at him. She put her hand behind his neck and pulled him close for another kiss.

She leaned back and giggled. "You passed," she whispered, grinning.

Voices broke their revelry. Foreign voices that sounded sharp and harsh. Soldiers in khaki uniforms paced near the edge of the bay. Rifles slung over their shoulders with bayonets attached, pointing toward the sky.

Emilia shrieked.

Johan clasped his hand across her mouth. Her eyes, wide with fear, fixed on the Russians across the wetland. He moved his hand slowly off of her mouth.

"Russkies!" Emilia whispered.

The Russians invaded the Karelian Isthmus. The rumor was that they wanted the warm water port Liminganlahti Bay offered. Now they were in Liminka.

"Emilia, look at me," Johan whispered, straining to remain calm.

She was shaking.

"Look at me," Johan waited to speak until she looked into his steel blue eyes. "They can't see us. We must crawl out of here. You first – that way." He motioned with his eyes and slight nod of his head. "Stay low. No sound. I'm right behind you. Now let's go."

Emilia slid onto her stomach again and snatched the bright handkerchief from her head. Her hair tumbled down around her face and she glanced back to Johan. He nodded for her to proceed. She started crawling, flat to the ground, dragging her skirts through the slick mud. Every few seconds, she glanced over to the Russians.

Johan whistled like a grebe and she looked back at him. He shook his head and pointed to the trees. There were tears in Emilia's eyes and she gulped back a sob but continued crawling.

Johan's back ached and the pain in his legs was excruciating. They had to cover the distance to the forest. Navigating their way through the bulrushes and tall sea grass soaked them to the skin. The cool breeze of fall blew over them, chilling the sweat on their necks.

Raucous voices rose. A shot fired into the air.

Emilia shrieked and jumped to her feet.

Johan lunged forward, catching her ankle and pulling her down into the mud again. He quickly huddled up next to her. "No," he whispered into her ear. "We can't run. They must not see us. They'll--"

"They'll kill us, won't they?" Emilia sobbed, stifling her tears with her handkerchief.

"Almost there," Johan whispered, pointing. "Just a little further."

"I can't, Johan," she gasped, touching her throat. She was having one of her breathing episodes.

"Breathe, Emilia," Johan ordered. "I'll be right beside you."

The voices were getting closer. Another shot fired into the air and drunken laughter erupted. Johan picked out the words "camp" and "shoot" but couldn't understand anything else. His right arm linked around Emilia's waist, half-pulling her forward. She peeked through the tall grass at the advancing soldiers; her breaths came short and fast.

"Breathe, Emilia."

Johan had seen her pass out before when her breathing became strained like this. Sometimes her lips would turn blue before she could be calmed down enough to take in air correctly. He had to get her to safety.

"Just breathe, love."

As he spoke these words, her full weight collapsed on his arm. She passed out. Now there was no other choice but to pull her onto his back and make a run for it. They couldn't stay in the grass to hide. When and if she awakened, she would vomit or cry out. They would be caught for sure.

"Oh Lord, help me," Johan fought panic as he pulled her arms over his shoulders. He stayed low and sprinted toward the forest. It didn't take long to draw the Russians' attention.

"Ostanovít!"

A shot fired into the air.

"Ostanovít!"

He kept running. Almost there. Every instinct in him wanted to cradle Emilia in his arms and protect her with his body from any gunfire. He couldn't stop now.

A shot fired into the grass near his right foot.

His boots sank in the mud and slowed him.

"Lord, help me!" he cried, between clenched teeth. His heart pounded with fear.

Another shot fired.

Pain! Horrible pain in his thigh!

He fell forward and Emilia's limp body landed on him.

"Augh!" he cried. Blood soaked the hole in his pants and his muscles cramped and burned around the wound. "Oh Lord, help us!" He grabbed Emilia around the waist with one arm. With the other arm, he dragged himself forward, grasping at tufts of sea grass. His attempts were futile.

The enemy cut off his escape to the forest. They stalked toward him with their black, leather boots sinking into the mud. They made a wall of khaki, blocking his retreat to the trees. Bayonets pointed at him from every direction.

Johan rolled onto his back, gritting his teeth from the pain in his leg. He clasped Emilia in his arms. Glancing down at her, he panicked. Her lips were blue and her face was blotchy and white. He put his ear to her mouth to listen for shallow breathing.

The soldiers laughed and poked each other. One soldier made kissing sounds to his comrade.

Johan couldn't hear even shallow breaths. He put his mouth to hers and blew some air into her lungs. The mocking from the Russians surrounded him but he didn't stop. She would die without air.

"Emilia!" he shouted, patting her face. "Emilia, breathe!"

One soldier stepped forward and kneeled on the ground next to them. He tried to pull Emilia out of Johan's arms.

"No!" Johan cried, shoving his hand away. "She's not breathing! Don't touch her!"

The soldier sat back on his heels and laughed. His comrades joined in again, pointing and jesting. Another soldier yanked Johan away from her. The first soldier reached down and dragged Emilia's limp body outside the circle of bayonets.

"You will kill her! No!" Johan screamed at them, fighting to get free.

A soldier took his heel and kicked into Johan's wounded leg.

He screamed in pain. Bursts of red and yellow splattered across Johan's vision. Little black spots blurred his eyes. He gasped from the torture.

Another soldier kicked him in the head.

All he tasted was blood. Still he had to see Emilia. He had to save her. He lunged forward to attempt to stand. "Emilia," he cried, spitting blood out as he spoke. He reached for her though everything was blurry.

A soldier stood in front of him with his rifle butt raised and hit him in the temple.

Everything went black.

The soft chirps of the swifts in the forest and constant tapping of a cuckoo woke Johan. *Where was he?* He shuddered with cold. He pressed his hand into the bed. *This wasn't a bed.* His hand sunk into something moist and thick.

Pain. Oh, the incredible pain throbbing in his leg. *What happened?* Soft rain was falling on his face. The lapping of the waves close by reminded him. He was at the bay. *Why was he here?*

Emilia! He was here with Emilia. The picnic. They were having a picnic for her birthday. Her eighteenth *vuotta.*

Johan opened his eyes and tried to focus them. Darkness hung in the sky and everything was blotchy and out of focus. He couldn't see. He reached up and touched his eye. He felt something squishy and wet. Johan held his fingers in front of his eyes. Blood. He wiped his mouth. More blood. He forced his head to look downward even with the pounding headache. His pants were saturated with blood. He felt dizzy. Black spots started clouding his vision again.

"No!" Johan cried. "Must get up. Can't stay here." Heat radiated from his leg. Uncontrollable shaking took over him. "Emilia! Where are you?"

He struggled to his feet and dragged his wounded right leg behind him. In the dusk, it was hard to see more than the shapes of the trees nearby.

"Emilia," he cried again. "Where are you?" Then he listened.

Silence.

Footprints littered the pathway before him. Large footprints. Then he remembered.

"*Russkies*! Emilia!" He was desperate now. They had taken her. She wasn't breathing. Horror filled him. A sob rose from his gut and he released it in a cry of pain and anguish. Hatred and horror invaded his thoughts. *She's gone forever. They took her. She is lost to you.*

"Oh Lord," he prayed, dragging himself closer to the woods. "Just let me find her." He followed the footprints into the forest. Then, in the darkness, he lost them. His head pounded as he tried to think of what to do. *I'm going to die if I don't get help. The closest house is a mile from here. Kepolas. Emilia's family. I must get there.*

The pressure of standing was too great for his injured leg. He fell to his knees and crawled, dragging the leg behind him. Every bump, every tree root was agony. Hand over hand, muscles straining, he pulled himself on and on through the pine needles and ferns.

Finally, a warm light glowed in the distance. *Kepola's house. Emilia's home. His future in-laws. Would she be there?* Johan pulled himself along with that hope.

Something flickered in the distance. The light wasn't coming from the house. The barn was on fire. *What are those bumps in the yard?* Johan pulled himself over the dirt and gravel of their road. The cows and horses were laying on the ground with their legs sprawled in every direction. The fire from the barn leapt onto the roof of the Kepola's house.

"Emilia! Fire!" Johan screamed.

The closer he got, the more clear everything became. The windows were smashed in. The door had been broken off its hinges and hung ajar. Blood from the livestock pooled around the dirt yard in front of the house. If the family was there, they were not alive. Mr. Kepola would never have allowed his home to be destroyed like this. If he didn't escape, he died trying to defend it.

Johan sobbed at the scene before him. His future family was gone. He had no one now. His father and uncle were lost at sea when he was young. As an only child, he cared for his mother as well as he could. When she became sick and died, not long after, he had gone to live with his neighbors, the Kepolas. They became his family. Their oldest daughter, Emilia, was the love of Johan's life. The day she consented to marry him was the first time that Johan felt whole since losing his parents.

Gone. They were all gone. He might as well die.

Johan dropped his head down onto the dirt of the road. Who cared if the rocks were cutting into his open sores?

This is it. Twenty-one vuotta and my life is over.

Just then, his father's voice filled his mind.

"Johan Nevala! Get up this instant! You will live and not die. You have *sisu* running through your veins. Your Finnish blood still pumps in your heart and you will fight to live. Get up! This is not the end. Get up, son!"

Someone was running toward him, yelling in Finnish. "We have a survivor here!"

CHAPTER TWO

*"Plowmen have plowed my back and made their furrows long.
But the Lord is righteous; He who cut me free from the cords of the
wicked."*
Psalms 129:3

November 1849
Johan stepped through the heavy wooden front door of
the Mattilas. It was Esa Mattila that rescued Johan at the
Kepola's farm. A fisherman by trade, he was returning from
fishing in the bay when the fire caught his attention. The
gravity of Johan's loss was heart-wrenching for Esa and his
wife, Aani, and their two boys. They took Johan into their
home that very night.

Johan begged them to take him with them to bury the
bodies. Even though he had not recovered from the shot in his
leg, he shoveled and piled rocks on the graves of his loved
ones. Now Johan worked with Esa gillnetting to try to move
on with his life.

"Johan," Aani called from the kitchen. She walked into
the living room, drying her hands on her apron. She reached
into the pocket on the front. "A letter came for you today."
She handed him a weathered envelope with his name on the
front.

The writing was not good. The address was wrong. But
his name stood bold in a scrawling print and Johan's heart
raced. His life was about to change. He could feel it in his gut.

"Go on, boy," Aani urged, hands clasped together.
"Open it. I've been anxious to see who it is from all day."

Johan tore it open and read the first three words.

"My dearest nephew…"

He gasped. His uncle was alive. All these years
everyone believed he died with his father. Johan's heart
skipped a beat and his hands began to sweat. He read on.

"I pray that this letter finds you and your mother in the best of health and happiness. You may wonder why it has taken me so long to contact you. After our boat went down at sea, I was rescued by a Finnish fishing ship headed to the Pacific Ocean. They saved my life in exchange for my services on board their ship. I have been crossing oceans ever since.

Last winter, I took ill offshore the Oregon Territory in America. They settled me into the Karhuvaara's Boardinghouse on Taylor Street in Astoria. The owners have cared for me and helped me to reach you. Come to America, Johan. Bring your mother.

There is much opportunity here for you. The Governor, George Abernathy, told us of a land gift from the American government, starting in January of next year. If we will build houses and farm the land around Astoria, they will give three hundred twenty acres to any man over twenty-one years! Imagine this, Johan. Land of your very own. If you are married, your wife can have an additional three hundred twenty acres. This nation gives away perfectly good land! You must come to America.

If farming is not for you, I can teach you to gillnet on the Columbia River. Your mother can own a boardinghouse and do quite well. She could open a bathhouse for the fishermen. The Karhuvaara's is always full to capacity.

There are some Finnish people here. More arrive every few months. It feels like home with the large evergreen trees and seasonal weather. The hunting is excellent – elk and deer are abundant. Trapping beavers and mink is a lucrative trade here as well. You can sell them to the American Fur Company and make a handsome profit.

It would be a great adventure for you. I could finally have family near again. How I have missed you and your mother all these years!

Enclosed is the money needed for passage for you and your mother. I understand if you can't come. You must have a life established there in Liminka. But if you need a new start, here is your chance. The Lord bless you, whatever you decide.

Until we see each other again,
Uncle Frans

Esa played the violin after dinner while his wife and sons danced on the hardwood floors. The roaring fire in the hearth made their shadows leap on the walls behind Johan. He sat at the rough-hewn table polished smooth with the years of food served on it. The letter was still clenched in his fist. His mind would not quiet.

Go to America. Stay here. Gillnet in America. Gillnet here. Leave everything I know. Stay here and build a life with people I know.

Emilia's face crossed his mind and a sharp pain stabbed his heart. His decision was made. There was no life left for him in Liminka. Johan knew what he had to do. He would visit the Kepolas' farm one last time. He had to say goodbye. A Finnish fishing vessel, the *Hai*, was leaving for the Pacific in two days. He would be on it. If his uncle wanted a new life for him in America, how much more did he want it?

Family. To have family again was beyond his dreams. He looked up at the Mattilas dancing around in a circle, laughing. This is what he wanted. He wanted a family of his own. They had taken him in and helped him heal. But the truth remained; he was a guest. There was nothing keeping him here now. It was time to go.

He stood to his feet and Esa stilled his fingers on his violin. The boys and Aani came to an abrupt halt in their dancing. They looked at Esa first then followed his gaze to Johan.

Aani held her boys' hands, her chin trembling. "You're leaving us, aren't you, Johan?"

Johan clenched his jaw and nodded once. He didn't trust himself to speak with the knot forming in his throat.

"Uncle Johan!" the little boys cried as they ran to his side. "You don't have to leave us. You can stay here forever."

Johan sat down on the bench beside the boys and wrapped his strong arms around each of them. He squeezed them tight until the giggles burst from them. "I have to go," he whispered. "My uncle is waiting for me in America."

"America!" the boys yelled in unison.

The oldest said, "Can you take me with you, Uncle Johan?"

Johan looked up at Esa and Aani. She dabbed her eyes with the corner of her apron. Esa gave him a weak smile and clenched his jaw.

"You're a good man, Johan," Esa said, straightening his shoulders. "You can do this. I believe the Lord is directing you to leave at this time. Go with our blessings." Aani smiled bravely, nodding in agreement.

Johan looked at each of the boys then at Esa and Aani. "You have been my family when I had no one. I'll never forget your kindness. Never."

*   *   *

The road to the Kepolas' farm seemed the longest Johan ever walked in his life. Each step brought dreadful memories. He remembered the burning barn, the slaughtered animals bleeding out on the ground. The frozen gravel under his feet and fog in the air felt like nothing compared to the cold heart of stone in his chest.

He stepped into the yard, leaning down to rub his aching leg. Glancing up, he noticed the house. The door was repaired and closed. The yard was clear of debris. The barn, or what was left of it, was a charred patch of ground. Five graves, marked with white crosses, rested under the large pine tree to the left of their home. A bed of pine needles and cones surrounded the graves and kept it clear from weeds growing over the markers.

A cool, chilling breeze blew up from the bay with the smell of the sea lingering on it. Johan breathed deeply, closing his eyes. He would miss the smells, the familiar paths of his hunting grounds in Liminka. But he would not miss the painful memories of his childhood and youth. It was time to say goodbye and start over.

He had a few minutes alone before his comrade would meet him here to board their ship. He strode, reverently, toward the graves. He took in a deep breath when he realized he wasn't breathing. First lay the father's grave, then the mother's, then Emilia's. His throat tightened with the truth that she was really gone forever. She was so young, so full of life. Her brothers lay next to her to the right. But Johan's attention was focused on the grave in the middle. It was fitting, really. She should be in the center. She was the center of his world. The center of all his dreams. Now he had to lay those dreams down.

He eased himself down onto the frigid ground at the foot of her grave. Even in his white sailor pants, he felt it was only right to kneel and pay his final respects. He was careful to not disturb even a leaf. He read her name over and over. Then he lifted his eyes to heaven.

"Father in heaven, hallowed be Thy name. Thy kingdom come, thy will be done..." That line choked him up. Was it God's will for Emilia to be murdered with her family? Anger rose in his spirit. No. What did the Good Book say? "God willed that none should perish but that all should have eternal life." The Kepola family may be dead but they certainly had not perished. They were in the loving arms of their Savior. Johan cleared his throat.

"On earth as it is in heaven. Give me this day, my daily bread. Forgive my trespasses as I forgive those who trespass against me." Again, his words froze on his tongue. The Russkies! He could never forgive them for what they had done. Drunken, wicked pagans with hearts as full of ice as the Siberian wasteland!

"Never, Lord! I can never forgive them! Kill them all, Lord! May they die a thousand deaths more gruesome than the ones they invoked on these innocent people!" Johan's tears streamed down his cheeks and neck, soaking the sailor's scarf tied around it. He shot his fist into the air. "Why Lord? Why did you take her? Why did you allow it?" He brought his fist down and slammed it into the hard, frozen ground beneath him. Pain shot up through his fingers and hand.

"Augh!" he cried, in disgust. He shook his hand and felt it over to see if anything was broken.

Suddenly a calm and peace came over him that stunned him. Everything fell silent, not a bird chirped, not a leaf fell from the trees. It was just him and his God and Johan knew it.

Johan, you must forgive those who have trespassed against you. You must forgive the Russians or you will be the one in pain for the rest of your life. It is a choice of your will. To be truly free, you must let this offense go. Leave your homeland a free man, not one strangling in the chains of hatred and unforgiveness. Be free, son.

Johan dropped his chin to his chest and wept. He covered his face with his hand that was broken and bruised. Oh, the pain was so great. Would he ever truly be happy? He took in a deep breath and let it out slowly.

"I forgive...," he whispered so quietly only God could hear.

His body shook with revulsion for the horrific acts of the Russians. Through clenched teeth, he repeated, "I forgive." He saw Emilia's blue lips and white face with the Russian soldier's arms around her. A sob escaped his throat. "I forgive, I forgive, I forgive, Lord." Suddenly the vision of Emilia changed. He saw her running through the sea grass again. Her face was rosy and her eyes danced as he chased her. Her long, chestnut hair flowed free behind her. She was so happy.

Johan sat back on his heels. His hands folded in his lap. This is how he would remember her. He closed his eyes and thought of her again. The same vision of her running came back to him. He let out a sigh of relief. He would not be tormented. From this point on, he would begin to heal.

A twig broke behind him. Johan started and jumped to his feet, wincing from the pain in his leg.

"Sorry, Johan," his sailing comrade said. He pointed to the bay. "The tide has changed. It's time to go."

Johan turned for one last look at the Kepolas' graves. *Emilia Kepola.* Her beautiful name and memory etched into a white cross. *I'll see you again someday, Emilia. But I must go, love. My tide has changed.*

CHAPTER THREE

"Early pioneers probably had the sheriff not too far behind chasing them."
(1850's quote)

November 3, 1849
> *Uncle Frans,*
> *I am grateful to take you up on your offer to come to America. I regret to tell you that my mother will not be coming with me. She died shortly after father was lost at sea. I recently lost everything. There is nothing keeping me here now. I believe it is Providence that your letter came when it did. I will be boarding a vessel, called the Hai, leaving Finland soon. The ship will cross the Atlantic and round the horn of South America. We will fish the Pacific all spring. We should arrive in Astoria around February for the salmon season. Hopefully you will receive this letter before I arrive.*
> *A friend of mine plans to jump ship in San Francisco for the gold rush. He said the best way to escape undetected is to "fall overboard" at night. The captains and officers won't come looking for me that way. They'll assume I got drunk and fell overboard in the dark, lost to the sea forever.*
> *If you could row out to the ship at night with no lights, I will watch for you each evening from the deck. I will lower a rope and slide down the side of the ship. Have some nets and canvas covers in the boat for me to hide under. A friend will pull the rope back up and we'll be off to safety. They'll never find me once I'm ashore. I'll lay low in Astoria until the ship weighs anchor and heads back to sea.*
> *The punishment is severe if I am caught. The risk is worth it to me. The hope of a new start and to be reunited with you is all that keeps me going each day.*
> > *Until I see you, your nephew,*
> > *Johan*

*   *   *

The wind whipped hard and the rope banged against the side of the ship. Johan winced and took one last look around him to make sure he wouldn't get caught.

"Godspeed to you, Johan, and the best of luck," Veli, his friend, whispered. "Don't fall."

Johan gripped the rope with one hand, holding the rail with the other. He swung his leg over and took a deep breath. He swung his other leg over the side and began to slide down the rope. His hands burned as the twine cut into his flesh.

Just a few more seconds...then freedom.

He used his feet to slow his descent down the thick rope. Almost there. In the pitch blackness, only the outline of a twenty-foot row-sail could be seen. Slowly he continued, careful to not bang against the side of the ship.

Voices! Someone was coming!

He flew down the rope with abandon. To be caught now would mean a whipping for himself and his comrade. His feet landed in the bottom of the boat. A strong hand grabbed his coat and pushed him under a pile of canvas tarps. The rope fell from the deck of the ship and splashed into the water beside them.

Under the tarps, Johan could hear the muffled voices of Veli and the night watch. The conversation grew heated then he heard laughter. He held his breath. The boat wasn't moving yet. Better to wait until the men above were gone and then slip away.

Silence.

The soft lapping of oars cutting through the water calmed him. He peeked out from under the canvas and saw a pair of large leather boots.

"Stay put, now, boy," the voice nearby whispered in Finnish.

Johan froze. He had not heard his uncle's voice since he was eight *vuotta.*

Minutes of silence passed with only the sound of the waves and splashing of the oars to be heard. Johan hugged his sailor's jacket tight around him and tried to breathe evenly. His heart pounded with the success of his escape. He wasn't free yet though. What seemed an eternity finally passed and he felt the familiar bump of the boat hitting a dock.

"Alright," Frans whispered. "All clear. Let's go."

Frans pulled back the tarp and motioned for Johan to follow him. He put his fingers to his lips for silence. It was so dark on the water, Johan could not see his uncle's face. The faint light of coal oil lamps from above lit their way up the ladder to the boardwalk. Behind the wooden ladder was a rocky seawall. No sandy beach greeted him here. But the familiar smell of rotting plants mixed with salt water filled his nostrils and that was enough to bring a smile to his face.

"This way," Frans motioned, hurrying up the ladder.

Johan reached the top wrung on the ladder and climbed up onto the boardwalk. He stood straight and stretched out his back. He smiled. *America*! He made it! He reached into his pocket and pulled out the contents. Exactly twenty-one dollars. One dollar for every one of his years. Johan smiled again. Wasn't it just like the Lord to give him such a unique beginning here.

He glanced over to the coal oil lamp. A street sign hung beside the light. *Eleventh Street*. Raucous laughter came from an establishment nearby. The front door flew open. A drunken man and woman came stumbling out arm in arm. The man held a demijohn in one hand and a woman in a red, silk gown in the other. Johan just stared.

"Johan!" his uncle hissed. "Come on, boy. Nothing to see here." He spoke in Finnish, his voice resembling Johan's father's voice.

Johan jumped and followed his uncle down the boardwalk. It had to be late. Maybe midnight. He looked up at the stars but it was too cloudy tonight. They trudged west down the boardwalk, passing boardinghouse after boardinghouse. Kuntas'. Karhuvaara's. Johan smiled at the familiar names. His uncle was right. He would love it here. As they passed Karhuvaara's, Johan stopped while his uncle kept walking.

"Uncle!" he called after him. "Isn't this your place?"

"Yes, but you won't stay here, boy." Frans whispered, over his shoulder. "We're going to hide you with a pioneer couple until your ship leaves."

Johan followed again. *Smart thinking, Uncle.* The first place they would look for him would be a Finnish boardinghouse. How foolish he was! He ran a few steps to keep up with his uncle's spry step.

"Just a few blocks more now," Frans said. He pointed to a large craftsman-style house beside the mill pond ahead. "There it is. That's the Emerson's place. They're a good couple with room to spare. They said they would keep you as long as we need. You'll have good food and a warm bed."

Just the thought of food made Johan's stomach grumble in protest. He could hardly eat his supper on board the ship earlier that evening. His nerves were as taut as a fishing line all day. Now here he was, almost free.

They walked up a stone pathway under six large walnut trees. Johan marveled at the size of them. The warm glow of a candle on the window sill lit the steps for them.

The door opened just a crack before they could even knock. Uncle Frans slipped through. Johan followed. Stepping into a dark, large foyer, Johan blinked to get his bearings. The door closed with a click behind him.

"Welcome," a woman said. "Tervetuloa," she giggled.

Johan turned to face a stout woman, who would have been close to his mother's age. She had rosy cheeks and curly brown hair framing her face. She clasped her hands together and smiled at him.

Johan just smiled back. He didn't know any English. His comrades on the ship tried to teach him a few words but they didn't know much either. He reached out his hand to the woman in greeting.

She took it between her own two hands and smiled warmly. "I'm Mrs. Emerson, but you can call me Bonnie." Turning to Frans, she said, "So, Frans, this is your nephew, Johan."

Frans squared his shoulders and nodded once. He finally looked Johan in the eye. He teared up and coughed.

Johan's shoulders sagged with relief and he looked back at his uncle. Now that he could see his uncle in the light, the resemblance to his father was acute. They shared the same square jaw, piercing blue eyes and brawny build. It was obvious they were related. Their blond, thick hair and beards matched. Johan choked back tears as well.

His uncle stepped forward and pulled Johan into an embrace. He spoke in Finnish. "You are home now," Frans said, patting his back. "Welcome to America, Johan."

*   *   *

The next morning, Johan woke to the smell of bacon wafting into his room. The feather pillow and firm cherry wood bed were a welcome change from his canvas hammock on the fishing ship. He glanced over to his jacket on the wooden chair beside his bed.

Johan Nevala. His name was stitched onto the inside of his collar. His first day in America and it would begin with bacon. A great start. His stomach growled and he jumped out of bed. He wore his pair of wool farming pants from home when he escaped from the ship. No sailor pants today, or any other day, if he could help it. He grabbed the wool sweater Aani knit for him hanging beside his jacket. His boots were under his bed but Mrs. Emerson told his uncle last night that she didn't want him to wear them in the house. Something about fish filth and mud on her clean floors. No mind. He had a place to live and food. He would do whatever the Pioneer woman wanted.

He cracked open his door just in time to meet another young man with flaming red hair in the upstairs hallway. The youth smiled at him.

"I'm Spurgeon," he said, reaching out his hand.

Johan shook it and smiled. "Johan." He said, pointing to himself. He didn't know any other words so he just smiled again.

Spurgeon pointed down the narrow hallway. "Come on," he said, leading the way.

Johan followed him and the smell of freshly baked bread drifting up from downstairs. Their feet padded down the wooden steps. They walked around a thick banister and back toward the front door. The dining room was to the left just off of the kitchen. A long oak table filled the dining room with eight chairs around it.

Bonnie bustled into the dining room carrying a heaping plate of bacon and a basket of rolls. She smiled when she saw Johan.

"Good morning," she said, smiling.

"Hyvää huomenta," Johan said back, with a crooked smile, his face flushed. He glanced around the dining room. A middle-aged, red-haired man sat at the head of the table. To his right sat a young man about twenty years old with a serious expression. He also had red hair. Next to him sat a boy of about sixteen years with freckles all over his face. His hair was so bright red that it shocked Johan.

The youngster stood halfway to his feet and thrust out his hand. "Howdy!"

Johan leaned over the table and shook it.

Bonnie set the food on the table and motioned to a chair next to hers. "Here, Johan. You can sit beside me." She pulled the chair out for him and patted the top of it. She began to pull her chair out when Johan stepped in quickly. He took it from her and motioned for her to sit.

"Well," Bonnie said, blushing. "There's a gentleman for ya." She looked at her boys across the table. "Take notes, Henry and Luther. This is how you treat a lady." She turned to her husband at the head of the table and pursed her lips. Mr. Emerson grumbled something and bowed his head to pray.

Johan followed cue, sat down and bowed his head. He didn't understand their words but he was pleased to have landed in a Christian home.

"Amen," they said in unison.

"Aamen," Johan said quietly.

Just then, a knock came at the front door. Johan started and gripped the edges of his chair. Before he could move, the door opened and his uncle entered.

"Hyvää huomenta, Johan," Frans said, grinning. "Good morning, Gus and Bonnie. Boys." He pulled off his boots and pulled out a chair across from Johan.

Bonnie motioned for the boys to pass him the food. Apparently, she was expecting him this morning. What a hospitable country this was!

Gus spoke up first. "So Frans, what word on the land deed from the governor?" He scooped some fried potatoes onto his plate.

Johan looked from his uncle to Mr. Emerson. He must learn English.

Frans took a roll from the basket and handed the basket to Johan, smiling. He said in English, "There are thousands of deeds available. Johan and I can each have our own, if we want. We just have to clear the land, begin building a home on it and plant crops."

Johan saw that his uncle was excited about something but didn't understand what he saying. He took a few bites of food but watched the conversation, trying to pick up anything that made sense.

"Incredible opportunity," Gus said, shaking his head. "Seems that you two arrived at just the right time in America." He looked over at Bonnie. "If I could talk the Misses into farming, we could have 640 acres of our own."

"We have farmed, dear," Bonnie said, not even looking up from her plate. "You made more money fishing and building those boats last year than we ever made in one year farming. I don't want to live out in the hills with the Indians. Besides, I need supplies close by."

"You just want to live near the few women we have here," Gus grumbled. "You are right, though. The money is in the fishing in Astoria."

Frans laughed and looked over at Johan. He translated a few words from the conversation into Finnish for him. He told him that the land was ready to be settled. They would go to the deed office at the Custom House, after his ship had sailed. They'd sign him up for his own plot of land.

Johan smiled. He wanted it all. Anything and everything this land had to offer, he wanted. He didn't care if he broke his back working for it. He would make a new life here and take the blessings America offered. He grinned back at his uncle and stuffed a bite of bacon into his mouth.

"Jumala siunatkoon yhteistyötämme Amerikan," Johan mumbled.

"What did he say?" Bonnie asked Frans.

"He said, 'God bless America,'" Frans said. They all laughed.

CHAPTER FOUR

"...mere description can give but little idea of the terrors of the bar of the Columbia...one of the most fearful sights that can possibly meet the eye of the sailor..."
– Commander Wilkes, US Navy, Circa 1860

Pacific Ocean, April 1853

"Emily, you worry about everything, dearest," Ronald said, cupping her face in his hands. "Don't you know by now that I will always protect you? Our new life together will exceed your fondest dreams."

Emily turned her face away, doubtful, and leaned on the rail of the *Sophia*. Their steamship had faithfully brought them from New York harbor around the horn of South America. Now with their strenuous journey nearing the end, Emily's fears grew as turbulent as the mighty Pacific Ocean. She watched the sun sink into the sea and her stomach lurched. Black clouds were coming upon them from the north. She shuddered.

"You believe me, don't you, Em?" Ronald's eyebrows furrowed. His eyes flickered with a moment of pain before he squared his shoulders. He dusted off his brown tweed suit and straightened his bowtie. "You'll just have to trust me, dearest. I can see that you are not convinced yet."

Suddenly, the ship pitched starboard, throwing her off balance. "Ronald-"

He caught her in his arms. "Careful," Ronald said. "We need to get you below deck. It's getting choppy out here. Let me take you to our cabin." He wrapped his arm around her waist to steady her.

Emily leaned into his trim frame and matched his steps to the stairway. He walked ahead of her down the stairs to make sure she didn't trip on the whale bone bell of her skirt. Opening their door, he motioned for her to enter first.

"Thank you," she said. She entered their miniscule cabin and perched on the edge of the bed. "Are you coming in?"

Ronald stood in the doorway, looking intently down the hall. "I think I'll just go check on something first," he mumbled. "Sorry, dear, but I'll be right back. Something doesn't seem right." With that, he was out the door and down the hall.

Emily scrambled over to the door. "Ronald, what's wrong?" she called after him, "Where are you going?" She hugged the doorway. A pain struck her in the side and she winced.

Ronald stopped halfway down the narrow, red-carpeted hallway. He plopped his top hat on his head and tapped it down. "I'll be right back, I promise." He flashed a grin and called, "See you in a minute, dearest." He was gone up the metal stairs that lead to the deck.

*   *   *

Emily woke with a start. *How long was she asleep?* Her cabin was dark and the room rolled hard to port. Suddenly, the room flashed with brilliant light. Lightning! A loud cracking sound was followed by the boom of thunder. The boat rolled back to starboard and Emily fell out of bed with a thud on the hardwood floor.

"Oh!" She grabbed her bruised shin and rubbed it. She tried to rise off the floor but her stomach tightened and threatened to be sick. *What was this?* She had recovered from seasickness after they rounded the horn of South America. As quickly as it came on, it ended. *Strange.* She breathed hard and pushed herself over onto her hands and knees, trying to stand. The boat rolled back to port and she sprawled across her bed again.

"Ronald!" The room lit up again. He wasn't in there. "Ronald, where are you?" Thunder boomed outside and shook the thin walls, rattling the crystals hanging from the oil lamps on the walls. Lightning flashed again, closer this time. She screamed. She clutched the brass rail on the end of the bed. "Ronald!" She had to find him. The boat rolled starboard and she stumbled over to the door. She threw it open to find the hall packed with passengers, their arms full of luggage. "What's happening?"

"There's a fire!" a woman cried, gripping the hand of her small daughter. "Hurry! Get your things. They're loading lifeboats."

"Oh Lord," Emily prayed, stumbling back into her room, groping around in the dark. "Oh Lord, help me." Her heart pounded with fear. *Where were they*? They weren't due to reach Astoria and the Columbia River Bar until the morning. She dropped to her knees and reached far under the bed for the small metal lockbox that contained all she and Ronald held dear. It held their wedding certificate, two thousand dollars and the deed to the land awaiting them in Astoria. Emily hit her head on the frame of the bed in her effort to get the lockbox. Just then her hand felt cool metal. She looped her fingers around the handle on top and yanked it out, scraping the hardwood floor. She threw it onto the sheet on the bed and tied the corners together. Then she took the two remaining corners and tied them around her neck in a sling to hold the precious box next to her so she wouldn't drop it. The ship rolled and she stumbled back to her door, falling hard against it. Her head hit the corner of the door as it flung open again.

Sharp pain pierced her forehead then a warm sensation. She held her foot against the door to keep it from swinging back again. She felt her forehead. Blood. "Ronald." She whispered, "I must find Ronald." She swung out into the crowded hallway and allowed herself to be pushed along toward the stairs that led to the upper deck.

Just then, a wave crashed hard against the boat and water spilled down the stairs. People screamed as the frigid water splashed over them in the dark. Children shrieked and cried with fear. The dismal oil lamps in the hallway flickered unevenly. Two men stood at the top of the stairs helping the mothers and children up toward the lifeboats. Emily gripped the rails and tromped up the stairs, the metal box banging her leg with each step.

Without warning, another wave poured down the stairway, drenching Emily to the skin. She gasped. The icy water stole her breath away.

"Hurry lady, please." A father pressed in behind her on the stairs, holding his son.

"Sorry. I'm sorry." She wiped the dripping hair out of her eyes and strained to see. It was so dark.

"Here Miss," one of the men at the top of the stairs called. "Grab my hand! There ya go!" He yanked her up the remaining two steps and she stumbled out onto the deck. Rain hit her face like needles. Tiny ice pellets mixed in with the water. The deck was slick and her leather high heel boots skidded across it. Her dark green skirt belled out at the bottom, bumping into those crushing around her. The lace on her collar clung to her skin, scratching her. With only her fitted dark green jacket and lace gloves to keep her warm, she began to tremble, chilled from the icy sea water.

She followed the crowd to where the lifeboats hung. The bright yellow and orange flames of the fire stunned her. Sailors and crewmen tried to smother the flames. *Where was the captain?* Emily realized the fire was raging on the captain's deck.

"Women and children first! Women and children first!"

"Sir, we're going to have to ask you to wait. Women and children first."

"That's my family! I'm not leaving them."

"You, Miss. You next." Emily felt a strong hand grip her upper arm, pulling her forward. She glanced to the side and one of the crewmen was dragging her to the lifeboat.

"No!" Emily screamed, struggling to pull away. "My husband! Ronald Davenport! I must find my husband!"

The boy sailor stepped in front of her. He spoke sternly, "Ma'am, please. We have no choice. Please go now. You may not have another chance."

With those words, Emily looked at the crowd of men and sailors around her. The light from the fire lit up their faces. The fear in their eyes confirmed that the sailor spoke the truth. She felt the air escape from her lungs and no words came out in protest. She allowed him to assist her into the lifeboat. She was the last one on, scrunched in between the side of the boat and the woman with the small daughter.

"I want my Daddy! Mommy, where's Daddy?" the little girl wailed.

"Shhhhhh, Nellie," coaxed the mother, wrapping her arms around her.

The crew lowered them toward the raging ocean. *How could this be the better choice for survival?*

"I am First Mate, David Hawthorne," an officer bellowed over the wind and storm. "If you listen to me and obey, I will get you to safety. You have to trust me. My fellow crew mates will row you to land. Please give them the room they need and remain calm, come what may."

Silence fell over the lifeboat. Only the roar of the ocean and the merciless wind whipping around them could be heard. Even the children hushed as the crew disconnected the ropes from the ship. They slipped away from the *Sophia* into open water. Huge waves lifted them up and away from the towering sides of the steamship. Emily turned to gaze back. Her eyes searched the deck for one glimpse of Ronald. The only light came from the fire raging. The splintering of wood and twisting steel echoed over the waves. Another lifeboat was lowering into the water. Emily turned around and could barely see two other lifeboats bobbing on the waves.

Rain pelted down upon them and she trembled, unable to control her shaking. Water dripped off her eyelashes, blurring her vision. Still she strained to see Ronald on the deck of the ship. Nothing. The sailors were just little specks moving in front of the blaze on deck. Ronald in his brown suit and hat would be invisible to her in this darkness.

Now the voices from the deck of the ship were drowned out with the wailing and whining of the wind. Wave after wave lifted them precariously high. Then they would sink far below the next wave. Then they would lift up again.

Emily stole quick glimpses of the other lifeboats when they rose. Then they would disappear out of sight. Fear gripped her chest. *Would they become separated? How would they stay together?*

At the other end of the boat, First Mate David Hawthorne made a spark and lit a candle inside a glass lantern. He fastened it onto a tall pole and stuck it into a hole in the end of the boat. Hope filled Emily. Their lifeboat rose on the next wave and light after light lit up on the other lifeboats.

"Mommy look!" the little girl cried. "We can see each other."

"Yes, Now shhhhhh, honey. We must stay quiet."

Emily glanced down at the little girl beside her. She was so small, maybe four or five years old. Emily clasped the sheet holding the metal box close to her chest, partly to cover her from the rain, mostly to keep it safe. It was her only hope now.

A sob rose in her throat and constricted her breathing. She put her hand over her mouth so the little girl wouldn't see her cry. Ronald was gone from her forever.

Emily felt sick to her stomach again. Her last meal was at lunch earlier that day. She slept through dinner and now was famished. *Where were they on this huge ocean? Would these waves swamp them or would they reach land first?*

Emily clutched the side of the lifeboat. Her lace gloves did nothing to protect her hands against the spray from each wave. Her fingernails dug through the thin gloves into the side of the wooden boat. Air wafted up her skirt because the thin bone bell stood straight up and down in front of her. She tried to hold it down with her other hand.

The little girl next to her kept watching her. Emily tried to smile at the little face staring up at her. It came out more like a grimace of agony, she could tell. The little girl hugged her mother more closely and glanced back at Emily again with caution.

"Ladies and gentlemen," the First Mate yelled above the ocean's roar. "We are nearing the mouth of the Columbia River. It is the most dangerous crossing in our nation even for a steamship much less a lifeboat. But mark my words, you will reach Astoria shortly or my name isn't David Hawthorne."

*   *   *

Bells rang from the docks in the middle of the night. Johan sat up in bed, rubbing his eyes. *Where was he?* Now he remembered, he had stayed the night at the Emersons. The catch today took longer to haul in than normal. Uncle Frans would take care of the animals and his farm. In return, he would get an early start on the next day's fishing and give his uncle a share. He heard a soft knock on his door.

"Johan," Gus called. "There's been a shipwreck out at sea. Lifeboats are struggling to get over the bar. Let's go!"

Johan leapt out of bed and grabbed his trousers from the chair in the corner of the room. He glanced out the tall, thin window overlooking the river. Faint lights from the lifeboats twinkled through the wind and rain. They glimmered softly then disappeared, then lit up again.

Johan pulled his undershirt over his head and shot his arms down the sleeves. He yanked his wool sweater over his body and pulled his wool cap low over his ears. He stuffed his bare feet into his leather boots. He didn't bother to lace them up as he threw open the door.

"That's a lad!" Gus beamed. His face was lit up with a candle in the narrow hallway. "The boys are downstairs. Let's get going!"

They tromped down the stairs two at a time. Grabbing their oilskin coats, they raced out the front door and headed east to the docks and their boats.

Johan tripped on his untied boots as he ran.

"Why didn't you lace those up?" Luther asked, punching him in the arm.

"If we go into the water tonight," Johan answered, "I won't want them weighing me down."

"Good point!" Luther cried. He stopped running and leaned over to untie his own boots.

"Come on now!" Gus yelled. "You'll have time to tie or untie your boots later!" He wiped his brow and put a fist in his side as he ran.

Johan reached the docks first and loosed the boats. He held the lines tight for fear that the whipping waves would pull them away. The spray from the huge waves crashed against the rock wall, soaking the men. Luther, Spurgeon and Henry jumped into their skiff. Gus lowered himself gingerly into his boat and Johan followed.

They were joined by the other gillnetters from Taylor and Bond Streets.

"See those lights! Row, men, row!" Gus yelled over the wind. "Innocent lives are on the line. Smoley Hokes! There's a storm blowing tonight!"

Johan rowed hard against the current of water pushing downstream.

"Straighten her out, boy," Gus ordered. "She'll cut through those waves like they're butter if you hit 'em right."

Johan adjusted slightly and felt the pressure ease with rowing. The wind and rain pelted his back as he pulled hard on the oars. He mumbled the Lord's Prayer in Finnish over and over to keep his rhythm. His boat pulled ahead of the others and the light of the first lifeboat came into view.

"There she is, Johan," Gus bellered. "A little more and we'll have them. Keep it up!"

Soon the cries of those on the lifeboat could be heard above the howling wind.

"Here! We are here!"

"Overshoot us a bit, sailor," a confident voice shouted.

Johan glanced over his shoulder and could see the outline of a sailor at the bow of the lifeboat. He passed them upriver and let the current pull his boat back to them.

"That's it, boy!" the sailor called.

The other boats from Astoria rowed past them to the next lifeboats coming over the bar. The waves rose and crashed hard against the boats.

One of the lifeboats was swamped by a huge wave.

"Save us!"

"There were children on board! Go there first!"

Luther, Spurgeon and Henry rowed hard to the edge of the bar. The tumultuous waves and pitch black of night made spotting the people in the water nearly impossible.

Just then, a massive wave rolled past Johan's boat nearly spilling it. It hit the lifeboat near him and turned it over in the water. All fifteen passengers popped up around the overturned lifeboat. Hands flailed above the water. Women screamed. The two sailors on board were pushing the women toward to lifeboat to hold on instead of being carried downriver with the current.

Johan stood up in his skiff. He surveyed the top of the water. One white hand with a lace glove shot up out of the water. He kicked off his boots and jumped in after it. Johan caught his breath as he emerged from his dive. The woman was nearby. He spun around searching for her. To the right, he heard some splashing sounds. He dove toward the sound and caught hold of an arm just below the surface. He kicked hard and pulled the body upward.

Long hair surrounded him in the water and his hands got caught in it as he tried to hold onto the woman. He found her waist in the water and lifted her up. They broke the surface and sucked in air.

The woman was coughing and gasping for air. She was desperately kicking but her dress was so heavy, it pulled her downward.

"I've got you, Miss," Johan shouted. "Relax and breathe. Just breathe."

His mind flashed back to holding Emilia at the bay. *Breathe, Emilia. Breathe.* He shook his head hard to clear it. He held the woman with her back to him. He pulled them through the water with his other arm toward Gus' boat.

"Come on, Johan," Gus yelled. "Over here, son!" Gus was pulling in another woman into his boat.

Johan followed the voice in the darkness and reached the side of the boat.

"Take her," Johan cried, exhausted.

Gus reached over and tried lifting the woman, but strained. "Her skirt, Johan! It's too heavy. It's getting caught."

Johan grabbed the waist of her skirt and tore it. Instantly, it sank and the woman lifted out of the water in her white petticoat and jacket. She fell into the bottom of the boat, gasping for breath.

Johan pulled himself up and over the side. He stumbled over the other passengers sitting on the benches. His survivor lay huddled in a pile of white lace in the middle of the boat. He crawled over to her and lifted her onto the middle bench. Water expelled from her lungs and she vomited all over Johan.

Johan straightened her up on the bench. He wiped her long, dark hair away from her face.

"Astoria?" she choked out. "Are we in Astoria?"

"Yes," Johan said, grabbing his oilskin coat off the floorboard to wrap around her.

"We made it," she said. "We're alive." She looked around the boat at the faces of the other survivors. "Did the mother and girl survive?"

"Yes," a woman nearby answered. "The First Mate got them into another boat. We all survived. Mr. Hawthorne was right. We all reached Astoria."

The young woman started sobbing. She buried her face in her hands.

Johan pulled the oilskin around her tighter. "You made it. You will be safe now."

She looked up at him in the darkness. "Thank you for saving my life. I don't know how you did it, but thank you."

They were trembling violently with cold as they stepped out of Gus' boat onto the docks. Bonnie met them at the top of the ladder.

"I have hot baths waiting for the ladies and children," she called over the storm. "You men go down to Kuntas' bathhouse for yours. I'll have hot soup ready when you return."

"Our boys?" Gus called after her.

"They will meet you at Kuntas'. They just arrived with their boat full of survivors as well," Bonnie cried. "Praise the Lord! He snatched these dear ones from the mouth of death tonight."

Johan helped the young woman out of the boat. He pulled his boots on quickly. She started to take off his oilskin coat when he stopped her. "No ma'am," he said. "Please keep it. I know where to find you…I mean it, the coat, tomorrow."

They climbed the ladder to the boardwalk. The dim lanterns above them cast a light over her. Johan could see what she looked like for the first time. Long, dark hair. White skin like porcelain. Large, blue eyes. She was beautiful. She was also freezing. He came to his senses.

"Follow Mrs. Emerson, ma'am," he said. "She'll see to your needs and get you settled. Everything will get sorted out in the morning." He turned to go.

"My box!" she shrieked, looking around. She leaned over the boardwalk rail to search Gus' boat.

Johan stood beside her, looking into the boat as well.

She turned to him, her eyes wide. "When you saved me, did I have a sheet with a box around my shoulders?"

"Uh…," Johan said, raking his fingers through his wet hair. "You could barely swim with that heavy skirt. I'm sure the sheet and box are gone."

"No!" she cried, sinking down to her knees onto the wooden boardwalk. "What am I going to do? I've lost everything!" She looked out over the river. It was a black abyss that stretched out for eternity. They couldn't even see the other side. There was no going back to find her treasures. Now they were lost, too.

The young woman's body trembled with cold and fatigue. Her lips were blue and her teeth chattered uncontrollably. Johan scooped her up into his arms and carried her down the boardwalk to Bond Street. The Emerson's home was near but she was in no condition to walk there now. He hugged her close to his chest. The oversized coat was cumbersome but it would have to do.

The woman laid her head on his shoulder and closed her eyes. Her long petticoat threatened to trip him a few times on the way but he got her to the Emerson's safely at last.

Bonnie met his knock on the front door.

"I thought I lost one on the way here," she said. "Hand-delivered, I see." She grinned at Johan with the warm lights of her sitting room behind her. "Bring her in and set her on the couch until I can see to her. She can warm up by the fire."

Johan set her on Bonnie's horsehair loveseat. He swung one end of the couch over so that she sat full in front of the fireplace. He tugged the soaked, oilskin coat off of her shoulders and hung it on a peg by the door. He grabbed the knitted blanket off of the back of the loveseat and wrapped it around her.

Bonnie hustled back into the room. "I better see to that, Casanova." Bonnie whispered, smirking.

Only then did Johan notice her skin through the thin petticoat. He blushed and ran out the door, snatching his oilskin on the way. He closed the door firmly behind him. Sauntering down the muddy, lantern-lit street to the Kuntas' bathhouse, Johan felt warm in spite of his soaked clothing. In fact, his heart was beating so hard it surprised him. Maybe it was the adrenaline from the rescue on the river tonight. Maybe it was coming so close to death. But he knew this feeling. He felt it the first time he saw Emilia in Milinka. He was in love.

CHAPTER FIVE

"Hunger is a great seasoning..." – Lewis and Clark

Johan tied off the gill net and worked the line thoughtlessly. He could fish with his eyes closed. He let his mind wander. This was what he loved and hated about this job. The time to think was a blessing and a curse. He didn't feel like himself after the long night rescuing the survivors. But he had to pay his way. His land wouldn't work itself. His home wouldn't be built for free. Every day on the river took him closer to his dream; owning his own place with enough room for a man to breathe.

Johan's head spun and grew hot. He shouldn't be out here yet.

"Johan? You alright?"

It was Henry Emerson. His parents named him Matthew Henry, after the great Bible commentator. He chose to go by Henry just to be able to fill his own shoes everyday. He purposely anchored his boat much closer than needed today to keep an eye on Johan.

Johan waved his hand at him, dismissing his concern. He plopped down hard on the bench and leaned on the oar.

He straightened out his net. The fish were huge and the owner of the Finnish fish market only accepted the best in his store. This was one thing Johan took pride in – his work ethic. *Good Finn roots.* He smiled and wiped the sweat off his brow. His work and his faith are what held him from throwing himself into the wretchedness of Astoria along with the other fisherman. Sometimes he was tempted, that was for sure. The pain would eat at him and not let up. That's when he would take a walk in the woods alone and find his peace with God. It was time for another long walk.

Johan sighed. He glanced over at Henry who waved back at him. Johan wiped the sweat beading on his brow again. *What would he have done without the Emersons?* Everyone needed a good friend or two in a town like Astoria. There were too many swindlers who'd take your last crust of bread if they thought they could get away with it.

The new girl he rescued the night before kept slipping into his thoughts. She was certainly pretty enough. Too pretty for the likes of Astoria. A single woman like that wouldn't last six months here without hitching up with the first desperate bachelor that could make her a good offer. He had seen it happen a few times in the last three years in Astoria.

Emily. That was her name, wasn't it? Those blue eyes were something else. They were blue like the sky on a hot, clear day over Liminka. He allowed himself to remember her face, her long thick eyelashes and her trim little waist.

A sick feeling hit his gut. It tasted like betrayal. What was he doing thinking about another woman? Emilia had been gone for less than four years. When he first arrived in Astoria, he vowed to never marry because there were so few women to choose from. It wasn't worth the hassle of looking. Astoria had only a few eligible brides but none that would marry a young fisherman like him. These gals were high society and could take their pick of gentlemen. There was no lack of gentlemen. More and more were showing up all the time to invest in this new land out west.

Emily was high society, no doubt. He could tell by her fine clothes…or what was left of them. Most likely she'd turn up her nose at him and find a man with deep pockets. She'd be a fool to try to survive out here without a large income to make it comfortable and worthwhile. There was nothing to keep her here in Astoria. She'd be leaving soon.

That thought made him feel a little melancholy.

Suddenly, out of the corner of his eye, Johan saw Henry stand up quickly in his boat and fall overboard. Johan secured his corkline to the front of his boat and stood up to search the murky water for him.

Henry submerged once and gasped for air then disappeared again.

Johan kicked off his boots, still wet from the night before. He dove into the bay and the freezing water shocked his frayed nerves. He pulled himself through the water and reached the side of Henry's boat. There was no sign of him. Desperation and adrenaline shot through Johan and he gulped a huge breath of air.

He dove down to the bottom. Henry's arms flailed on the bay floor and his eyes were wide open. His arm was caught in his corkline and he couldn't break free. Johan pulled a knife from his belt and quickly cut through the line. The men pushed off the muddy bottom of the bay and kicked hard for the surface. Gasping for air, Johan shoved Henry toward his boat and to safety.

Henry gripped the side of his row-sail and pulled himself back on board. He turned and pulled in Johan after him.

Johan sputtered and his body shook violently. "What...what are you doing, man? Trying to get us killed?"

Henry shook the water from his red hair. "Sorry, Johan...got caught and...couldn't get free...free."

Johan shook his head. "Where's your knife, Henry? If I wasn't here with mine, that would have been it for you."

Henry hung his head sheepishly. "I forgot it."

"Again?" Johan stuttered. "You owe me, friend. I wasn't ready to jump into that water again so soon."

Henry put his hand on Johan's shoulder. "You don't look so good..."

CHAPTER SIX

"One always has the idea of a stupid man as perfectly healthy and ordinary,
and of illness as making one refined and clever and unusual." -
Thomas Mann

Emily stayed near the toasty fire at the Emersons'. It seemed that she could not get warm in this wet, moss-covered place. She sat at Bonnie's writing desk, trying to put into words the tragic events for her family. Tears streamed down her face and kept falling onto the parchment and fresh ink.

"The Emerson's home is chaotic with the survivors from the steamship. All day, their door slams open and shut with noisy fishermen or neighbors bringing food and supplies..."

As if on cue, the door flew open with a bang against the wall. Emily jumped to her feet, dropping her blanket and quill on the floor. Her oversized skirt from Bonnie almost slipped right off her hips but she grabbed it just in time. She cinched it up with one hand and ran over to the door.

Gus stumbled in backward. "Bonnie! Come quickly!"

"She isn't here," said Emily, holding the door open. The men shoved their way in from the rain and cold. They were carrying a large man who appeared unconscious. She caught a glimpse of blond hair as they rushed by her. "She stepped out to help Mrs. Veith with something," Emily said.

The men paused in the entryway trying to figure out where to put the sick man.

"Emilia," the man mumbled, his blood shot eyes barely open. He reached his arm toward Emily and let it drop when he didn't have the strength to hold it up. "Emilia," he groaned. He struggled in the men's arms. "Stay, Emilia. Please stay."

Emily's face flushed and looked to Gus, not understanding.

"Go fetch your Momma quick, Spurgeon," Gus commanded. His son dropped the leg he was holding and trumped back out into the rain. "Let's take this boy upstairs. He's bad. He's real bad."

The sick man locked his eyes on Emily as though his life depended on it. "No, wait! Stop! Don't take her from me," he slurred. Then he mumbled on in some foreign language.

The men clambered up the narrow stairs to Henry's bedroom.

Emily stood clutching her skirt and closed the door. It barely closed before it flew open again and another draft of cold air blustered in.

"He's burning up real bad, Momma," Spurgeon said, ushering his mother in, forgetting to close the door behind him.

Bonnie hung up her shawl on a peg. She tossed her sewing basket on the wooden bench beside the door. She waddled up the stairs as fast as her stout legs would carry her.

Spurgeon turned to Emily, "Evening, ma'am." Then he shucked off his boots and followed close behind his mother upstairs.

Emily stood in the entryway, shocked. *Who was this man?* Her heart filled with pity for the delirious man upstairs. How could he know her name was Emily? But he said Emilia. Odd. It was strange that she felt like she knew him. She had just arrived and knew no one except the Emersons. She was all alone in this God-forsaken place.

A gun shot echoed outside a short distance away. Emily slammed the door.

*   *   *

Johan lay bare-chested and Bonnie applied another cold, wet towel. His blond, thick hair clung to the sides of his head, dripping with sweat.

"Oh Lord, this fever has got to break," Bonnie prayed, squeezing out another towel into the bucket. "Another towel, Emily."

Emily jumped, realizing that she had been staring at the stranger. She flushed and grabbed another towel to soak. "Here you are, ma'am."

"Thank you, dear." Bonnie said, applying the new towel.

"Is this your son?" Emily asked.

"Oh no," Bonnie said, looking back at her. "This is Johan Nevala. He came over from Finland a few years ago. You don't remember him?"

"Remember him?" Emily blushed, feeling foolish.

"This young man saved your life last night," Bonnie said, brushing his hair off his forehead.

Emily studied his face. He looked different without his wool cap. "Oh, yes. Johan Nevala is his name?"

"Yes, that's right. Came here all alone. Dropped into our laps late one night. Just like you did. Wouldn't trade this one for anything." Bonnie looked around her for another towel.

Emily turned to see how she could help but felt suddenly dizzy. She eased into the closest chair hoping that the room would quit spinning. Her face flushed hot then cold and clammy all at once.

"Hand me another washcloth, dear." Bonnie said, putting her hand out. She turned to Emily, "Now what's happened to you? You look awful. Not much for nursing, eh?"

"Mrs. Emerson, I don't feel very well," Emily said, pressing her cold hand against her cheek.

"Not you, too," Bonnie said, turning to her and feeling her forehead. "You both must have caught fever in that cold, night air. Just sit there and rest a minute, dear."

"I'm so sorry," Emily said, leaning her head back on the chair. "I want to be of help to you. You've been so kind to let me stay here...while I get my business matters settled, anyway."

Bonnie spun on her chair and turned to Emily. She put her fist on her hip. "Darling," she said, pursing her lips. "Here in Astoria, we take care of our own. You washed up here so you're one of us now. You stay as long as you need."

Emily felt a lump in her throat and swallowed hard. "Thank you again. I...I lost my land deed, all our money and our marriage certificate in the river. The box must have slipped away from me when our boat was swamped." Heat flooded through Emily again and she had to close her eyes to ward off another attack of nausea.

"Don't you fret," Bonnie said, tucking in the bed sheets around Johan. "We'll go to see Mr. Shively, the postmaster. If he can't give us some direction, then we'll go see Mr. Conrad Boelling. He's good with business and should be able to give you a hand."

"I've starting writing a letter home to my parents," Emily said, pressing her cold hand against her cheek. "They will send for me as soon as they know what has happened." Emily leaned on the arm of the chair with her hand covering her mouth.

"Did you and your--" Bonnie paused. "I mean, do you have any connections here in Astoria otherwise. What was your business here?"

"My husband, Ronald, and I were going to build a home uptown," said Emily. "Ronald's family invested in the fur trade with Mr. Astor. With that trade diminishing, Ronald came westward with hopes of making a fortune in the hotel industry. He wanted to be part of building up Astoria like San Francisco."

"Well, you can certainly make your fortune by selling whiskey here," Bonnie said. "Not sure a hotel would do as well. Astoria is known for two things – the saloons and brothels of Swilltown."

"My mother warned me about the corruption here," Emily said. "She begged me not to come. When I married, there was no stopping us from coming west. Now I see how foolish that decision was. I just wanted out from under my parent's roof. I wanted a life of my own. What were we thinking coming here?" Emily buried her face in her hands.

"Well, if I know anything, it's that everything happens for a reason," Bonnie said, laying a hand on Emily's shoulder. "You're not here by mistake. We'll just take one day at a time and get your things in order. Everything will be fine, you'll see."

Emily looked up at Bonnie's face. Her sweet smile and gentle nod settled Emily's heart.

A groan came from the bed.

"My, but he's burning up." Bonnie turned back to Johan. She took the dry towel from his forehead and soaked it in cold water again. She rolled it and put it back on his forehead. "This fever has to break. Can you hand me that metal cup, dear?"

Emily handed Bonnie the tin cup of water, who tried pouring some into Johan's parched lips. He sputtered and coughed, trying to swallow.

"Dear, will you run down to the kitchen to bring up some broth? He has to keep his strength up," Bonnie said.

Emily stood quickly and black spots filled her vision. "Mrs. Emerson, I--"

*   *   *

Emily opened her eyes to the green and white brocade wallpaper of the sitting room. She blinked hard and tried to figure out how she got there. Then she focused on Bonnie sitting across the room.

Bonnie smiled and shook her head. "Well, are you trying to give me heart problems? First Johan, now you! You fainted dead away in there, dear. He wasn't even bleeding." Bonnie's motherly concern showed through the fear in her voice.

"What? What happened?" Emily blinked hard.

"I had Henry carry you down here. Couldn't leave you lying on the floor up there, now could I?"

"Everything went black. I don't know what happened. What's wrong with me?"

"I have my guesses," Bonnie whispered, looking around her to make sure no one was listening. The other guests were settled at the dining room table playing cards. A curl of a smile appeared at the corners of Bonnie's mouth and her dimples showed. "Why don't you tell me what you think happened first?"

"I felt dizzy and didn't feel well. It was hot and cold all at once."

"Hmmmm. Not feeling well, huh?"

"Ma'am, I'm so sorry I didn't help you..."

"Mrs. Davenport-"

"Please call me Emily."

"Alright, but only if you call me Bonnie." She tilted her head and her tight curls flopped onto her shoulder. "Have you been sick for a while?"

Emily hesitated. Maybe they wouldn't let her stay if she was ill. Her heart pounded with fear. *Where would she go?* She turned her face away from Bonnie.

Bonnie slid her chair closer to Emily's and took her hand. "My dear, I think you are with child."

Emily's eyes shot back to Bonnie's face. "I don't know. I suppose I could be. I'm not sure." Her brave façade melted and the tears escaped. "I don't want to be a burden to you and your family. You have been so generous already. How can I ever repay you? If only Ronald--"

"Shhh, dear. That's enough. This is your home now for as long as you need it."

A sob escaped Emily's throat and she pressed the back of her hand against her mouth to hold it in. "My husband will never know--"

"Emily, look at me."

The mention of her name stilled Emily.

"You have nothing to fear. You and your baby can stay as long you need."

Another sob broke out. "You are too kind, Bonnie." She threw her arms around Bonnie and accepted the embrace in return.

"All will be well, you'll see." She wiped some whisps of Emily's long hair back from her face and tucked them behind her ear. "Now, get some rest."

"What about the boy upstairs? Don't you need help?" Emily started to rise from the couch.

"No, dear." Bonnie tucked her curls under her cap. "My sons will help me with Johan. He may be young but he's no boy." Bonnie looked toward the stairs and rose to her feet. "He'll pull through. He's done it before and he'll do it again." She smiled through the tears in her own eyes and let out a sigh. She shook out her skirt and clapped her hands together with a giggle. "Now you sleep. That little one needs you to get your rest."

Emily sat up quickly, clutching Bonnie's hand. "Please don't tell anyone, Bonnie. Not yet anyway."

"Of course not, dear. Don't worry, just rest."

*　　　*　　　*

Emily woke early to the birds singing in the tree outside her window. A red-breasted robin chirped its heart out as the sun rose. Bonnie settled her in a room of her own. She smoothed her oversized skirt and tiptoed down to the kitchen in search of Bonnie. She was eager to help this morning after last night's drama.

The kitchen was chilly. The fire needed stoking. Bonnie must have had a long night. Emily boiled the water for coffee for the men. She mixed up some porridge to help start breakfast. When it was ready, she put some in a bowl on a tray and carried it up to Johan's room with a glass of water.

The door stood ajar. She tapped it with her toe and it opened with a creak. Early morning light flooded the room and the light rain tapped on the thin, glass windows. It felt serene. Bonnie lay fast asleep in her rocker in the corner. The boys must have brought it up for her last night. Emily smiled. What a good woman Bonnie was. She stayed up all night watching over everyone.

Emily set the tray down on a nearby dresser. Turning her eyes to Johan, Emily stepped up for a closer look. His face was strong. His square jaw and thick neck sat defined on broad shoulders. His chest was broad. His arms were covered in thick, curly blond hair. His hands rested on his chest. Emily stared at the size of them. His fingers weren't manicured and delicate like Ronald's. These hands had scars and calluses. She liked them. She smiled and looked back at his face.

His eyes were open.

Emilia? Am I dreaming? He blinked again. No, this vision before him was very real. *How did he know her? Where was he?*

He glanced around him. Henry's room. He was at the Emerson's. His head pounded. He closed his eyes tight and sucked in a breath. He had been holding it without realizing it. He relaxed and breathed in and out a few times. He ventured to open his eyes again, focusing on the figure in front of him. Tiny waist, full skirt, trim figure, pretty face, blue eyes. This woman had blue eyes. His Emilia had dark brown eyes. A pain hit his chest near his heart. It was familiar and didn't alarm him. He was used to it by now. Every thought of Emilia had that effect on him. Johan groaned and closed his eyes tight.

"Sir? How can I help you?"

He felt a cool hand on his forehead and opened his eyes a sliver.

"Are you thirsty? Could you drink some water?"

He nodded, suddenly very parched. His tongue felt dry and stuck to the top of his mouth. The fever dehydrated him. "Yes please," he croaked. His voice shocked him. It was raspy and rough. He knew the fever broke last night but his muscles and bones ached inside him. It hurt to move. The fever took hold when he was out on his row-sail. He didn't remember much after that.

The young woman was back at his side with a cup of water. She slid her arm under his pillow to lift his head. With the other hand, holding the water, she put it to his cracked lips. Some water dribbled down into his beard before it cooled his mouth and slid down his dry throat. He coughed.

"I'm so sorry," she said. She quickly set the cup down on the dresser and grabbed a dry cloth. Gently, she dabbed his mouth and beard.

Johan meant to save his dignity and take the cloth to dry his own mouth. His hand touched hers instead of the cloth and froze. Her skin was soft and delicate. It felt like silk, it was so smooth. He was suddenly aware of how rough his own hands were touching hers.

She froze, eyes wide, but didn't withdraw her hand.

"Excuse me, Miss," he stammered.

She seemed unsure of how to proceed. She handed him the cloth and reached for the water again.

"Would you like to try to drink some more?" she whispered.

"Please." He propped himself up on his elbows, amazed at the aching sensation running the length of his body. He winced. Suddenly he felt her support his pillow again. When he opened his eyes, her face was close to his. She didn't look at him, but focused on helping him drink. She bit her bottom lip as she tilted the glass toward him again. He drank deeply, emptying the glass.

"My! Shall I get you some more?" She seemed pleased to not soak him this time. "I guess you were thirsty. Are you hungry? Would you take some porridge?"

She laid his head back gently and stood over him. She wasn't overly tall. An average height for a woman. Johan nodded just as his stomach growled. The girl giggled and turned to get the bowl of porridge.

He looked down and realized his chest was exposed. He quickly drew up the blanket to cover himself. She turned just in time to see. Her cheeks flushed.

"I'm sorry I didn't know you were cold."

"I'm fine." He didn't want to stare at her but his eyes were drawn to her face. She put the warm porridge in his hands with a spoon. It didn't look like Bonnie's porridge. It was pale gray and didn't have the cinnamon and sugar on top.

"Do you need help eating?"

He glanced up at her face. Her eyes were mesmerizing. Blue was so different to him.

"Shall I pull over a chair and help you?"

"No ma'am." He didn't want this woman helping him any more than she needed to. He was a man. He could certainly feed himself.

She seemed disappointed and wiped her hands on the front of her skirt to dry them. "Alright then, I'll just go check on...something downstairs... then." She smiled and swirled out of the room. Her skirt hugged the corner as she went around it to go downstairs. He could hear her light step touch each stair, the click of the front door opening and the click of it closing again.

He tasted the porridge. Whew! Terrible stuff. Maybe Gus cooked breakfast because Bonnie was up here caring for him. He would have to poke some fun at him.

*   *   *

Emily retched into the privy and black spots filled her vision. No, not again. Not here. The smell was bad enough to empty her stomach even on a good day. *Lord, have mercy on me, please.* Another wave came over her. She spat. Opening the door and stepping onto the muddy lawn, Emily put her hands on her hips to steady herself and drew in a deep breath. Her skin felt clammy and cold. She glanced up just in time to see the puzzled expression on Henry's face.

CHAPTER SEVEN

"Where'er a noble deed is wrought,
Where'er is spoken a noble thought,
Our hearts in glad surprise,
To higher levels rise"
-Henry Wadsworth Longfellow

May 1853

"Bonnie, you really outdid yourself," Gus said, kissing his wife's cheek, as he scuffled to his seat. The table lay heaped with two dressed pheasants, potatoes, canned beans and a cranberry chutney. It looked like Thanksgiving but it was only the spring.

"Well, we needed to celebrate and thank the good Lord for a prosperous spring," she said, shooing him away. "Come on in, everyone. Please be seated."

She motioned for Emily to sit beside Henry. Johan was to sit across from her beside Spurgeon and Luther and Frans. Gus said grace. Johan peeked across the table at Emily who obediently closed her eyes tight.

"Amen."

She glanced up and caught Johan looking at her. She smiled.

"Please pass the taters," Luther said.

"They're coming, son. Have patience." Bonnie said, smiling at her youngest. "Why is it the youngest is always so worried the taters will be gone before they get to him?"

Everyone laughed, knowing it to be true of Luther. He didn't seem to think it was so funny.

"Do you have brothers and sisters, Emily?" Bonnie asked, taking a bite of meat.

"Yes, I have one brother, Aaron, back in New York," Emily said. "He was the youngest, too, Luther. Don't worry, you're not alone. He always worried that the pudding would never make it to him either."

Luther broke into a smile, obviously grateful for some small connection to Emily.

"Johan," Gus said, wiping his beard with his napkin. "You started lookin' more like yourself out there today. How ya' feeling?"

"Well, Gus," Johan said, quietly, keeping his eyes on his plate. "You were practically standing in my boat, so I guess you'd notice that I'm fine."

"Gus," Bonnie said, putting down her silverware. "I told you to give that boy some space. He's gonna be alright. I swear you hem and haw after him like he was one of your own." She smiled warmly at Johan. "You do look well and we're so grateful."

"This is delicious, Bonnie." Johan said, taking another bite of potatoes. "Much better than Gus's cooking, that's for sure."

"Gus's cooking?" Bonnie said, confused. "He never cooks."

"I think he did some cooking the other day," Johan teased, a crooked smile on his lips.

"That man is not allowed near my stove and he knows it," Bonnie chided, her face growing red.

"What did I make?" Gus asked, amused now.

"I believe you tried to make some porridge, Gus." Johan chuckled but Gus looked confused. Johan looked around the table at blank stares. Only Emily's face turned white and she set down her napkin quickly.

"Excuse me," she said, scooting back her chair to leave.

Understanding hit Johan and he swallowed hard. "Emily made the porridge," he whispered. Bonnie nodded, biting her lip.

Emily went outside and closed the front door quietly behind her.

"I never thought- -I was just going to tease Gus. Excuse me." Johan left the table and ran out the door after her.

Johan walked up beside Emily near the Emerson's fence. She was batting her hand at a bunch of Scotch broom. "Ma'am?" He couldn't even look at her, he was so embarrassed.

She turned her back toward him and quickly wiped her face.

"Please forgive me. I meant to tease Gus. I didn't mean to hurt your feelings."

Emily mumbled something behind her hanky.

"Sorry, ma'am. I didn't catch that," Johan said, coming around to see her face.

Emily rolled her eyes and suppressed a sob. "I never learned..." She grabbed a tuft of Scotch broom and played with it.

"Ma'am?"

"I never learned to cook. I didn't have to. We always had servants. I thought it couldn't be that hard but I guess I'm terrible at it." Emily dabbed her eyes and nose. "I feel so foolish. I didn't mean to make a scene." She looked back at the house with the warm lamplights glowing out from the dining room.

"Miss Davenport?"

Emily looked straight at him, blushing. "Actually, it's Mrs. Davenport. I'm a widow...now." She pursed her lips to keep them from trembling.

Johan took a deep breath. *Could he dig this hole any deeper?*

"I'm sorry," he said, his face red and avoiding her eyes. "It looks like those rain clouds are not going to hold much longer. Will you come back inside?" He motioned toward the front door.

She hesitated then took Johan's arm, much to his surprise. She wrapped her hand around his wool sleeve. Even through the thick fabric, he could feel the warmth of her hand and it sent a shock through him. He hadn't had a girl on his arm for a long time. It felt good and comforting. He led her to the front door and opened it when she stopped suddenly.

She whispered, "I know I'm a silly woman, but are my eyes all puffy?"

Johan broke into a smile.

She giggled and smiled.

"No, Mrs. Davenport," he said, averting his eyes to the ground. "You look just fine." He glanced back at her face and motioned for her to enter first.

Her clear voice called out, "Luther, did you save me any of those taters?" Laughter filled the dining room and the evening was saved.

Johan let out a sigh of relief. She wasn't entirely uptight. It was too soon to know if she was a gold digger. But what was the point? This girl wouldn't be around long enough for him to find out.

*   *   *

Johan stretched out his back, folding his arms over the end of his rake and looking up into the clear blue sky. His muscles pulled and ached. Only his shoulders fared well as he was used to pulling in his nets. He wasn't accustomed to bending over to weed and pick out rocks from his land. He grabbed a handkerchief from his back overall pocket and wiped his brow. For May, the sun was warm and baking down on him and his uncle in the open field.

"Come on boy, those weeds won't pull themselves!" Frans called from a few rows over. "You getting soft on me? Sitting out in that boat isn't making you weak, is it? This *tapiola* won't turn itself into a farm."

Johan shook his head at the teasing and shoved the handkerchief back in his pocket. His uncle could still almost outwork him at double his age. Impressive. The Finnish work ethic was something to be proud of. They came from good stock. But the bad side of it was trying to shut his mind down at the end of the night. Many times, he'd crawl out of the bunk in his shed to walk out under the stars. His land was becoming an obsession to him. It was his. He would pass it down to his children one day. The Russians wouldn't come and take it from him over here.

Suddenly, two bare feet stood before him in the mud. He glanced up, shocked.

Johan sighed with relief, recognizing his visitor. He extended his hand to the native Nehalem man. "Wah-tat-kum," he said.

The chief took Johan's hand in one of his own and held up a chunk of skinned deer carcass in the other. He grinned, revealing some missing teeth. Around the chief's neck hung a heavy dentalium shell necklace, showing off his wealth. His soft deerskin pants and tunic had his special tribal symbols painted on them.

Johan took the carcass, grateful for the meal he would enjoy that night. "Thank you," Johan said, grinning. He patted his stomach to show his pleasure at the gift.

The chief grinned back at him. He pointed to the ground. "What plant?"

"Same as last year," Johan said, smiling. "Corn, squash, wheat…"

"Good, good," the chief said, surveying Johan's land. "This winter…cold."

Johan raised his eyebrows in surprise. "Colder than last year?" Disappointment must have shown on his face. The chief grinned and patted him on the back.

"Get much deer," he said, serious again. "Skin…dry with salt."

Johan glanced over to his uncle who was bartering with the chief's friends. Johan chuckled at the intensity of the negotiations. One native was trying to keep Uncle Frans' hat. He had it on his own head and began walking away with it.

"Hey there!" Frans called out to him. "Don't be taking that!"

Johan and the chief exchanged knowing glances and walked over to the scuffle.

The chief raised his hand and spoke loudly. "Ka-ta-ta! Give...him." Then the chief proceeded to speak more in his own language to reinforce his order. His brave turned and reluctantly handed the hat back to Frans.

"Thank you," Frans said, patting it down hard on his head. Frans handed the brave their extra ax. The native handed Frans a scraper for skinning deer and elk hides. The brave also pulled a stone knife from his waistband and gave it to Frans.

Nodding his approval, Frans took the gift.

"Must return to longhouse," Wah-tat-kum said, waving to his men. He nodded toward the deer carcass and smiled at Johan and Frans.

"Thank you, Wah-tat-kum," they said, bowing their heads in respect.

Frans turned to Johan and chuckled. "Gifts from the Lord come in strange packages sometimes, don't they, boy?"

CHAPTER EIGHT

"If you step on a stone or billet of wood,
ten to one you measure your length on the ground;
everything is slippery with green moss…"
(Dec 24, Alexander Henry JR. Journal entry)

May 1853

"But I must do something to pay my way," Emily said, pushing her chair back from the Emerson's dining room table.

Gus folded his arms over his chest. "Well, I don't like it. A little woman like you working in the cannery. It ain't right. What would your father say? I'll tell you, he'd say we aren't taking care of you right. That's what he'd say."

Bonnie clucked her tongue. "Quite right. Emily, you need to understand that no respectable woman sets her foot on Taylor Street." She raised her eyebrows for effect.

"Mrs. Emerson, I can't sew. I can't cook. I am not a good nurse, as you have seen. The only school in town already has a teacher, so I can't even teach." Emily perched on the edge of her chair. "I will not take your charity a day longer. If I am to live here, I must contribute. Bonnie, you have your hands full with your family and cooking. I am only under your feet."

"Nonsense, Em. You…set the table wonderfully," Bonnie said, nodding her head and looking to Gus.

He sat back in his chair, disgusted. "I can't believe I'm saying this but I will take you down there this morning."

Emily clapped her hands in victory.

"I'll check in on her at lunchtime, Bonnie," said Gus. "Pack her a lunch pail and let's see how she does."

Bonnie shook her head in disapproval.

Emily walked with her head held high down Taylor Street next to Gus. Bonnie tied a flowery apron on her front to protect her jacket. She tried to secure Emily's skirt on both sides, promising to sew her one that fit soon. Emily's outfit was ridiculous. In New York, she would never have gone out in public in it. But here in Astoria, it was just another symbol of her survival and she didn't care. She was going to work today. Her parents would be on the next ship westward if they knew!

Gus stole a sideways glance and chuckled under his breath.

Emily shot him a teasing glare.

"Ok, stay to this side of the street from here on, Mrs. Em," Gus said, moving to her left side. "You don't want to walk near those, uh, businesses."

A shrill whistle sounded from the other side of the street.

"Who you got there, Emerson?"

"What would Bonnie think, Gus?"

"She's a little young for ya, don't ya think?"

Gus' face matched his red beard. "That's it!" He pounded one fist into the other.

"No, Gus," Emily pleaded, grabbing his arm. "Let's just go to the cannery. Then everything will be fine."

"You can think that, if you want to," Gus mumbled. He wiped his nose on his sleeve. He put his hand on her lower back, hurrying her along.

The huge, square building ahead wafted with the smell of salmon a block away.

"Whew! Fishy!" Emily complained, pinching her nose.

Gus pulled her hand down. "You ain't gonna want to do that, dear. Breathe it in 'cuz that's where you'll be workin'. The sooner your little nose gets used to that, the better."

Emily breathed in deep and coughed. "It's really, uh, something, isn't it?" Her eyes watered with the acrid smell of fish guts and stale salt water.

Gus led her to the door where a tall man stood wearing a bloody apron. His rotund belly blocked the entrance.

"George! How are you?" Gus shook the man's hand with a firm pump. "Emily, this is George Bell, Astoria's cooper. He builds the barrels for the fish you're gonna slime."

"Slime?" Emily gasped. "Mrs. Emerson said I would be cutting them up. She said nothing about slime." Her face went white.

George folded his arms across his chest and howled. "What little nymph is this, Gus?"

"She's, uh, well her name's Mrs. Davenport," Gus said. "She'd like to work for ya. She's one of the survivors of the *Sophia*. Her, uh, husband didn't make it."

George looked over at Emily. She set her jaw and held her chin high.

"This young lady would like to work until her affairs are settled, it seems," Gus said, looking to Emily.

"That's right," Emily said. "If you will teach me, I'll work hard, Mr. Bell."

"It's going to be a lot of hard work. It's going to be long hours. It's going to be wet and cold. It won't always be fun, but it is fun sometimes." George smiled. "You'll be cleanin', guttin' and packin' these fish." He stopped to examine her face. Emily nodded once and set her jaw. "We rub the salmon down with salt and pack 'em in those wooden barrels. Well, let's give it a try, shall we?" George led Emily into the dark cannery. Gus stood at the door and watched her stand at the first table piled high with salmon.

Emily pressed her fist to her mouth then squared her shoulders.

"So, you're gonna cut, scrape and clean these fish here. See this incomplete fin cut. That blood has got to go. You gotta wash it out real good like," George told her.

"Oh Lord, help her," Gus mouthed. He turned on his heel and headed for the boathouse where he worked with his neighbors, Charles Veith, and Job Aitkem.

Emily's fingers froze to the bone. She sliced one with the razor sharp knife. She tore some material off the end of her shirtwaist to wrap it. It bled through in less than a minute. Her lower back ached from standing on the hardwood floors all morning. The chill blasting through the building froze her to the core. She tried to focus on her work in front of her. The pile of fish would keep her busy for a week, much less today. But most distracting were the sideways glances and snickers from the other men and women working.

"Prinsessa..." snickered the young woman next to her.

"Siistia..." another man whispered. The girl worker next to him giggled. She was looking at Emily until their eyes met then she glanced away.

"Hajua koten lohen..."

"That's enough," grumbled George, walking down the aisle. He stopped in the middle of the warehouse and looked over his workers. Everyone dropped their heads and went on sliming.

One woman, two tables over, snorted back a giggle. Emily lost it. She ran through the cannery, out the back door to the docks. She stood at the railing above the river and dug her nails into the wood. Nausea overtook her and she emptied her stomach into the river. She spit and was about to wipe her mouth when another wave of sickness came over her. The stench from the cannery made her head spin.

"Hey there, girl. You alright?" A sailor called from down the boardwalk. He had his arm slung over a woman in a red and black taffeta dress.

Emily blushed and turned away from them. She wiped her mouth on the edge of her flowery apron. Blood and fish guts covered most of it. "Oh, I ruined it," she murmured, wiping her hands on the sides of her skirt.

"Thanks for feeding the fish," called a voice below her.

Emily glanced down. Another sailor had his row-sail tied up not far from her vomit on the top of the water. A swarm of fish tumbled over each other where she had gotten sick.

"Oh!" Emily stepped back, disgusted.

The sailor bent over, laughing.

Emily's face flashed red. She turned hard on her heel, determined to finish her day. She bumped into the bloody apron of Mr. Bell.

"How you doin', Mrs. Davenport?" he said, examining her face. "You 'bout done yet?"

"No sir," Emily whispered, trying not to upset her queasy stomach. "I will finish my work."

"Atta girl," he said, smiling. "And don't you worry 'bout those Finns. They mean you no harm. They just ain't seen nobody like you in the cannery before. They aren't a mean sort of folk, understand."

"Thank you, Mr. Bell," Emily said. She put her shoulders back and walked through the doors. "If you would have told me three months ago that I would be here, I would have called you crazy," she mumbled. She strode past the Finns' stares to her table. She grabbed her knife and got back to work.

*   *   *

"Mr. Bell," Emily said, as she opened the Emerson's front door. "What brings you here?"

"Well, dear," said Mr. Bell, handing her a few dollars and odd cents. "I'm gonna have to let you go."

Emily put her hand to her chest. "But why? I know I'm not as fast as the other workers but that's because I'm new."

Mr. Bell just smiled and shook his head. "Ma'am, you did your best, there's no doubt about that." He chuckled and coughed. "You'll just die of starvation if I keep you on."

Emily blushed. He was referring to her vomiting all day. "I'm sure I will get used to the smell, sir."

Mr. Bell laughed. "You been there all week. No change, ma'am. I'm sure there's something work-wise better fitted for you in Astoria. Sliming is a tough job. I don't want to be the employer responsible for your lost fingers." He chuckled.

Emily hid her bandaged fingers behind her apron and flushed red. She gripped her wages in one hand, and extended her other to Mr. Bell. "Thank you for the opportunity, Mr. Bell. I'm sorry it didn't work out."

He shook her hand and walked back down the front stone path. He reached the end and looked back at her. "You'll do fine here, ma'am. Just don't give up."

Emily didn't trust herself to speak. She just waved. Then she stepped inside and closed the door. Sinking onto the loveseat, she held her few dollars in her lap.

Just then, the front door opened. Gus and his boys came in.

"What was Mr. Bell doing over here?" asked Spurgeon.

"Kinda unlike him to come down all this way, ain't it?" Luther said.

"*Isn't* it!" chimed in Bonnie from the kitchen.

"Isn't it?" Luther repeated, shucking off his boots by the door. "Hey, Mrs. Em! I didn't see you there."

"Hi Spurgeon, Gus, Luther, Henry." Emily smiled weakly. She set her money on the seat next to her. Her filthy apron still covered her skirt. She stood and pulled it over her shoulders and rolled it up.

Gus pulled off his boots and padded over to her in his wool socks. "There, there, girl," he said. "You made a good go of it. I tried to warn you."

Emily reached down and took her wages off the couch. She handed the money to Gus. "I know it's not much, but please take it. It's all I can do to repay you for your kindness right now. When my letter reaches my parents, I'll be able to do more."

Gus folded her hand back over the money. "You just hang on to this for a bit. Looks like you could use a few things." He glanced down at her ill-fitting skirt and smiled.

"I am a sight, aren't I?" Emily giggled through tears, in spite of herself. She drew in a deep breath. "Well, at least I can wash out this apron." Emily called to the kitchen, "Point me to the lye and washboard, Bonnie. I'll have this done in no time."

"Back porch, dear," Bonnie called back. "Dinner in a few minutes. I made salmon!"

Emily shot a look at Gus, then the boys, and ran out the front door. She threw up in the rose bush beside the path. "I'm so sorry," she said, still hunched over.

Gus and the boys just laughed.

CHAPTER NINE

"...to our shame, the moral aspects of Seattle are quite similar to those of Astoria, the liquor prevails, and religious influences stand in the background, as with us. Saloons and tippling shops are met with on almost every corner. There must, however, come a day of reckoning..."
- The Weekly Astorian – March 31, 1877

May 1853

The Emerson boys strolled ahead of Emily, Bonnie and Gus, along the docks. Heading to church, they stopped to watch some children paddling around below them in little boats made out of fish boxes. Emily stared in amazement at how these contraptions could even float. Gus leaned over the wooden rail of the boardwalk and chuckled.

"They lather tar on the bottom of the box to make it waterproof," he said.

Emily smiled at the playful splashes of the youngsters with their homemade oars. "Aren't you worried they'll drown?"

"Nah," Gus said, smiling. "Those boys will paddle all over this river before we get out of church today."

"Their parents won't take them to church?" Emily asked, turning to Bonnie.

"Fishermen put in some long hours at work," Bonnie said, shaking her head in disapproval. "Some are trying to send for sweethearts back east. Some are just trying to forget the life they had before Astoria. Either way, this is not a real church-going town. We're fortunate to have Reverend Malcolm. He only arrived last year."

"Nice young fella," Gus said, straightening and grabbing Bonnie's hand to continue their walk. "Kind of conservative and uppity, if you ask me, though."

"Gus," Bonnie shushed him. "We're blessed to have some religious training here at all. We'd have to go to the Lutheran church if Reverend Malcolm didn't start the Methodist one for us."

"Now, now," Gus chided. "Johan attends the Lutheran church and enjoys it just fine." He leaned over Bonnie to speak to Emily. "A town of three hundred people and we still have our divisions of religion. Cryin' shame, ain't it?"

"Isn't it," Bonnie murmured.

"What?"

"Never mind."

Emily snickered into her handkerchief and lifted her skirt front as they climbed the hill.

"Watch your step now, little lady," Gus said. "Mind those patches of moss. They'll surprise ya and you'll be on your backside before ya know it!"

Emily always enjoyed attending church but this service was very different from her own church in New York City. This service, with the common hymn singing and short sermon was a pleasant surprise. Even though both churches were Methodist, they couldn't have been more opposite.

Her church back home had long pews and high vaulted ceilings. The music of a pipe organ filled the huge cathedral and made the walls shake. Floor to ceiling stained glass windows lined the walls.

Meanwhile, the dark walls and hardwood floors of this church in Astoria felt rustic but cozy. The small choir of faithful congregants filled the chapel with sincere, but not-so-polished melody. But at the front there was a large stained-glass window displaying Peter, the disciple, holding a fishing net. The sun's rays broke through a cloud behind the disciple. The window captivated Emily. Next to this window was another one with a fishing boat. The mast made a large cross in the background with an open sail in front of it. Emily was taken with the beautiful artwork of these pieces. They didn't seem to fit in Astoria at all. She stared at the artwork throughout the whole sermon catching little pieces of the message here and there.

Emily glanced around during the hymn singing to see if the church had a piano. Ever since she was a child, she regularly sang for the services and played piano, when needed. There was no piano in this church yet. *Pity.* Perhaps she would donate one if she sold her property. It would be an honor to help advance religion in this town. Enough people, certainly, advanced the corruption.

"Are you ready, dear?" Bonnie tapped Emily's arm.

"Oh yes, pardon me," Emily said, startled. "Over already?"

"Yes," Bonnie whispered. "One of the Methodist church's blessings is that the Reverend isn't long-winded."

"Thank the Lord," Gus chuckled.

Reverend Malcolm, a young man, who looked to be in his late twenties, approached them. He wore a trim black suit, crisp white shirt with a black clerical collar. It matched his nearly black hair. "Mr. and Mrs. Emerson," he smiled, heartily shaking Gus' hand. He turned to Emily. "Mrs. Davenport, how are you today?"

Emily blushed at the title which seemed more fitting for her mother-in-law than for herself. She felt her cheeks grow warm under the Reverend's gaze. "Very well, thank you, Reverend," she said.

"Please call me Daniel," he said. "Surely, the formalities can go by the wayside. We're all friends here."

He smiled warmly and Emily felt increasingly warm. The air suddenly seemed muggy in the building and she was ready to be outside. Emily stood and straightened her skirts and slid out of the pew to the aisle. "My," she said, dabbing her upper lip with her handkerchief. "Is it normally this warm here in the spring? I could use a cool breeze from the ocean right now." She smiled and excused herself and headed up the short aisle and out the door.

Gus and Bonnie and the Reverend followed her out with the other parishioners. Small families began to disperse and head home. Emily noticed that there were no young women her age who attended. The members were well-dressed upper class businessmen and their wives. A few children were part of the service but were relatively quiet and well-behaved. It seemed that Reverend Malcolm was the only candidate from church to be a friend to her.

Henry, Spurgeon and Luther spoke with the Reverend and he seemed to loosen up a bit when they conversed. As soon as an older person came near, the Reverend put on his pastor role and kept to serious conversation.

"Daniel?" Emily asked. "Where did you obtain the stained-glass windows from? They're lovely."

"I noticed you admiring them," he said. "We had them put in shortly after I arrived in Astoria."

Gus piped up. "What the Reverend isn't telling you is that he made the windows himself."

Emily glanced from Gus to Daniel. "Is that true? They are wonderful," she said. "How did you learn to make them?"

"My grandfather taught me. He raised me." He shrugged. "You could say I followed in his footsteps in more than one way. He was also a Methodist preacher."

"He must have been sorry to see you come to Astoria," Emily said, wincing a bit at the memory of leaving her own parents. "What brought you here?"

Daniel glanced over to Gus and Bonnie. "Well, it's kind of a long story. Maybe for another time?"

"If you will walk Emily home to Kuntas', we'll go on ahead," Gus said, smiling. "Mrs. Kuntas invited everyone over for Sunday dinner."

"Come along, if you like, Reverend," Bonnie said.

"I'd be happy to," Daniel said, beaming. "We'll follow you shortly."

Emily watched the Emersons walk down Fifteenth Avenue. The boys kept glancing back at her and she waved. A breeze blew up from the bay and the cries of sea gulls filled the air. The sun shone full in the sky and not a cloud could be seen.

"I know it's not the weather that brought you here," Emily teased. "This is the first clear day we've had since I arrived last month."

"Definitely not," Daniel said, tapping the toe of his boot on the step. "I actually felt *called* here."

"Well, it is the 'ends of the earth'," Emily said. "The fields are ripe for harvest...most definitely." She clasped her hands in front of her.

"The fishermen put in such long hours working. When they have time off, they frequent the saloons and dance halls."

Emily jumped in, "Bonnie calls them *hurdy gurdy* houses." She giggled.

"Well, they are certainly no place for respectable folk," he said, hanging his head. "This town is gaining the reputation as one of the most wicked cities in the world. Men disappear suddenly from the bars, never to be seen or heard from again. There's murder in the streets. They lose all of their hard-earned money in one night of revelry."

Emily's face went white and she pressed her handkerchief to her lips.

"Pardon me," Daniel said. "I'm speaking too freely." He glanced out over the river and ran his fingers through his hair. "The devil comes to steal, kill and destroy. He is doing very well in this town so far." He clenched his teeth. "I aim to change that. I don't believe it's a coincidence that these lost fishermen use our church's steeple as their guide to get home from out at sea. My hope is that eventually they will realize their spiritual need and come here." He motioned toward the church building. It was plain and stark white but not entirely uninviting. Spring flowers bloomed all around the building.

Emily nodded in agreement, leaning against the rail to the steps. "You seem determined and like you said, you feel called."

Daniel smiled back at her. He stooped to pick one of the red geraniums beside the steps and handed it to Emily. "The question is, do you feel called here?"

"I...don't know yet." Emily turned away from him and looked up the hill at her property just a block away. Her land was situated on 15th and Franklin Avenue near the Methodist Church. The tall spruce and Douglas fir trees on her lot seemed to beckon her. It was a pretty piece of land. But was it for her? "There's much to decide on whether I go or stay."

"If it would be pleasing to you," he said, tentatively, "I would love to teach you how to make stained-glass windows."

Emily turned back to the preacher. "Really? I would like to learn. I need something to keep me busy. There's not much I know how to do here it seems."

"I plan on putting them in around the whole building." Daniel surveyed the side of the building. "So few things point to the Lord, I'd like to tell the story of salvation with the windows. That way, any passerby will see the Gospel without even stepping foot in the church."

"What a wonderful idea, Reverend," Emily said. "Genius, in fact." She smiled her approval.

His whole face lit up. "Well, I bet you are ready for your Sunday dinner." He extended his elbow. "Shall we?"

They started down Fourteenth Avenue just as two rough-looking characters made their way up the hill.

"Hey Preacha!" one man called in a drunken drawl.

"I'm gonna tell him what you did last night, Riley!" the other man said, shoving his friend hard.

The first man stumbled backward and shook with rage. "If I done told you once, I done told you a thousand times, Red, don't-touch-me!" He pulled a knife from his pocket and the blade gleamed in the sunlight.

"Oh Reverend!" Emily shrieked. "He's going to cut him!"

Daniel pushed Emily behind him and held his hands out to the men. "Gentlemen, please, stop this right now."

The man named Red spun around to face the Reverend. He held his hands up in mock surrender. "There ain't nothing to be concerned with here." A string of spittle dripped from his mouth and he wiped it on his sleeve.

Emily turned away in disgust.

At that moment, Riley charged Red with the knife and stabbed it into his side.

"No! Stop!" Daniel cried, grabbing the armed man and pulling him off the other. "For goodness' sake, stop!"

Red fell to the ground in pain, clutching his wound. Blood seeped through his stained chambray shirt. Daniel held his opponent away and tried wrestling the knife from his hand. Though the man was drunk, he was no amateur with a knife. He snapped it closed and pushed past Daniel to get to the man lying in the dust.

"Get off of him!" Daniel shouted. "Get out of here!"

Emily stumbled backward toward the church, never taking her eyes off of the horrific scene in front of her. Just then, she felt two strong hands on the sides of her arms. She shrieked with fear.

"Emily! It's just me," Johan said. He led her back a few more steps, depositing her safely on the church steps. Then he ran to the brawl in the street. With one well-landed blow from Johan, Riley slumped to the dusty street and didn't move. Next Johan grabbed the Reverend's hand and pulled him to his feet.

Daniel's black suit was covered with dirt. Blood stained his Sunday white shirt. "Oh bother," he muttered, dusting himself off.

Johan turned to the wounded man on the ground next. He lifted his shirt up to assess the extent of the wound.

"Will he…die?" Emily called, her eyes wide with fear. She gripped the rail beside the stairs.

"Oh no," Johan said. "He will need some cleaning up and stitches, though. I bet Bonnie would see to it."

"She's on her way to Kuntas' for Sunday dinner," Emily said, wringing her hands. "Daniel and I were just on our way there now when *this* happened."

Johan shot a quick glance over at the preacher when Emily mentioned his Christian name.

Daniel swatted the dirt off his pants and walked gingerly over to Emily. She still clutched her flower between her fists. The petals were strewn all over the ground around her. "So much for a lovely, Sunday afternoon stroll," he said, with a crooked smile. He exhaled and gave her his arm again. "Shall we try to get you home in one piece, Emily?"

"What about that man, Daniel?" Emily gasped, avoiding his gesture. She ran to Johan's side and stooped beside the wounded man. "Johan, will you need help with him? What can we do?"

Johan straightened. "Reverend, if you could take one arm. I'll take the other. We need to get him some help."

"What about Mrs. Davenport?" Daniel rebutted. "Who will look after her, may I ask?"

Johan looked over at Emily and smiled. "I'm pretty sure that she is quite capable of looking after herself." He dropped his eyes to the ground and she blushed.

Emily felt her pulse quicken and she cleared her throat. "He's right," she said, tossing her flower to the side. "I'll be fine. This man needs help. Let's go."

The disappointment that crossed Daniel's face spoke volumes. Neither Johan or Emily missed it but both chose to ignore it as they carried Red down the hill. Riley would have to wake up on his own and face the headache Johan Nevala blessed him with.

Emily walked beside Johan down the hill while Daniel took the other side. "So, Mr. Nevala," Emily said, teasing. "I'm glad to see you made it to church this morning."

CHAPTER TEN

*"If you have run with footmen and they have wearied you,
then how can you contend with horses?"*
Jeremiah 12:5

Mrs. Kuntas swung open her back door and gasped. She started rattling off in Finnish. "Come in, come in," she said to Johan. "Take him up these back stairs to the last room on the right. Is the Reverend hurt too?"

Johan spoke back in Finnish. "No, just the man. Would you have Bonnie come up and help us?" He was already heading toward the stairs.

Mrs. Kuntas grabbed Emily's arm before she followed. She spoke in broken English, "You, wait here minute." She pulled some clean towels and a sewing basket off a shelf and put them in Emily's arms. "I bring up hot water and candle for needle."

Emily stood there, confused.

"You go now. Follow boys." Mrs. Kuntas waved her away and Emily jumped to obey.

She tiptoed up the back stairs and almost ran into a sailor coming down them.

"Well, hello there," he said, leaning against the wall to let her pass. "What's yer name?"

"Excuse me," Emily said, sliding past him. He reeked like the docks, the stench of alcohol and vomit. It turned her stomach. She pressed her nose into the towels until she reached the top of the stairs.

"Tommy!" the sailor on the stairs called behind her. "Look what's coming! The Wigwam don't got any girl like the one we got here at Kuntas."

Emily glanced back down the stairs to make sure the sailor didn't follow her. She bumped into someone and spun around. Another raunchy sailor barred the hallway. He leaned on one wall and crossed his feet against the other wall, blocking her way.

Emily flushed crimson and her heart began to race. Men made their rude remarks on the street but she was never this close to them. The sweet smell of chewing tobacco reached her nostrils and her stomach threatened to throw up. "Please excuse me," she whispered, afraid she would be sick.

The sailor leaned against the other wall. But just as Emily tried to pass him, he reached his hand across again, blocking her way.

She stepped back, now angry and afraid. "There's a hurt man down there. Please move, sir." She said more firmly. She set her jaw and clutched the bundle in her arms.

"Old Red'll be fine," the sailor sneered. "I'm the one that needs some attention, little lady." He reached for her and Emily stepped back. Her foot teetered on the top step and she reached for the wall to steady herself.

"Whoops!" the first sailor said from behind her. "You almost fell. Here let me help you." He put his hands on Emily's waist.

"Help! Johan!" she cried and scrunched down to the floor to escape their groping hands and foul breath. She spilled the clean towels and the sewing basket tipped and dumped.

The door opened down the hallway. Johan reached the sailors in two steps. He yanked the first one away from Emily and into an open doorway. The hard crack and thud of his fist was all Emily heard before he was back in the hallway for the next sailor.

"I didn't mean nuthin'," the sailor shrieked as he ran down the stairs. The back door opened and slammed shut.

Johan stooped to help Emily up. She leaned against the wall, shaking. He tossed the sewing basket items back into it and grabbed the towels in his other hand. "Come on now," he motioned her to walk before him. "You better stay near me today. Seems the whole town had a little too much to drink last night."

They walked into the small room with Red lying on the bed, soaking the clean sheets with his blood.

"Gruesome, isn't it?" Daniel Malcolm said, as they entered. "He passed out a moment ago. We've got to stop this bleeding or this poor soul will be in dire straits. Did you say Mrs. Emerson is on her way up?" Daniel's face was white and clammy.

Johan looked between him and Emily who was pretty shaken up from the incident in the hallway. "You two sit…or head downstairs to dinner. I'll go get Bonnie and see to Red," he said.

"I'll stay and help," Emily said, clenching her jaw and straightening the front of her dress.

"Of course I'll stay and help, too," Daniel said. He offered the one chair in the room to Emily and stood in the corner with his arms crossed tightly over his chest. "I'll pray for the poor fellow."

Emily pulled the chair closer to the bed, grabbed a towel and began applying pressure to the wound to stop the bleeding. "I'll pray, too," she said.

Johan nodded and ducked out the door and down the back stairs.

"Emily?" Daniel asked.

"Yes?"

"This is what I meant about this town," he said. "Those who are pure of heart are few and far between here. It might be best if you remarried so you have some protection and covering here."

Emily gulped hard and felt the heat rising up her neck. "Reverend Malcolm, it has only been a month since my husband died. I hardly feel ready to remarry yet." Her face flushed and she concentrated on the patient in front of her. "I don't know if I'll even stay here."

"Of course," he said. "I didn't mean to impose anything on you. I simply wanted to advice you in case no one else has spoken to you about these things."

Emily cleared her throat and stifled a laugh. "Everyone...no *almost* everyone has already spoken to me about these things. Every person I talk to has great advice about what I should do. I could remarry here. I could remarry in New York. But you know what? I don't know if I ever will remarry. Maybe I will build a house out on Tongue Point and live like a recluse with the Indians. That's it! I'll learn to live like the natives and no one will bother me."

"Pardon me, ma'am," Daniel Malcolm said, his voice tight. "I didn't mean to offend you. I just want you to know that I would be honored to help you in any way I can."

Emily looked down at the floor, embarrassed for her outburst. "Please excuse me for my emotions," she said. "I haven't really been myself today. This town is insane."

Daniel Malcolm snorted, trying to hold in his laughter. Emily giggled in return.

Just then, Bonnie walked through the door with Johan following. They stopped short, seeing them laughing. "I didn't realize stitching up a patient was so much fun," she said, frowning. "How bad is he?" Emily stood and offered Bonnie her chair beside the wounded man. "Whew! That's a lot of blood." She lifted the towels and let out a whistle. "I've seen worse. There was this time on the wagon train coming out west that Gus took a tumble. Seems that he fell asleep..." Bonnie rambled on to Daniel about stitching up Gus' head while she worked on Red's wound.

Emily turned away so she didn't have to watch the needle going in and out of Red's skin. Johan stood beside her, keeping an eye on Emily's face to make sure she didn't faint. "Is he doing alright?" Emily asked Johan. "Does Bonnie need me to go fetch anything? More towels?"

"He's fine," Johan said. He barely got the words of out of his mouth when Red sat up in the bed and howled.

"What you doin' to me, woman?" he cried. "Trying to kill me?" He tried swatting the needle out of Bonnie's hands.

Johan lunged forward and grabbed Red's hand and held it to the bed. "Sit still," Johan ordered. "She's just putting you back together." He turned to Daniel. "He's going to need some whiskey. Will you go get some from Mrs. Kuntas?"

"Don't you think he's had enough, Mr. Nevala?" Daniel asked, throwing his hands up in the air.

Johan dropped his head and took a deep breath, trying to hold the struggling man. "Reverend," he said, in a strained voice. "Would you want to be stitched like this without some help?"

Daniel shook his head once and said, "No, I suppose not. I'll be back in a moment." He disappeared out the door in search of Mrs. Kuntas' whiskey.

Red flailed on the bed in pain.

"You're only making this worse, Red," Johan said, pinning him down. Blood spurted out from the wound. "Please hold still for Bonnie."

Tears escaped Red's eyes and Emily felt compassion for him. He was dirty and scruffy and reeked from a night in the saloon but he was a human being in pain. Her heart hurt for him. She began to pray when the door opened again.

Mrs. Kuntas held her glass bottle of Scotch whiskey and a shot glass in her hand. "Like I say, Reverend," she said in her thick Finnish accent, "this only for emergencies."

"I'm sure it is, Mrs. Kuntas," Daniel mumbled. He walked over to the window and opened it partially for some fresh air. The room was growing warm and the air was stagnate with all the bodies in there.

Mrs. Kuntas was giving Red a whiskey shot when a loud cry came from outside. Everyone in the room froze and Daniel threw the window fully open. He stuck his head outside to see what the commotion was about.

"A man just fell from the upstairs window!" he cried, pulling his head back in.

Emily ran over to his side and looked out as well. A sailor lay on his back in the thick mud of the river. The tide was out so he was in no danger of drowning. He narrowly missed the rocks below his window at Karhuvaara's Boardinghouse. Raucous laughter came from the upstairs window across from them.

"Jimmy! This is the second time this month you done fell out this window! You crazy coot!"

"You gonna break yo neck one of these times!"

"You be nuttier than a squirrel on gin, Jimmy!"

The boy in the mud looked no older than Emily. He folded his arms behind his head and laughed as he sank into the black muck.

Daniel and Emily looked at each other in disbelief. "God will judge this town for its wickedness, mark my words," Daniel said.

Mrs. Kuntas looked up from the patient who was now relaxing. "I make kala soppa, rieska and kaali kaaryle for dinner. Reverend, why don't you go eat with men? Miss Emily, you hungry, dear?" Mrs. Kuntas continued, "Johan, I need you stay and hold crazy man. Kylla?"

"Kylla. I mean yes, ma'am," Johan said, smiling at Emily.

Emily made hand motions behind Mrs. Kuntas asking what she said in Finnish. "She just said that fish stew, bread and cabbage rolls are ready downstairs," Johan whispered. "Go eat. We'll be fine." Red let out a scream and started sobbing. Johan grimaced. "Yep, we'll be just fine. Mrs. Kuntas, why don't you give him another shot."

CHAPTER ELEVEN

"There is no medicine like hope, no incentive so great, and no tonic so powerful as expectation of something better tomorrow."
- Orison Swett Marden

Bonnie stepped into Emily's bedroom. "Emily, this is Sikkus," she said, smiling. "She is the midwife I told you about."

Sikkus Lattie, the Native American widow of Alexander Lattie, stepped into Emily's bedroom. Through the feverish sweating of her morning sickness, Emily tried to sit up for her visitor. But the dark-skinned woman hurried forward and placed a gentle hand on Emily's shoulder and shook her head. She removed her deer skin cape and set it on the chair nearby. She removed her cedar cone-shaped hat on top of it. Her dress resembled Emily's own simple frock with the fitted top and gathered waist. But to Emily's surprise, the woman wore no shoes or boots. Her broad barefoot feet plodded silently across the floor as she turned back to her patient.

Bonnie put her hand on Sikkus' shoulder and smiled. "There is no one better to help you right now, dear." She turned to Sikkus. "Here is your basket and some hot water."

Bonnie set the tea pot and cup on a towel on the dressing table and Sikkus went to work. The native woman took a mortar and pestle from her basket and began grinding up raspberry leaves, dried mint and goldenrod together. The dentalium shell beads from her necklace jingled while she worked. When the leaves ground to a fine powder, she took a pinch and rubbed it between her fingers. She turned to Emily and smiled broadly. "This help you."

Emily just nodded and smiled through the queasiness in her stomach. A wave of nausea hit her and she leaned over the side of the bed and emptied her stomach into the pewter bedpan. A cold sweat broke out on her brow and she leaned back in bed with a sigh.

Sikkus clucked her tongue and shook her head. "She not good," she said to Bonnie. She pinched the skin on Emily's arm and released it. "Need more water. Too thin."

Bonnie nodded in agreement. "She can't keep anything down lately. That is why I called you here." Bonnie furrowed her eyebrows and pursed her lips. "You think this fusion will help?"

"Yes, will help," Sikkus said, sternly. She put a few pinches of her concoction into the tea cup and poured hot water over it. She swirled the liquid in the cup around a few times and smiled. "This good and strong."

Bonnie helped Emily sit up against her pillow. Emily smelled the tea and smiled weakly. "Smells good," she whispered, still not trusting her stomach to behave. It grumbled in protest. Closing her eyes, she sipped a bit of the tea. Mint filled her nostrils with a hint of raspberry. It was delicious. She waited for it to settle in her stomach before trying more.

"Drink whole cup." Sikkus said to Emily, with her fists on her hips. "Any time feel sick. Make more." She grinned approvingly at how Emily's face relaxed. "Good, yeah?"

Emily sipped a bit more. "Yes," she said, reaching for Sikkus' hand. "It's very good. It's helping already."

Sikkus turned to Bonnie. "She need more fat. Too thin. Baby need fat. Feed her meat. Make bigger. Lots of salmon."

Emily's face turned green. She retched into the bed pan again, surprising Sikkus.

Bonnie chuckled. "Salmon is not such a good idea. Maybe chicken and venison?"

Sikkus watched Emily's face and grinned. "Fish not good, yeah? Deer good. Elk. She need meat and milk stuff."

Emily wiped her mouth with her small hand towel. "No, fish not good." She leaned back against her pillow again and closed her eyes.

"Check baby?" Sikkus directed her question to Bonnie.

"Emily?" Bonnie said, touching her hand. "Sikkus wants to check the baby, just to make sure everything is coming along fine. Is that all right with you?"

Emily nodded her approval without opening her eyes.

Sikkus pulled up a small wicker chair to the bedside. She folded the covers back and rubbed her hands together to warm them. Placing one hand on the left side and the other on the right side of Emily's abdomen, Sikkus closed her eyes and pushed in gently. "Mmmmmm," she murmured. "Uh-huh." She moved her hands around expertly, pressing here and there. After a minute or so, she opened her eyes and grinned. "All good. Baby be fine." Sikkus stood and put her chair back. "I leave with you, Miss Bonnie." She motioned to the basket of herbs. "I bring more later. Next week."

"Thank you, Sikkus," Bonnie said, walking around the bed to take her hand. "Our poor girl needed some help. She'll do fine now."

Emily opened her eyes and stretched her lips into a thin smile. "Thank you so much," she whispered, reaching for Sikkus' hand. The native woman took it and squeezed. "You have healthy boy. You see."

Emily's eyebrows arched in surprise. "A boy?" She shot a glance to Bonnie and back to Sikkus. "How can you know it's a boy?"

Sikkus tapped her forehead and her heart. "Me just know." She tilted her head and grinned. "You see." She pulled on her cape and hat. Turning to Emily, she smiled and said, "See soon."

"Thank you, Mrs. Lattie," Emily said, her hands on her abdomen.

"You call me Sikkus. We friend now." With that, the Clatsop woman was out the door and padding down the stairs with Bonnie following.

Emily took another sip of the hot drink and looked out her window. Spring rain started tapping on the plate glass windows. The cherry tree outside swayed gently with the wind kicking up from the river. A few blossoms broke free and swirled away on the breeze. *A boy?* Was she really carrying a boy? Her husband would have been so proud. He would never know. She pressed her fist to her mouth to stifle the sob threatening to come out. How would she raise a boy without a husband? She didn't know the first thing about training a son. She would have to ask Bonnie. Bonnie's sons were respectful, hard workers. But Bonnie had Gus to help raise them. Who did she have? No one.

Suddenly, Johan's face came to mind. Emily's heart skipped a beat. How dare she think about Johan to raise her son! Yes, he was capable at everything he did but she could not expect him to raise another man's child.

She thought back to her society friends in New York. She always had plenty of suitors before Ronald married her. Surely, there would still be a gentleman who could be a stepfather for her child when she returned home. But the idea repulsed her. She wanted her son to learn how to survive by his wits and skills not just by his family connections, the way Ronald had. A tinge of guilt filled her for feeling this way. There was nothing wrong with Ronald's upbringing. He was well-educated and had all the relationships he needed to set out on his own in Astoria. He did possess a desire for adventure which led them here, after all. Emily shook her head. He would have been shocked at the roughness of Astoria and the immorality. Would he have fit in like the other gentlemen in town after some time? Spending his time divided between Swilltown and a proper home on the hill? Emily wanted none of that kind of a life for her son.

She didn't want to live in town. She decided that she would never build the house on Fifteenth and Franklin as she and Ronald had planned. If she stayed in Astoria, her son would live further away from the corruption of Swilltown.

Johan and his uncle had property just outside of town. Maybe she would visit it with Bonnie and see if they would sell her part of their land for a good price. That is, if she decided to stay in Astoria. Emily put her hands to her warm cheeks. She couldn't believe she was actually considering staying here.

CHAPTER TWELVE

"The soul should always stand ajar. Ready to welcome the ecstatic experience."
Emily Dickinson (1830-1886)

June 1853

Bonnie chuckled while she stirred a huge cast iron pot of beans. "I think it is time to spill the beans, Em."

"Is it that obvious?"

"Your trips to the privy alone would give you away, my dear. You're either pregnant or you really enjoy spending time out there."

Emily changed three shades of red. "I don't want to make the boys uncomfortable. We've become such good friends."

"Friends, huh?"

"Yes, especially Henry and I. He's almost like a brother to me now." Emily looked out the window at the boys chopping firewood in the back yard. They took turns pounding an awl deeper and deeper into an unfortunate redwood. She turned to look at Bonnie when the kitchen grew strangely quiet.

"Brother, huh?" Bonnie held her wooden spoon aloft and had the other fist on her hip. "Do you honestly think my Henry thinks of you as a *sister*?"

"Oh yes," Emily said, surprised. "He told me so the other day on our walk to the market."

"He did, did he?" Bonnie seemed amused. "What did he say exactly?"

"Well," Emily said, leaning on the windowsill. "I believe he said that 'if he ever had a woman in his family, he would want it to be me.'"

"And you think he meant as a *sister*?" Bonnie chuckled and went back to stirring her beans. "Oh shoot, they're burning on the bottom."

Emily felt the heat rise in her chest and face. "Oh Bonnie, you don't think he likes me like that, do you? How could he? He's younger than me and I'm a widow already! Oh dear!" Emily pressed one hand against her neck. "I would never mislead him, Bonnie. I promise you."

"Don't fret now. He's just gonna have a big surprise tonight when he hears your news, that's all. We'll see if that cools some flames a little." Bonnie reached over and grabbed Emily's hand and dragged her near. "You have nothing to be ashamed of. This baby is a wonderful blessing. God will use this child to be a comfort to you."

"A comfort?"

"Don't think I don't hear you crying yourself to sleep at night. I know you're still missing that man of yours."

Emily gasped and flushed crimson. Her eyes burned with sudden tears.

"No one else knows. Men certainly don't pick up on these things but another woman knows. I can tell when your eyes drift off to that man of yours and it's like a storm moving in."

"I've never wanted to seem ungrateful or discontent." Emily sucked in hard and held her breath. "Sometimes I want so badly to go home, Bonnie." She burst into tears. "My mother won't be here when the baby comes."

"I'll be here. Or if you don't want me, there's always Frederika Veith across the way," Bonnie teased.

"No! Lord, no! Not Mrs. Veith. I'd be afraid," Emily sobbed.

Bonnie took her face in her hands. "I'm not used to having a daughter. I'm sorry that I tease when I should just shut my mouth." She smoothed Emily's hair with her hand. "I will be here through it all because your momma cannot. It's an honor." Bonnie stirred her beans a few times.

"What will I do when you go away again?" Bonnie said, her chin trembling.

Emily wrapped her arm around Bonnie's waist and laid her head on her shoulder. "Can I take you with me? You still need to teach me to cook."

"Don't tempt me, child. I just might do it. Leave these men to their own devices." Bonnie waddled over to the window and tapped loud. The boys jerked their heads up. "Dinner!" They took off around the corner of the house.

Bonnie turned around and put her hands on her hips. "They are not gonna take too kindly to you ever leaving, I suspect, especially if that baby is a boy or a girl."

"You said 'boy or girl,'" Emily said, giggling, wiping her tears away. "What would they like better?"

"It won't matter," Bonnie said. "Just parting from you won't be easy, Emmy Lou."

Emily smiled at the new nickname.

"Now taste this," Bonnie held up the spoon for her to sample the beans.

Emily tasted the tip and closed her eyes to savor it. "That's delicious."

"That's what beans are supposed to taste like. Don't let Mrs. Veith tell you any different!" Bonnie grabbed the pot with a huff and whisked it to the table. "Bring those cold cuts and bread and butter, Em."

"Gentlemen," Bonnie said, placing her hands on the table beside her plate. "We have an announcement."

The men kept right on eating and talking amongst themselves.

"That twine is too thin. It won't work, Spurgeon."

"Nonsense, just try it."

"It broke again today. I did try it. It doesn't work. It's too weak."

Bonnie cleared her throat once.

"Henry, pass me some more of those beans, would you, son?"

"Yes sir."

"Father, maybe we should move out into the bay where there ain't so many lines. I think we'll have more luck."

Bonnie cleared her throat again.

Emily blushed and giggled.

"You go too far out and ya got nothing to anchor to, Luther."

"Would you pass me some butter?"

Bonnie started talking in spite of the men. "So Emily?"

"Yes, Bonnie, what is it?"

"When you have the baby, what will you name it?"

Emily giggled and said loudly, "Um, I was thinking of Methusaleh or Hepzabid. What do you think?"

Gus scooped more beans on Luther's plate. "Son, how many helpings have you had?"

"Not but five or six, Father."

"This is it. We'll never make it through the winter with you boys eating like this." Gus ran his hand over his beard.

Emily smiled at Bonnie who was trying to remain calm. Emily winked and said, "Perhaps we should try this New York style." She took her fork and gently tapped the side of her pewter goblet, making a clear bell sound. Instantly, it was quiet. All eyes were on her.

Emily motioned to Bonnie with her hand. "Bonnie, could you?"

"We were trying to tell you that there is going to be a change in this household," Bonnie began.

Gus suddenly rose out of his chair. He pounded his fist on the table. "I am *not* doing my own laundry again, woman."

"Relax, you old goat. I mean…dear," Bonnie smiled and winked at him. "We will have a new addition in a few months."

"Quite right, Mother. I completely agree," Henry said, glancing between his mother and Emily.

Emily raised her eyebrows in confusion.

"Emily needs a bigger room of her very own," Henry said. "This business of her living in that small boardingroom is absurd. I offered her my room more than once but she refused. She needs her own." Henry folded his arms and seemed very pleased with himself. "And I'm going to build it for her. I will cover all the expenses myself."

"Henry, please," Emily protested. This was not going well at all.

Gus stroked his beard, then nodded. "I think that's a wonderful idea. Seeing as how she fits in so well. Bonnie has the daughter she's always wanted. I think that — "

Bonnie stood to her feet and pounded her fat, little fist onto the tabletop. Dishes jumped in protest. "Emily is going to have a baby!"

Emily flushed crimson and put her napkin to her lips.

Henry went white and just stared at her.

Spurgeon, Gus and Luther sat frozen with their jaws resting on the floorboards.

"How did that happen?" Luther asked, looking from his father to his mother.

Gus slid his hand over his face and looked at his youngest son. "Luther, be still."

"A baby? Emily is having a baby?" Spurgeon slapped his hand on his thigh and jumped to his feet. He ran over to her chair and pulled her up. Throwing his arms around Emily, he swung her around. "Congratulations, Em. That's wonderful!"

Henry stood to his feet, resting his fingertips on the table. He straightened his shoulders and walked around the table. He took Emily's hand in his own and kissed it. "Congratulations, Emily. I'll help you however I can. Just ask."

Luther was still confused. "But she's not married, Father."

Gus turned his whole body toward Luther and spoke in a low voice. "She's a widow, son. Her husband died. This is her dead husband's baby."

"Oh." Luther snapped his mouth shut. He whispered, "Sorry, Emily. I forgot you were married."

Emily smiled back at him. "It's alright, Luther. You never got to meet my husband. He would have loved all of you. If he could thank you for your kindness to me, he surely would."

Just then the front door opened and Johan hung his hat on the rack.

Luther jumped to his feet and shouted, "Emily's having a baby!"

Johan's face blanched and he glanced over at Emily and Henry who was still holding her hand. "Congratulations," Johan whispered, avoiding looking at them. He stood there awkwardly for a few seconds. Then he gulped down hard and walked to the door, snatching his hat on his way out.

Bonnie bustled after him, grabbing the back of his flannel shirt before he could leave the porch. "You get back here, Johan Nevala. Don't you dare leave like that. This little lady needs our support right now. All of us."

Johan squared his shoulders and turned to come back in. Whatever Emily needed, he would do. But Henry, now that was another matter! His face went crimson with anger.

Bonnie stopped him by the bench and planted a hand in his chest. "What's the matter with you?"

"How can you stand for this, Bonnie?" Johan whispered hoarsely. "It's not right. Not in the eyes of God."

"You make no sense. Are you still ill?" Bonnie's fists were on her hips. "She's having a baby. She's about five months along. It's starting to show. We wanted the family to know."

"Five months?" Johan was confused. She only came to Astoria three months before. He threw his head back and slapped his hand on his forehead. "I'm a fool."

"Yes, you are behaving very foolish." Bonnie peeked around the corner. Her family was busy planning Emily's "new addition." They were engrossed in talk of the right wood, nails, and wallpaper for her room. "She would never."

"She doesn't think I thought—"

"No, now compose yourself and congratulate this poor girl. This is hard enough as it is. Being a widow and pregnant. Without us, she'd be in dire straits."

They turned the corner to come back in the dining room. Emily looked up expectantly at Johan and Bonnie. She stood clasping her hands in front of her.

"I know this is all so sudden," she said. "I'm still trying to get used to it myself." She shrugged her shoulders and blushed.

Johan went over to her and bowed his head, respectfully. "Congratulations, Mrs. Davenport. That's wonderful news about your baby."

Emily looked to Bonnie who just shrugged and shook her head. Muttering, she took herself to the kitchen to fetch something.

"Thank you, *Mr. Nevala*." Emily said, trying to keep the sarcasm from creeping in too much. "Please take my seat. I'll go grab you a clean plate and silverware. Just a moment."

Johan sank into her seat, still in shock.

"We're gonna be uncles!" Luther wore a silly grin.

Henry was in a pensive mood. He was mumbling about the cost of lumber to build Emily's room.

Spurgeon sat across from Johan, staring at him.

"What, Spurgeon?" Johan smiled, trying to lighten his mood.

"Aren't you happy for her?"

*   *   *

Aren't you happy for her? That question plagued his mind the whole way home. Ginger, his horse, kept stopping and eating grass.

"Come on, girl. It's late. Let's go." He kicked her sides and she whinnied. *Am I happy for her?* She's having a baby. She's a mother. He thought of her differently. She really had been married. She really was a widow. She was carrying *his* baby. Johan felt something rise in his spirit. He wanted to protect her. Instincts came out in him that he never felt before. He wanted to make sure her room was dry and safe and beautiful.

Henry made it clear that he would take care of everything and Johan knew why. Poor boy. He loved her. How could he not? He watched Bonnie tonight and Gus. They did nothing to discourage Henry in his plans. Maybe they were for a match between them. Couldn't they see that Emily was too much of a lady to ever fit in here? She didn't belong here. She wouldn't stay.

That thought hit him like a ton of bricks. *She's not going to stay.* She's only stayed this long because she can't travel now.

What did he care? She'd only been here three months. She'll only stay nine months more, at the very most. She would probably wait until the baby was a few months old to travel. She came from money. Her family would want her back. What would keep her here? Nothing. Absolutely nothing.

Johan rode onto his land. He had ten acres clear cut with a small shed at one end of the clearing for his home. It wasn't much but it was all he needed. He cooked outside over a fire pit. He slept inside on a cot. At least it was dry. But for the first time, Johan looked at his land how Emily would see it. Rugged, unkempt, unworked. No garden, no home. She needed a home, not a room or a shed. She needed real hand-blown glass windows and a flower garden. She needed an ice house and a privy, a crib, a table, chairs and so much more.

Johan Nevala set his jaw and slid off of his horse. It was time to quit living in the past and make something of his future. If he wanted Emily in it, he had some changes to make and fast. Nine months was not enough time but it would have to be. Then there was the matter of Henry. It was time to show this girl that she needed a man, not a boy.

CHAPTER THIRTEEN

"the man who clears an acre of this land builds himself a monument..."
P. W. Gillette – drawn to Oregon by the free land act

"And here we are," Frans said, pulling his wagon to a halt on Johan's property. "Where's Johan? He seems to have forgotten that Sunday should be a day of rest. Nephew," he called, looping his reins around a hook on the seat. "I've brought you some guests!"

The cracking of splitting wood ceased from behind the shed. Johan strode out, pulling his shirt over his head. He tugged it on quickly and tucked in his tails. Bonnie and Emily looked away for a moment. "I...I wasn't expecting company," Johan said quietly to his uncle.

"Well, boy," Frans mumbled back, "If you were in church this morning like you should have been, you would have known that Emily wanted to see our properties. I met up with the Emersons after their service and they asked to come for a drive." Frans turned back to the women and smiled. "They have come bearing gifts."

Bonnie reached behind her on the bench seat and pulled a basket with a gingham napkin on top.

"Bless you, Bonnie," Johan chuckled. "I'm starving. I haven't eaten today."

"But it's almost three o'clock," Emily retorted. "I've never seen people work so hard in all my life." She stood to step down from the wagon. Johan was before her in an instant to help her down.

Frans and Bonnie shared a knowing look. "What are you working on so hard, Johan?" Bonnie asked, looking around. Frans helped her down from the wagon.

"He's splitting beams for the home he's building," Frans answered for him.

"You're building a new home?" Emily asked, glancing over at his shed. "This isn't your home?"

Johan flushed. "No, ma'am. I mean, it is for now. But it's time for a real home." He motioned for her to follow him. "Come with me, I'll show you." They walked around the shed and the smell of freshly chopped cedar still hung in the air.

"It smells wonderful," Emily said. "What kind of tree is that?"

Johan pointed to his first pile. "There's the Port Orford Cedar for the framing. Over there is some Douglas Fir for the ceilings and floors."

"You've been busy," Emily praised. "When did you find time to do all this?"

"My uncle has been helping me in the evenings," Johan said, smiling. As if on cue, Uncle Frans came around the corner of the shed with Bonnie.

"Johan!" Bonnie said, with a fist on her hip. "You will kill yourself with all this work! Why the sudden rush?"

Johan's neck grew red and it crept up to his cheeks. "I...need to get the roof on before summer is over and the rainy season hits."

Uncle Frans wrapped his arm around Johan's shoulder and grinned. "We'll get it done, all right. But not without missing a few Sundays, I suppose." With his other fist, he rubbed Johan in the ribs and doubled him over. "Just remember, God honors those who honor Him, nephew." He tossled his hair and they laughed.

"I'm starving. Do you mind sitting out here while we eat?" Johan asked, eyeing the basket Bonnie held.

Emily and Bonnie made themselves comfortable on the stacked pile of cedar beams. Uncle Frans and Johan sprawled out on the wood chips to eat. They made short work of the fried chicken and buttermilk biscuits with huckleberry jelly. Uncle Frans and Bonnie discussed their vegetable gardens. Johan stood and wiped his hands on his dungarees.

"Would you care to walk around my property?" Johan asked Emily, extending his hand to help her up.

"I'd love to," Emily said, taking his hand. "Where will you build your home? I see you've got this cleared here. How many acres is this open area?"

"I've cleared about ten acres so far," Johan began, strolling slowly beside Emily. "I'd like to build the foundation for the house in that far corner." He pointed to the southeast corner of his property. "I like the view from there and it's closest to the stream for water."

"How long will it take you to build a foundation?" Emily asked, looking over to the future location. "Do you have more help than just your uncle? And how much will it cost to build it altogether? Do you like it out here?"

"Well..." Johan began.

"How big will it be? Oh, and how much work is it to clear a garden spot?" Emily asked, her eyes wide.

"Now let's see, where to begin," Johan laughed. "You sure seem interested in all this. I have to admit that I didn't expect that."

Emily giggled. "I've never built a home before. I'm curious as to what I'm getting into."

"You? You are building a home?" Johan shot a glance over to his uncle and Bonnie, then back to Emily. "I didn't know that."

"I own a lot in town," Emily said, clasping her hands together. "I wanted to come out here today to see how different it is living outside of town. There's no reason I can't sell my lot and live further out, if I'd like to, is there?"

"No, it's a great idea," Johan said, confused. "But why do you want to live out here? Not alone, right? That's not safe, Em."

"You live out here alone and the Indians don't bother you," Emily began. "Why would they harm a woman and her child? I mean them no trouble. In fact, I am friends with an Indian woman named Sikkus. Do you know her?"

"Yes, I know her. She's a very kind woman," Johan said, his eyebrows furrowed. "Do you plan on staying in Astoria then? Even without--"

Emily turned partially away from Johan and blushed. "I am just exploring my options, I guess." She surveyed the different types of trees on his property. "It's really beautiful here. I enjoy the change in seasons." Emily turned back to Johan. "It reminds me of home." She dropped her eyes and looked at her feet. "I don't know what I'll do for sure. I'm still waiting to hear from my parents."

"It's been three months," Johan said. "You will hear from your family soon. Don't worry. Did you tell them about your...uh...baby?"

Emily blushed. "Yes, by the time I sent the second letter I knew." She crossed her arms and sighed. "I know what they'll say. They'll tell me to come right home so they can take care of me. Well, they've done that my whole life. I want to make it on my own. If I sell my property, I'll have some money and my independence."

"You really want that, don't you?" Johan asked, keeping his eyes on his boots. "It's hard without some help though, ma'am." Emily glanced over at him. "I mean, having the money to do what you want is a great thing. But knowing where you want to end up is more important I think. What is it that you want out of life?"

Emily straightened and pursed her lips as tears formed in her eyes. "No one has ever asked me that," she whispered. "Not even my parents or my late husband. They always told me what they thought was best for me but never waited to hear my opinion."

"Well?" Johan asked, meeting her eye now. He smiled and crossed his arms.

Emily brushed away a stray tear and straightened her shoulders. "I want a home of my own with a vegetable garden to one side and a flower garden on the other side," Emily spun around as if looking for inspiration. "I want at least three rooms. One room for my boys, one room for my girls and a big room for me and my..." Emily's face grew red. "Oh goodness, I'm so silly, aren't I? I'm talking to you like one of my school girl friends. I'm sorry."

"No, I like to hear about your dream," Johan said. "If you can't say it out loud to someone, then it might never happen. Don't be afraid. Anything is possible with hard work." He smiled and Emily returned it. "Reminds me of what Gus always says."

"What is that?" Emily asked, tilting her head to one side.

"Emersons' family saying: "beginning is always difficult, work is our joy, and industry overcomes bad luck," Johan said, with a grin.

"My industry *brings* me bad luck," Emily said, giggling. "I've never been more sick than when I tried to be industrious. Maybe under different conditions, I'd do better." Emily placed a hand on her abdomen and patted it.

Johan felt a sudden urge to take her in his arms and hold her and the baby. There was no way he could tell her that the home he was building could be for her, if she would only have him. The timing was all wrong. He couldn't say anything yet. As long as she was willing to stay in Astoria, he would keep building. Now he had a better idea of what it should look like. Three bedrooms and space for gardens. He wouldn't forget.

"Johan?" Emily asked. "If I could sell my lot, would you consider selling me a parcel of your property?"

Johan was so shocked, he didn't know what to say.

"Is that a ridiculous request?" Emily said, suddenly embarrassed. "Here you've worked so hard just to get where you are and some city woman wants a piece of it."

"I hope so," Johan said, quickly.

"Pardon me?" Emily said.

"I meant to say that it would be my pleasure to share part of my land with you, Em." Johan said, grinning. "You're not the type to shoot off shotguns in the middle of the night, are you?"

Emily laughed. "Not usually," she said. "Only when someone gets too close to my rose garden. Then a woman has to do what a woman has to do." She put her fists on her hips.

Johan's eyes were drawn to her tiny waist. It was hard to believe that she was with child. There was not much evidence of it yet.

The practical side of her request was that it wouldn't be accepted socially. No one would approve of a young woman like her living outside of town near two bachelors. But this was Astoria, after all. Many things happened everyday that brought ill repute to the town. No one could raise an eyebrow to an innocent request like Emily's.

"Emily!" Bonnie called from across the clearing. "We'll need to get going soon, dear."

Uncle Frans was helping Bonnie up into the wagon when Johan and Emily reached them. "Time to go, ladies." Frans said. "Did you find out what you wanted to know, Em?"

"I believe so," Emily said, smiling at Johan. "Johan is willing to sell me a parcel, if that's what I'd like to do." She turned to shake his hand. "Thank you for your time and please excuse our invasion of your privacy."

"Any time, ladies," Johan said. "Bonnie knows that I excuse a whole lot of inconvenience with a basket full of good food and some good company." He helped Emily up into the wagon with ease. She turned and placed her hands in her lap. "I'll be praying for you to have wisdom with your business matters," Johan said, with his hand resting on the wagon seat. "You have some big decisions ahead of you."

Emily nodded once. She glanced over at Bonnie and Frans. "Yes, but this is the first time in my life when I feel like I have the support I need no matter what direction I choose. Thank you, Frans, for bringing us out here today. Thank you, Johan, for your generosity. Thank you, Bonnie, for teaching me how to cook and survive out here. It's starting to feel more like home to me. Now let's see what my parents will say..."

CHAPTER FOURTEEN

SwillTown Defined: an unsavory part of Astoria where if one discharged a double barrel gun at close range at any time in the night, he would hit a thief with the contents of one barrel and a prostitute with the other."
- J.F. Halloran reminisces

June 1853
  Bonnie and Emily walked arm in arm east on Bond Street to the Boelling Hotel. Emily wore her dark green jacket and lace blouse with a new black wool skirt with layers of pleats. Bonnie finished her skirt that morning, just in time for her appointment regarding her land. Emily's waistline was changing but no one would be able to tell for another month at least. Right now she felt as put together as she ever had on a New York street. Never mind the saloons lining up one after another, with Female Boardinghouses tucked in between. The burlesques were labeled in large letters as "FB's" as if the men couldn't figure it out on their own.
  The Columbia Bar, the Monitor and the Bonita were already open for the day. Music poured out their doors. A woman peeked out from her "crib" behind red curtains above the Wigwam Saloon.
  "Mr. Boelling seems the logical businessman to ask about your property," said Bonnie, puffing along beside Emily. "He already owns the hotel, a beautiful home and has plans for another school. He and his wife came from Ohio on the Oregon Trail in '47."
  "He's certainly ambitious," said Emily. She gripped Bonnie's arm a bit tighter. "Without the deed to my land, I'm not sure what he can do, though."

"Well, we will see what can be done," Bonnie said, patting the girl's hand. They arrived at the hotel and opened the heavy wooden door with the brass handle. A bell dinged as they stepped into a lovely foyer with coal oil lamps on the walls. The owner's mahogany desk stood in front of them and a handsome, middle-aged man waited.

"Mr. Boelling, I presume?" Emily asked, extending her hand.

"Mrs. Davenport," he answered, with a smile. "The Emersons mentioned that you might come by. How can I help you?"

Emily leaned in and spoke quietly. "I have a few questions about my land here in Astoria." She didn't want to not draw attention from the other guests in the dining room.

"I'll see how I can help," Mr. Boelling said. He stepped out from behind the counter and motioned for the ladies to follow him. They crossed opposite the dining room into a spacious sitting room with Empire couches. "Please, take a seat." He motioned to a plush couch for the ladies while he took the matching chair close by.

Emily sat very straight and tucked one ankle behind the other. She cleared her throat to gain her composure. Her heart was pounding. *If Mr. Boelling couldn't help her, who could?* "Mr. Boelling, as I said, I own some property here in Astoria. It's in my husband's name, Ronald Davenport. It's located on Fifteenth and Franklin. Are you familiar with that lot?"

"Of course," he said, with a smile. "It's a lovely piece of land. I was looking into buying it myself."

"You were?" Emily gasped, turning to Bonnie.

"Yes, it has a few tall trees left on it. Most of the hillside has been stripped of its taller trees to make room for the homes going in." Mr. Boelling leaned in and spoke in a hushed tone. "You wouldn't be interested in selling, now would you, Mrs. Davenport?"

Emily felt her face turn pink. "I...I don't know what I want to do, sir." She suddenly felt warm. "I just lost my husband and we were going to build our home there. Without him, I don't see how I can keep the land." She glanced over at Bonnie. "I can't build the house now. I lost our money at sea when the lifeboat spilled..." Emily felt hot tears fill her eyes and was frustrated with her emotions.

"There, there, dear," Bonnie whispered, touching her arm. "Does she need to sell it right away, Mr. Boelling? There's no harm in taking some time to decide, is there?"

"Of course not," Mr. Boelling said. "You are free to do with your land as you like. John Shively, the county surveyor, here in Astoria is aware of your husband's interests and property. We can check at the customhouse on your husband's other assets. As to the money to build, I'm so sorry that was lost. I don't see how it can be replaced or recovered. Do you have family that can send you more money to build?"

"That's just it," Emily said, slowly. "I don't know if I'll be staying in Astoria now that my husband is gone." She shot a glance over at Bonnie. Bonnie just gave a knowing smile and nodded. "I can't work. I've tried that. I could teach but-" Emily dropped her eyes from Mr. Boelling and her face burned hot.

"May I?" Bonnie asked, squeezing Emily's hand.

"Yes, please." Emily said, pressing her fist to her mouth.

"She is with child, Mr. Boelling," Bonnie beamed. "She won't be able to work but for a few months before the wee one arrives."

"Congratulations, Mrs. Davenport," Mr. Boelling said, patting her arm. "How wonderful! I believe this will be the first baby born in town this year. With only one woman to every three men, there aren't many families here yet. It will be wonderful to see another child around...for a while, anyway. Will you return to New York then?"

"I don't know yet," Emily said, nervously. "The Emersons have been so gracious to let me stay at their place. Their son, Henry, has even added on to the back of it for the baby and I."

"Oh, I see," Mr. Boelling said, nodding to Bonnie. "Well, your property is safe for now. When you know more about what you want, come see me again. The city leaders and I will help you in any way we can." He stood and extended his hand to Emily. She put her gloved hand in his and shook it firmly. He held it for a moment. "Congratulations, ma'am. A baby will be a wonderful blessing to this small community. Maybe it will remind some of our less moral city-dwellers to tie the knot and do things right." He touched his nose and winked.

Emily blushed and smiled. "Thank you so much for your help, Mr. Boelling. I hear you are going to open another school soon, is that right?"

"As soon as I can," he said. "Too bad you will have your hands full. We are looking for the right teacher for our children. You would have been ideal. Good day to you, ladies." He motioned them to the door.

"Thank you again," Emily said, stepping out the door after Bonnie. It closed behind them and Emily let out a sigh of relief. "My land is safe at least." She smiled. "I might even have him as a buyer, if need be."

"What did you expect, dear?" Bonnie said, giggled. "We are not completely uncivilized here. There is some semblance of order. There is some honor among the businessmen of Astoria."

Just then, a gentlemen, in a top hat, stepped out of bawdy house with a blond woman on his arm. Their voices carried over the street to Bonnie and Emily. "Daphne Delight, huh?" the drunk man said, laughing. "Just don't tell my wife..." The woman giggled and leaned over to kiss him right there in the street.

Emily gasped. "Is that man who I think it is? That's the husband of Mrs. — "

"Shhh!" Bonnie grabbed her arm and wheeled her around toward home.

"Does his wife know, Bonnie?" Emily glanced over her shoulder and felt sick.

"Some of the wives know," Bonnie whispered. "But there's nothing they can do about it. These men run the town and pay for their big houses up on the hill. They won't complain too loud."

"Oh Bonnie," Emily said, putting her hand over her mouth. Bile rose in her throat. She leaned over an azalea bush nearby and lost her breakfast. She spat as ladylike as she could and looked at Bonnie with sheepish eyes. "That just makes me sick."

Bonnie chuckled. "I know, dear, me too. Mark my words, if Mr. Emerson ever thought he could get away with anything like that, he would be sleeping in the boathouse on a pile of wood."

"I believe you," Emily laughed. She looped her arm through Bonnie's. They strolled home and the stress she felt that morning lifted. Her land was safe. She glanced over her shoulder at the gentleman with the prostitute. Deep in her heart, Emily resolved that she would not remarry any man if this is how they chose to live. She couldn't bear it if her husband was unfaithful to her. She'd rather not remarry. Who cares if it was considered acceptable to the social class here? She could not and would not accept it for herself or her baby. There had to be something better for their future.

"I think Henry will finish your new addition this week," Bonnie said, with a sideways glance.

CHAPTER FIFTEEN

"There's a romance to fishing, watching the sails out on the horizon with the sun setting behind them – like huge birds flying over the waves...until it starts raining, then the romance is gone. People go inside and earnestly hope, as they are closing their shudders and pulling curtains shut tight, that no boat capsizes. Women and children pray that their father's boat won't drift in the fog outside the bar."

"You're sure this won't upset your stomach?" Johan asked, holding out his hand to help Emily into his boat. The early morning mist still hung over the water and docks.

"Well, I never know for sure, but I have felt better lately," Emily smiled and stepped gingerly into the bottom of the row-sail. She was instantly grateful that her new cotton, burgundy dress did not have the whale bone hoop in it. She almost lost her life due to that silly, oversized skirt. "Are you sure you want me to help you sail this? I've never sailed before. To be honest, I'm a little nervous...since the Sophia sank."

"I rescued you once," Johan said, smiling. "I can rescue you again, if needed."

Emily stood to her feet and started to get back out of the boat when Johan caught her hand and made her sit opposite him.

"I'm teasing you," he said, more seriously. "I would never let anything happen to you. Look over there, by the horizon. You can tell by the sky that the weather will be clear today. It's a perfect day to be on the water. You're going to love this."

"I hope so," Emily said. "If I don't like it, I'll be stuck out here for hours. Good thing I brought a book, just in case." She grinned and patted the satchel slung over her shoulder.

"You won't have time for that out here," Johan said, untying them from the docks at Baker's Bay. The morning chill hung over them as the wind caught in the sails and pulled them out onto the water. The waves lapped softly on the side of the boat. Johan pulled at the oars to propel them more quickly ahead of the other boats leaving the dock.

"Is this a race?" Emily whispered. "You seem determined to win the prize spot out here."

Johan grinned at her between strokes and glanced behind him to check on their progress. "We're going to fish with the tides like everyone else does," he said. "We'll drift down and back up and then we'll go home for the day."

"You make it sound so easy," Emily said, smiling. "Maybe I could have given you the day off and taken care of this for you."

Johan dropped his chin and chuckled before resuming his rowing rhythm. "It's not quite that simple, I guess." He looked out past the bay at the ocean. "You have to know the tide table. You must know which nets to use with the different fishing seasons. Today we're catching Chinook Salmon. Beautiful fish."

"I've never thought of a fish as being beautiful," Emily said, scrunching up her nose. "I guess it takes a man to appreciate their unique…beauty."

Johan laughed. "Almost there. We'll start spreading out our nets right over there."

"Good thing you hurried," Emily said, craning her neck to see where he pointed. "It looks like a good spot."

"Oh, no one would take my spot here," Johan said, straightening his back.

"Why is that?" Emily asked.

"Henry and I cleared the debris from here, that's why," he said with confidence.

"How nice of you to clean up after yourselves," Emily said, giggling.

"No, I mean that we dove down last summer and got rid of the debris and branches off the bottom for our nets." He waited for her to understand. She furrowed her eyebrows, confused. "He who cleans up the area, gets the area. If anyone else tries to fish here, it's called *corking*. This drift is mine. I worked hard to clear it with Henry's help. Newer fishermen have tried invading this space but I just pull ahead of them on the drift tide and take all the fish before the fish can reach their nets. They learn pretty quickly that they're not welcome. There are plenty of drifts on the river and in the bay, there's no need to fight over them."

"Have you ever had to fight someone over your drift?" Emily asked, concerned.

"I've been challenged a few times, but no one wants to come to blows." Johan chuckled. "Most guys are a lot of hot air and foul words, but they leave me alone."

"Especially since I'm with you today," Emily teased. "They wouldn't dare cross me. I'm too intimidating," she said, sitting tall and crossing her arms in front of her.

"You're intimidating, all right," Johan said, smirking. "Most of these rogues will stay away from you because they don't know how to speak to a lady." He avoided her eyes and his cheeks flushed. "Here we are. Will you hand me that end of the net, please?" He held out his hand and Emily pulled the closest end of the net over to him. Their fingers touched just briefly. "That's it, keep it straight. We don't want tangles. It should just lay out on the water."

"How big are these fish today?" Emily asked, noticing the size of mesh in the net. "These holes seem pretty big."

"You should see our sturgeon nets," Johan said, tossing the net over the side of the boat. "This is nothing compared to the monsters we pull in with those."

"Am I going to have to beat something on its head? You never said I'd have to fight for my life today," Emily said, wide-eyed.

"No, you'll be fine. That dress might get a little dirty but I'll do all the killing for you." Johan turned and surveyed his bobbers on the top of the water. "So far, so good. Just a bit more net and we'll be ready."

"How is this going to catch the fish? Don't you need hooks on it?" Emily looked past him at the line with bobbers. She pulled an apron from her satchel and tied it over her dress.

"That's the corkline there on top of the water," Johan said. "The bottom line that rests down at about fifteen feet is the leadline." Johan put his hand through the mesh. "When the fish come in on the tide, they get caught by their gills in the net, trying to swim past it. They can't pull themselves back out and the next thing they know, they're on Mrs. Emerson's table with a bowl of butter. Or they end up in Mr. Bell's barrel packed with salt."

Emily's face turned green at the mention of Mr. Bell's cannery. She put a hand to her stomach.

"Uh oh. Wrong thing to say."

Emily turned her face, closed her eyes and took in a few deep breaths. She reached into her satchel and pulled out a piece of dry toast. After taking a few bites, she broke off a piece and handed it to Johan.

"No thanks," he said. "You seem to need it more than I do. I'm fine. I had a big breakfast with my uncle. Eggs, steak…"

Emily went pale and leaned over the side, emptying her stomach. When she was done, she sat down gingerly and wiped her mouth with her apron.

"Sorry, Em," Johan said.

She just nodded and smiled but didn't trust herself to speak yet. She put one hand on her stomach and felt it begin to settle. "So, what is the largest fish you have ever brought in? Just so I know what to be ready for," she said, attempting a smile.

"Oh, I haven't pulled in anything close to what Mr. Veith brought in last year. He and his son, Hugh, were sturgeon fishing and they thought they hit a snag." Johan smiled in recollection. "Hugh was just about to jump into the river when he spotted a huge, dark shadow under their boat."

Emily shuddered partly from the cool morning and partly from Johan's story.

He continued, "Mr. Veith decided to pull in their nets and see what they were dealing with. They pulled hard. Caught in the net was the largest sturgeon anyone in this area has ever seen. The nose on that monster was six feet long before they even saw its eyes."

"Stop," Emily cried. "You might not want to tell me anymore or I'll be no good to you out here. I'll be so scared I'll refuse to help you pull anything in the boat."

Johan just laughed. "Time to get to work. This will get your mind off of the sturgeon. Hand me the end of that corkline. I'll tie it off up here."

Emily held on tight to the line pulling hard in her hands. She carefully passed it off to Johan. Their fingers touched again as she gave it to him and it sent warmth up her hand. Her face went red and she turned away while he worked.

"Now we wait for the tides," he said. "It won't be long now." He looked out over the bay to the ocean. "This place is like the Garden of Eden."

"Why do you say that?" Emily said, giggling. "This place feels nothing like paradise to me. This is only one of a few mild mornings since I've been here. I confess that I almost backed out three or four times before today."

"I'm glad you didn't," he said, catching her eye. "You would miss all the fun."

"Did you fish in Finland?" Emily asked, pulling her shawl more tightly around her shoulders.

"Yes," Johan said, testing his line. "Every boy fishes in Finland. I lived along a bay much like this one. Gillnetting is second-nature to me. My father showed me how when I was just barely big enough to walk. I've done it ever since."

"That's wonderful," Emily said. "To have a trade to support yourself must be a wonderful thing." She dropped her eyes and wrung her hands in her lap.

"If a man doesn't work…" Johan began.

"Neither shall he eat," Emily finished quickly, smiling at him.

"Right." Johan turned in his seat and checked over his nets. "The best thing about this land is that I'm free. I can make as much money as I can. I can work my land with my own two hands without fear of invasion." His voice caught and he cleared his throat.

"Well," Emily whispered. "What about the natives? Don't they invade sometimes?"

"Not me or uncle, they don't," Johan retorted. "They know we won't hurt them. They don't hurt us. I've learned more about how to survive from them than any white man." Johan glanced over his shoulder toward the shore. The bay was covered with row-sails casting out their nets. The water resembled a broad petal with many butterflies perched on top of it.

Emily followed his gaze. "It's really beautiful, isn't it?"

Johan smiled in return. "Look over there." He pointed along the shore.

Emily strained her eyes and finally caught some movement in the trees. "What is that?"

"Those are some of the Indian women," he said. "They gather berries this time of year to prepare for winter. Every season has its own provision to help them get through the next one. These women will pick huckleberries, salal berries, strawberries and wappato for the winter."

"How will the food keep that long?" Emily asked. "Do they make jelly like we do?"

"Sometimes they make a cake from the mashed down berries," Johan said. "The dry out much of their food to store it until the weather turns cold."

"This isn't cold?" Emily teased, shivering.

"Oh no," Johan said, smiling. "This is about as good as it's going to get here. Enjoy today, it won't last."

Emily nodded and looked out to the ocean. It was breathtaking. This view from the water was entirely different than the view from the church or the shore. She loved it despite the chilly breeze and salty musk from the water.

"Get ready," Johan said, sitting up more straight.

"For what?" Emily asked, looking at him first then following his eyes. "What is that?"

"That's dinner!" Johan said, shooting her a grin. He put a hand on his corkline. "Hang on, we're going to get really busy for a few minutes." He laughed at the incredulous look on Emily's face when the salmon hit the nets. The water frothed around them with the catch.

She broke out into laughter and bounced in her seat. "I've never seen anything like this!" She glanced over to the next boat near them. The tide hit them and they sat ready with their nets as well but their eyes were on her. Emily turned away and shifted in her seat. "Johan, you have to tell me what to do. I want to help you."

He smiled at her and handed her a sharp knife. "Just be ready for any mutinous fish that want to jump ship." The shock on Emily's face made him laugh.

Hours later, Johan and Emily sat in the same spot as they had that morning. The sun was threatening to sink into the ocean and disappear on them for the day.

"It's really breathtaking, isn't it?" Emily said, mesmerized by the glow and warmth of the sunset.

"This part of the day is always my favorite," Johan said. "We'll stay just a little longer after sunset then we'll pull in our catch for the day. You have held up very well. I'm proud of you."

Emily beamed at the compliment. The sky darkened and a few stars began to twinkle over them. Muted voices and clanking equipment could be heard above the lapping of the waves. The water was relatively low and calm and the breeze was still warm from the heat of the day. As the sun inched lower in the sky, the chill crept over the top of the water from the east. Fifty kerosene lamps lit up the night and reflected off the water. The smell of strong coffee and tobacco drifted on the breeze.

Suddenly, an odd sound came from a row-sail across the bay. A Greek, who had not been in Astoria but a few days, stood up in his boat and plucked the strings of his violin to tune it. Some laughter erupted from the boat near by. A scraggly-bearded fisherman bellowed, "Hey Greek! You got some Mozart over there or Beethoven?"

His burly friend piped up, "I'm in the mood for some Bach! Nice little romantic evening we have going on here." He was looking over at Johan and Emily. They blushed at the comment and turned away.

The Greek paid his mockers no attention and laid his bow expertly across the strings a few times. The effect was hypnotizing on the crude fishermen. The sound carried over the water and it was as if the bay were an amphitheatre. Then he began to play, soft and sweet, at first.

The strains of music sent chills down Emily's spine, it was so lovely. She clasped her hands in her lap and closed her eyes to enjoy it more fully. A scale cascaded and descended on his instrument. Even the orchestra and opera in New York City didn't hold a candle to the enchantment of the violinist's song.

Emily opened her eyes to find Johan staring at her. He smiled quickly and looked back at the Greek. The rhythm of the lines rubbing against the boats, the swishing of the waves and the stars above made the moment feel like a dream. She vowed to remember it always.

CHAPTER SIXTEEN

"The spirit of a man is the lamp of the Lord, searching all the inner depths of his heart."

Proverbs 20:27

SUNDAY, July 1853

Emily stood at the edge of Coxcomb Hill near the cliff overlooking Baker's Bay. A sigh escaped her lips. *Oh, for a small patch of sunlight between all these gray clouds.* Her spirit sagged each morning with the lack of sun. But there was always a distraction of some kind at the Emerson household, especially with the "addition" coming.

Henry ordered the final wood and nails needed to finish her new room. She didn't have the heart to tell him that it was unnecessary as she wasn't sure that she would stay long enough to enjoy it. Just this week she leaned more toward going home than staying in Astoria. The baby fluttering in her belly made her ache for her family. The Emersons wanted her to be comfortable and feel a part of their family. But the truth remained, she was an outsider to this small city and sometimes wanted to keep it that way. The idea of staying here forever made her heart race and grow fearful.

Who would marry her now? A widow with a child no less? In New York, she had been the belle of the debutante balls. She had many offers to choose from. Ronald was her parent's choice for her. She trusted them and grew to love Ronald but he was never her ideal. She felt guilty for that now. She placed her hands on her growing abdomen and took in a deep breath. Those beaus from the past wouldn't have her now.

"Are you alone up here, Em?" Johan called.

Emily jumped to see Johan some distance behind her. She immediately smiled to disarm his worry. "I'm fine, Johan, I was just thinking…" She looked back out over the bay.

"What brings you up here today? It's quite a hike. I was surprised to see you here."

"Peace. Quiet. Time to think."

Johan strolled toward her tentatively. "Sometimes it helps to have someone listen." He smiled and his eyes showed his concern.

Emily smiled back but didn't speak right away. She didn't want to seem ungrateful for how she was feeling especially in light of how kind everyone had been.

"Bonnie knows you're here?" Johan asked, trying not to sound meddlesome.

Emily turned slightly to him and grinned, "Of course. I can't leave the house without an estimated return time, the proper chaperone, and so on."

"How did you sneak out today?"

"I said I needed to pray and that God would put His angels around me," Emily said. "Bonnie seemed satisfied with that answer. Who can argue with that anyway?" Emily giggled.

"True." Johan smiled and looked out at the valley below them. He wasn't leaving. He wasn't prying but he wasn't in a hurry to go.

Emily swallowed hard. She could trust Johan. "I don't know what to do." She turned to Johan and shrugged her shoulders. "If I go home, I'll never know what life could be like on my own. I'll be dragged right back into the humdrum society I couldn't wait to leave."

Johan nodded and kept gazing out at the bay.

She continued, "If I stay, I will need to provide for myself and my child. That will mean hard work with skills I don't have." Emily turned to Johan. "I don't sew but I can knit. I can hardly cook though I'm learning from Bonnie but I can orchestrate a dinner party for one hundred guests. I am educated so I could be a teacher. But who would care for my child while I'm working?" She clasped her hands together.

Johan glanced over at her and his smile faded. "You have some big decisions to make, that's for sure."

Emily hugged her arms around herself to keep warm. "At least here I feel like I can choose my future. I'm just Em, not Emily Davenport of the New York Davenports." She looked down at the few rows of houses at the bottom of the hill. "No one cares."

Johan looked down at his boots. He cleared his throat. "My fiancé's name was Emilia. I guess it's hard to say your name sometimes because it reminds me…"

"I'm sorry. I didn't know…Johan."

At the mention of his name, Johan looked up at her. He held her gaze until the silence became uncomfortable.

"You could stay if you wanted to…Emily," he said. He cleared his voice then looked away, avoiding her eyes. "Would you stay if there was someone to take care of you and the baby?"

Emily laughed, exasperated. "Not you, too!" She playfully swatted at him. "Did Bonnie put you up to this? It's no secret that Henry would marry me, if I wanted him to. It's not that I don't care for him as a person, understand. It's just that I need someone like…"

"Me." Johan said, resolutely. He didn't look at her. He set his jaw and focused his gaze out to the ocean. Then he turned to her. "You need someone like me. Someone not afraid of this land or its difficulties. Someone to build a new life with. Someone who understands your loss. I do." His face flushed crimson at those last two words.

Emily blushed. "Are you proposing to me, *Mr. Nevala*? Right here on this hill?"

"Yes."

Emily coughed. "You are serious? Johan, you still don't really know me." She pressed her lace glove against her throat.

"I know what I need to know."

"And what is that?"

"I know you can't cook." He smiled crookedly.

Emily furrowed her eyebrows and pursed her lips.

"I know you are willing to learn."

She cast her eyes downward and nodded.

"I know you aren't afraid of work. You just haven't had the opportunity to see what you can do." Johan turned toward her but kept his hands in his pockets. "There is a side to you that wants the freedom of this land more than anything else. I want it, too."

She tilted her head sideways and nodded once in agreement.

He continued, "I know that you could love me."

Emily gasped. "How could you be so bold to presume that!"

He stopped her mouth with a kiss. Not just any kiss. Not a prudent, tentative one like Ronald had given her at their engagement. This was a heart-stopping, blood-pressure raising kiss that made Emily's toes tingle in her boots. He didn't let go. He held her waist gently and cupped her neck in his strong hand. He held her to him until she pushed away.

"Mr. Nevala!" Emily gasped and put both hands on his chest. Her cheeks were flushed and she wafted her shawl to cool herself off. "You, sir, do not know as much about me as you think. If you think that--"

"I'll tell you what I think, Emily," Johan said, quietly. "I think you need one of those kisses everyday for the rest of your life...from me. And I think you'll stay."

"You presume to know things you can't possibly know," Emily said, breathlessly, stepping backward from him. "I must go."

"I just wanted you to have all the information you need to make your choice, Emily," Johan said, with a gleam in his eye.

"Well, that's fine. Uh—thank you." Emily stumbled on a tree root as she retreated down the pathway.

"Careful, Em," Johan called, reaching toward her.

Emily stopped suddenly. "I think you better continue to call me Mrs. Davenport. We are friends. I appreciated the pleasant day fishing with you. It was lovely but we are not this close of friends, Mr. Nevala."

He smiled crookedly, avoiding her eye. "Yet."

Emily turned and straightened her cap, tucking her loose hairs in the sides. She glanced back at him and almost tripped again.

"Careful, Emily," he whispered. "Careful. You have the power to crush me if you are not careful."

*   *   *

Dearest Emily,

We expect you home as soon as you and the baby are able to travel. The Wild West is no place for a woman of your position in society. Come home and we will help you with the baby. You can have your old room. Our maid can be a nurse-maid for the child until he or she reaches school age. We can send the child to boarding school when they are of age and you will be able to remarry. You will still be young enough to attract a suitable gentleman.

Our daily concern is for your welfare in that God-forsaken place. If we had known that Ronald was going to whisk you away to that immoral town, we would have never allowed him to marry you. How our hearts froze when we heard the news of the "Sophia" sinking at sea! You were lost to us once. We won't lose you again. Come home, Emily. Come home as soon as you can.

All our love,

Emily's mouth went dry. With the note was enough money for her boat ticket back east. She bowed her head to the cushioned arm of the couch and wept. Her shoulders still shook every few seconds as the remnant of tears dried up.

"Uh-hmmm."

Emily glanced up quickly to see Henry's face contorted with concern. She sighed. "Yes, Henry. Can I help you?"

"That was my question, Emily. Can I help you?"

"I'm fine, thank you."

"I don't think you are, ma'am."

Emily leveled her eyes at him. "You wouldn't understand this because you don't have sisters, Henry. But I really am fine. Girls just need to cry sometimes. I need to cry often." She pointed to her abdomen and raised her eyebrows.

"A baby is nothing to feel bad about, Emily. It's a blessing from God."

"I know that, Henry." Emily's patience was wearing thin. First Johan. Now Henry. Too many concerned men were not a blessing. "I just received a letter from my family."

"You miss them?"

"Yes, very much."

"Well, tell them that you are well-taken care of here. You're gonna be just fine."

"Yes, Henry," Emily replied, exasperated. "I'll let them know."

Henry left and scooped up his hammer and nails by the door. He turned and called over his shoulder, "Your room is ready for you to move in. I just finished it." He grinned, pleased with himself. "How about that, little lady?"

Emily wiped her eyes and straightened her shoulders. She left home so she could begin to make some decisions for her own life. What was the lesser of two evils? To be told what to do while living in comfort of the city? Or to take control of her life in the squalor of Astoria? To raise her child in the city with overbearing grandparents? To raise her child in the filth and immorality of the west? Could she do it alone? It wasn't conventional but she could make it on her own, couldn't she? It was time to see Mr. Shively at the customhouse and see where her affairs stood. She had some decisions to make that would determine the rest of her life. Now it wasn't only herself that she had to consider. What was best for her baby? She needed answers.

CHAPTER SEVENTEEN

"Should you seek great things for yourself. Seek them not."
- Jeremiah 45:5

August 1853

"Could you believe all that nonsense?" Emily said to
Bonnie, Daniel Malcolm and Sikkus. She leaned back on the
grass by the Skipanon River and pulled her legs under her
skirt. "Poor Mrs. Kuntas! I didn't think we'd ever be invited
over again!"

They all laughed. The warm summer wind cooled the
picnickers and the distant roar of the ocean made the setting
serene. Bees flew around the smoked fish, fried chicken,
apples and bread.

"You'd think those boys wouldn't want to fish on their
day off," Bonnie complained. "We finally have a church picnic
and the men want to be out on the river."

"They have fun," Sikkus chided. "Look." She pointed
down the river to Luther and Spurgeon wrestling in a small
skiff. Gus had his hands on either side of the boat and was
rocking it hard back and forth. The boys let out a yelp and
both landed in the river on opposite sides of the boat. Gus sat
back and howled with laughter.

Bonnie clucked her tongue and looked around. "Have
you seen Henry, Frans and Johan? They were supposed to
meet us here today." She lowered her voice to a whisper. "It's
Johan's birthday so I made him a cake." She grinned from ear
to ear.

"You might as well just call him Johan Emerson,"
Emily teased. "He's as good as adopted by you, Bonnie." She
reached over and squeezed her friend's hand.

"Some lads need someone to look after them," Daniel said. He squinted his eyes from the sun bearing down on them. "It's good to have some authority figures around to help them stay out of trouble in town." He tugged at his necktie to loosen it.

Emily and Bonnie and Sikkus shared a smirk between them. Emily spoke first. "I don't think Mr. Nevala is the type who needs anyone to look after him," she said. "He's too busy gillnetting, farming and building his house to get into any mischief."

"I certainly hope that is the case, Emily." Daniel stood and dusted off his black slacks and dress boots. "I'm going to go stretch these old legs. Emily, would you care to join me?" He extended his hand to her but instead of taking it, Emily covered her eyes with her free hand.

"I think I'll rest here for a bit longer, Daniel," she said. "Thank you for the offer, though." She smiled sweetly and turned back to Sikkus and Bonnie.

Daniel bowed curtly and turned on his heel. He walked over to another group of picnickers from the church.

Sikkus and Bonnie giggled. "He's sweet on you, honey," Bonnie teased. Sikkus hid her smile behind her gingham napkin but nodded in agreement.

Emily glanced over at him and back at the ladies. "You two are worse than my friends back home. For goodness' sake, I feel as big as a cow right now. Any man in his right mind wouldn't want me in this emotional, uncomfortable condition." She fanned herself with her free hand. "Thank goodness I'm not nine months along or this sun would be unbearable." She eyed the food. "I can't stop eating. Is this normal?"

Bonnie and Sikkus laughed again. "You could eat this whole picnic and still be fine, dear," Bonnie said.

"You look better, Miss Em," Sikkus said, patting her hand. "Sickness gone now?"

"Yes, finally," Emily said, smiling.

"What's *finally*?" Frans called, as he and Johan and Henry walked up.

"You finally arrived!" Bonnie teased them. "You'll have to eat up quickly. Emily will finish this picnic off herself."

Emily gasped and swatted Bonnie playfully. "I will not!" she said, laughing. "Come take a seat with us. We have a surprise for you, Johan."

Henry quickly sat down next to Emily. Frans grabbed a chicken wing but continued standing. "If I sit way down there," he said. "I'll never get up again." He patted Johan on the back. "This boy had me chopping beams late into the night. Said I had to for his birthday present," He chuckled. "Made me miss church this morning, too. Shame on him!"

Johan's cheeks flushed. "Uncle, I apologized," he whispered, turning his face away from the women.

"Not again, Johan," Bonnie said, sternly. "You need a day of rest and some fun, especially on your birthday. Spurgeon and Luther are swimming. Gus is out in the boat there. No work allowed today. This might be our last summer day to enjoy for quite a while." Bonnie pushed her straw bonnet off her face and brushed her curls back from her pink cheeks.

Emily glanced over at Johan. He stood by his uncle with a chicken thigh in one hand and an apple in the other. He was laughing and wiped his mouth on his rolled-up sleeve just in time to see Emily watching him. He smiled like a boy getting caught misbehaving. His eyes twinkled and it made Emily's heart skip a beat. Heat filled her cheeks and she glanced away quickly.

Suddenly, the baby kicked hard inside her. "Oh!" Emily said, putting her hand on her side. She covered her mouth, embarrassed at her outburst.

Bonnie was beside her in an instant. "What is it, dear? Are you alright?" she asked.

Emily laughed. "I think the baby just wanted some attention," she said. The baby kicked again. She moved her hand to feel the spot.

Emily glanced over at Henry who had a look of amazement on his face. It made Emily giggle. Henry shook his head. "He's kicking?"

Sikkus scooted across the blanket to Emily's other side. "It's about time for him to move alot. This a good sign, Miss Emily." She was beaming with pride, taking Emily's hand in hers. "He will be healthy and strong."

The baby kicked again.

"I saw it that time," Bonnie said, giggling with joy. "Men, you should go hike or something. Take the food with you." She dismissed them and they took the hint...and the food.

The women sat and talked about babies and what to expect in the coming months. Emily got the full story on each of Henry, Luther and Spurgeon's births. No detail left untold. By the time the women were done talking, their back sides were sore from sitting so long. Their sides ached from laughing.

"Let's get you up and moving," Bonnie said. "We'll need to head back soon. It will get cold out here come sundown." Sikkus and Bonnie helped Emily up.

"I'd like to walk by the river for a few minutes," Emily said. "I'll be with you ladies soon." The women waved her on while they cleaned up. She stretched her legs. Her ankles felt swollen in her leather boots. The grass looked so inviting and cool. She glanced around her and saw no one so she slipped her boots and stockings off. The grass felt wonderful under her toes. She walked over to the edge of the river between the cattails. Holding onto a low hanging branch of a Sitka spruce tree, Emily dipped her toes in the water.

"Am I going to have to pull you out of there?" Johan said, behind her, biting into another piece of birthday cake.

Emily squealed and almost lost her balance from surprise. "You scared me," she said, giggling. She put her hand to her chest and tried to hide her toes under her dress. Sikkus had braided her hair into a long braid and it swung over her shoulder.

"I like it," he said, smiling and picking up the end of her braid. "You're a little bit New York and a little bit Astoria now." He grinned.

Emily liked his clean shaven look for summer time. His skin was smooth and tanned from the long hours out fishing. His hair was bleached blond, almost white, by the sun. He let go of her braid and stepped back, putting his hands in his pockets. He ducked below the branch and pointed out to the river. "Look there, Em."

She held onto the branch above her and followed his finger. "Oh, they're darling," she said. Two river otters swam on their backs, floating down the river. One held a small fish between its paws and nibbled away while it floated. "Wouldn't that be nice?" Emily said, laughing. "Cooling off while eating some food."

Johan stepped up to the edge near Emily and sat down on the bank. He let his feet dangle over the edge. He pulled off his boots and stuffed his socks inside them on the bank. "Keep your eyes open for bald eagles," he said, looking up into the sky. "There are a handful of them around these parts. Amazing birds. I can see why Americans named them as the symbol for their nation."

Emily felt rooted in her spot, holding on to her branch. The last time she was alone with Johan, he stole a kiss. A wonderful kiss that she thought about often but a stolen one, none the less. She wasn't going to make it too easy for him to take another one. People might get the wrong idea about her and she valued her reputation too much. She wanted to put her shoes back on but that would seem rude so she stayed put.

"Do you want to sit down?" he asked, glancing up at her.

He smiled and it made Em's heart race. How could this man have this much influence on her when they really did not know each other very well?

He patted the ground next to him. "Sit and cool your feet with me," he said.

"It's really not very appropriate for a lady-"

"Em," Johan said, grinning at her. "Your parents aren't here. There's no one to get in trouble with. You can relax."

"Pardon me, Mr. Nevala," Emily said, sitting down beside him. "But I think I have every reason to be careful around you, sir." She straightened her skirt and hid her toes below the water. He was right, though. Cooling off felt wonderful. "All we need is more of that birthday cake," she murmured.

Johan chuckled, then grew serious. "You are doing well?"

Emily looked over at him and smiled blissfully. "Very well. Thank you. I'm not sick anymore. I've been able to help Bonnie with more of the laundry and cooking. They keep saying they will pay me but I would never take a cent. They saved my life. Well--" Emily blushed and turned to Johan. "I mean, *you* saved my life. But they have taken such good care of me since I came here. I don't think I would have survived."

"Emily," he said, looking away from her. "You don't owe me or *anyone*, for that matter, anything for saving you. The Emersons love you and want to see that you'll be provided for, that's all."

Emily quickly put her hands in her lap. She felt a bit of regret that Johan kept his distance. It was nice to be alone with him. It felt safe like when her late husband would hold her hand while they walked or sat together in the evenings. She missed a man's touch even though she only had it for a few months. She bit her lip and glanced over at Johan. He leaned back and rested on his elbows in the grass, completely relaxed. She envied his calm and peace. He was easy to be with, unlike the Daniel who was kind but too uptight. She could never sit here with Daniel Malcolm, dangling her toes in the river.

"I won't see you for a while, Em," Johan said, quietly, keeping his eyes straight up on the clouds overhead.

Emily's heart sank. "Why? Are you going somewhere?" she asked. She turned toward him and swatted a pesky mosquito away.

"I won't be in town throughout the fall," Johan said.

"What about your row-sail? How will you make your living?" Emily asked, biting a nail.

Johan chuckled. "Henry will borrow it while I'm gone. I've made enough this year to last me through the winter and into next spring," he said. He looked over at her, following the line of her cheek with his eyes. "I need to finish the home I'm building. I figured out what still needs to be done before the rainy weather sets in and I can't work in town and finish it in time." He shrugged his shoulders.

"So, you won't come to church? Or to dinner at the Emerson's?" Emily's shoulders drooped. Forget good posture, she felt depressed at Johan's announcement. "You and Uncle Frans are the bright spot in our week." She looked out at the river and sulked. She gasped. "You won't turn into a heathen, will you? Promise you won't, Johan."

He laughed. "No, Em. I won't be wicked like the rest of the men in Astoria. You don't ever have to worry about that." He played with the grass between them. "If I was going that route, it would have happened a long time ago."

"I'm glad you didn't," Emily said, watching the sky for eagles. "I think that you and Reverend Malcolm must be the only two decent men in all of Astoria."

Silence.

Emily glanced over at Johan who was looking up at her. He searched her face and looked ready to say something but decided against it. He looked...disappointed.

"I'm sorry. Did I say something wrong?" Emily asked, swinging her braid over her shoulder. "I meant that as a compliment. Did you misunderstand me?" She held his gaze for what seemed a long time.

Slowly, Johan leaned toward her and she remained perfectly still. He put his hand on her cheek and studied her face. Emily didn't move but her heart pounded in her chest. His gaze stopped on her lips and Emily held her breath. *He wouldn't kiss her again, would he?*

"I'll see you soon, Em," he said, softly. Then he kissed her forehead and stood up suddenly. Grabbing his boots, Johan walked away in his bare feet.

Emily heard Henry calling to Johan. They spoke just quiet enough that Emily couldn't hear. Johan pointed to where Emily was and walked away. She followed him with her eyes until he disappeared from sight.

"Em!" Henry called, waving her over. "We need to get going."

She pulled her feet from the water and dried them with the edge of her dress. She slipped her stockings back on and laced up her boots. It felt like prison for her feet after the refreshing water from the stream. Maybe she felt so sorely because of the disappointing news Johan left her with. *What did she say wrong?* She felt guilty for hoping he would actually kiss her again. Stumbling to her feet, she went over to Henry.

"Just found out Johan's getting married," Henry said. "She'll be a lucky girl."

"What?" Emily gasped. She felt heat and anger rise up for the innocent kiss he just gave her. What business did he have kissing her, even on the forehead, if he was getting married to someone else? "How do you know this, Henry?" Emily asked, feeling her throat tighten with each word.

"Uncle Frans told Ma that he's finishing the house so he can get married," Henry said.

"He didn't say *who* Johan was marrying?" Emily asked, searching Henry's face. She knew she had no claim to Johan but jealousy rose up in her unbidden.

"Something about someone from back east," Henry said, furrowing his eyebrows as if to remember better. "Some of the men send for mail-order brides. Maybe that's his plan. Not a bad one, I think." He turned to Emily and smiled warmly. "Course I don't need to think that way."

Emily put her fists on her hips. "Not a bad plan, Henry?" she chided. "He'll have no idea what he's going to get. Some strange woman from who knows where. Why would he do that?"

"Well, Em, in case you haven't noticed, there aren't too many eligible women that just wash ashore on the West coast." Henry put his arm around her and led her over to the waiting wagon. "Maybe he needs to find a wife some other way."

CHAPTER EIGHTEEN

"Cold from fishing? Come have a 10 cent cup of coffee – it will neither make ya, break ya, not set ya up in business, but it will get you a cup of Frank Fabre's celebrated coffee – pigs' feet, ham and eggs, and oysters in every style, to order at the same place. Open day and night. Special attention paid to ladies."
Fabre's Coffeehouse – Main St. June 6, 1880 advertisement

September 1853

"Lesson number one," said Daniel. "This is exciting, isn't it?" He set out the tools to work on the stained-glass windows in front of them.

Emily smiled in return and glanced around Daniel's kitchen in the church parsonage. It was pleasantly decorated. Nothing too fancy but definitely a step up from the Emerson's humble home. It was nowhere close to being as richly furnished as her parent's home in New York but it was comfortable. There was a wash basin with a pump. A large cutting board stood in the middle on stout legs. A metal rack hung on the wall with pots and pans hanging from it. Obviously, he could cook and take care of himself just fine.

"What do you think about this design, Emily?"

At the mention of her name, Emily turned back to him. He had a large piece of white linen cloth laid out on the table. It was a simple but beautiful depiction of Mary with Jesus as a baby.

"The first step in the Gospel message," Daniel said. "The Virgin Birth."

"It's lovely," Emily said, leaning over the drawing, studying each part of it. "I like the red poinsettas in the corners of it. It reminds me of Christmas."

"That was my thought, exactly," Daniel said, beaming. "So you think this will do? Shall we begin it today?"

Emily wiped her hands on her apron which protruded out more with each week. Daniel glanced over at her and smiled. "What can I do to help?" she asked, anxious to keep herself busy today. Any idle time she had, her thoughts seemed to drift back to Johan and it was depressing. This was the third Sunday in a row that he did not meet up with them after service. He warned her that he would not see her for a while but she didn't expect this emptiness at the loss of his company.

"Why don't you stir that glue that I have warming on the stove there?" Daniel pointed to a copper pot on his new Alpine wood stove. A bucket of wood and kindling sat stocked next to it. Emily walked over to it, took the wooden spoon and gave the gray mixture a few good stirs. The smell of it gave her a headache.

"Watch the front of that stove with the soldering irons," Daniel said, quickly. "I'd hate for you to catch your dress on them."

"I'll be careful," Emily said back, pulling her skirt to the side. The heat from the stove felt comforting as the weather outside was foggy and growing colder by the day. She stirred the glue again to keep it from burning on the bottom. *Careful Emily. Be careful.* As she mindlessly stirred the glue, Johan's words from Coxcomb Hill kept coming back to her. *How dare he tell her to be careful when he was the one toying with her?*

She glanced over at Daniel Malcolm. His white sleeves were rolled up to his elbows showing his masculine forearms and hands. Unlike Johan, he had dark hair on his arms. His skin was more olive than tanned like Johan's. But he wasn't unattractive, Emily reasoned. His tie was gone and he had his top button open. He was relaxed and smiled easily, truly engrossed in his work and enjoying every minute of it. But did he enjoy working with Emily? He seemed to favor her company more than anyone else's, even in her condition. Stir, stir, stir. The baby kicked a few times bringing a smile to Emily's face.

"What is it?" Daniel asked, looking up at her.

"Oh," Emily said, covering her mouth with her hand. "It's just the baby. He's letting me know he's hungry again, apparently." She smiled and stirred some more.

"That glue should be nice and smooth now," Daniel said. "Come over here, Em. I want you to see how I cut the glass. I'd like you to do most of the cutting and I'll place the pieces and solder them. I think it will go more quickly if we work together."

Emily stood next to him and their arms brushed against each other when he turned to grab the first piece of glass. He faced her and froze, mesmerized by her. He studied her face and hair. Emily held her breath and felt heat fill her cheeks under his gaze.

"Inspiration!" he cried. Suddenly he turned and picked up a small piece of glass from the pile by his door. He carried it back to the table and turned to Emily. "We are going to pattern Mary after you."

Emily gasped, "Me?" Her hand was on her side and she realized the reason for his inspiration. "I'm hardly the Virgin Mary, Daniel," Emily laughed, dismissing the idea.

"Your dark hair and soft complexion is perfect," he began. "I'll hand paint the pieces myself and copy that expression you just had. Only, in your arms, will be baby Jesus. It will be the most beautiful piece I've ever created." He turned back to the glass pieces and searched through them for the right sizes to cut first. "It will be stunning. We will have it done for the Christmas Eve service, Emily. We will work tirelessly on it until it's done…you and I. It will be our Christmas gift to this small, heathen community."

"Sounds…" Emily began, then choked, "like a lot of work and some long hours."

"It will be worth it, you'll see," Daniel said, patting her on the arm. "Anything worth having will cost you something but it's always worth it."

He handed Emily a cutting tool and took a larger one in his own hands. "See our template here." He pointed to the largest pieces first. "We'll cut these ones then we'll move on to the more intricate ones when we have the knack of it. Now watch me first." He placed the edge of the glass as close to his line as he could as to not waste even a bit of the precious material. Then he expertly scored the edge along his template. He pressed ever so gently with a towel and a weight along the score and the glass broke along the line.

"We always cut the most difficult cuts first, after having cut off the extra glass," Daniel went on. "Inside cuts first, outside cuts next, straight lines last." Emily watched him score the inside cuts of his piece. He placed a rounded button underneath it at its center and then placed a flat weight perpendicular to the button on top of the glass.

Emily winced at the snap of cracking glass but to her surprise saw a perfectly cut curve. "That's amazing!" she said. "May I try?"

"Of course," Daniel said, equally enthused. "The sooner you master this, the sooner it will be done. Let's see you cut the opposite side." He stepped back and let Emily score the glass. She extended her line beyond the template as he had. She pressed down firmly and glanced up at Daniel for approval.

"Fine. You're doing fine," he said, urging her on. "Now the button and the weight."

Emily put the button under the glass and the weight on top as he had. She hesitated to press down on it.

"Nothing ventured, nothing gained, Emily," he said, grinning.

She closed her eyes and pressed down on the piece of glass. It snapped and she opened her eyes to a perfect cut. "I did it," she cried.

"On to the outside curves," Daniel said, placing his hand on her waist as he moved around her to check on the glue.

The heat from his touch caught Emily off guard. He had never been that familiar with her. They walked arm in arm occasionally but this touch was so casual that Emily didn't think he even realized he did it. Maybe she was wrong about the uptight preacher. Maybe he could be more than a friend to her. His zeal for the Lord was a given. But to be a preacher's wife wasn't something Emily ever considered. Not that he was asking her. He was being kind and friendly and teaching her a hobby. But what kind of a father and husband could he be?

Emily scored the next piece, placed the button and weight and pressed on it. Snap! Piece after piece came together until they lined up on the template. Daniel and Emily worked side by side, leaning over the table, placing them like puzzle pieces. They straightened and stood back to admire their handiwork. Most of the Virgin Mary pieces were cut and placed when Daniel put his hand on Emily's and patted it.

"Time for a break," he said. "Let's have some tea in my parlor and rest your feet." He smiled and wiped back his hair from his forehead. Beads of perspiration dotted his brow. He took out a handkerchief from his pocket and dabbed them.

Emily took the edge of her apron and did the same. She used her hand as a fan when she suddenly felt warm from her work.

"Come, sit down here," Daniel led her to a plush armchair and footstool in front of a large, leaded glass window overlooking the river from Fourteenth Street. "We're losing daylight. We won't be able to do much more today. I'll need to walk you home after our tea." He seemed disappointed. He went back to the kitchen and returned with a teapot and two teacups and saucers on a tray. "Would you like to pour or shall I?" he asked.

"This is something I can do, Daniel," Emily said, with a giggle. "Allow me, please. You've been so kind and patient with me today. It's the least I can do." She smiled at him as he sank into his arm chair opposite her. "Sugar?"

"I take mine plain," he said. "I brought it out for you, just in case." He smiled at her.

"Very thoughtful," Emily said. "Again, thank you for today."

"I hope we can do this again…very soon," Daniel said, looking down at his tea and saucer. "I enjoy your company, Emily. We work well together. You are a very amiable and lovely person." He stole a quick glance at her then looked back out the window.

Emily smiled and sipped her tea. Her feet ached from standing in her tall leather boots all afternoon. She tried stretching her feet inside them but to no avail. She would try to enjoy her tea and relax back at the Emersons. Her heart skipped a beat. It was Sunday evening, Frans and Johan always stayed for Sunday dinner and supper. Perhaps he was there now. She suddenly felt anxious to get home. She sipped her tea more quickly to Daniel's amusement.

"I'm sorry, Emily, I must not have been a good host," he said, chuckling.

"Why would you say that?" Emily asked, confused.

"You must be hungry and tired. Would you like more tea?" he asked.

Emily giggled and gently set down her tea cup and saucer on the small table between them. "You were a wonderful host, Daniel. I just realized that I do need to be going now. I must be careful not to overdo it."

"Of course," he said, standing and walking over to her. He gave her his hand to help her up. They stood face to face for a moment with her hand still clasped in his. He brought it to his lips and kissed it so softly that Emily barely felt it. "I'm glad you came to Astoria, Emily," he said, in a whisper. "I hope you will find it in your heart to stay. It wouldn't be the same here without you."

CHAPTER NINETEEN

"Time is
Too slow for those who wait
Too swift for those who fear
Too long for those who grieve
Too short for those who rejoice
But for those who love
Time is not"
- Henry VanDyke (1852-1933)

"She's spending a lot of time with the preacher, Johan," Frans said, straightening after chopping a cedar beam. He wiped his brow with the back of his hand. "You might need to take a trip into town to remind her that you haven't been lost at sea."

"I told her I would be gone for some time, Uncle," Johan said. He attacked a branch with fury and almost hit his leg with his ax.

"Careful there, boy," Frans chuckled. "I'm not suggesting you feign an injury for Bonnie to stitch up. That reverend likes her and she needs a reason not to marry him."

Johan sat down hard on the pile of lumber he and uncle split that day. He dropped his head in his hand and breathed hard. "I don't know if I can do this. I'm running out of time." Johan looked up to the sky which was threatening to rain again. "Shively mentioned the other day that she sold her property to Boelling." He wiped his brow on his rolled up sleeve. "That means one of two things. She's either going home as soon as the baby can travel. Two – she means to stay here in Astoria. Probably remarry and settle down. Uncle, I don't think I can stay here if she marries the Reverend."

"Now, now, he's a good man," Frans said, dusting off his britches with his hand. "If you haven't made your intentions clear to Em and she hasn't reciprocated then she's fair game. Have you ever told her that this home is for her? She might need to know that."

Uncle Frans had a point there. But he had proposed on Coxcomb Hill. That kiss and declaration should have made it clear how he felt about her. Telling her that she could buy part of his land should have made things abundantly clear about his wishes. Maybe not. Apparently, Emily needed a good reminder of what they could have together. He wasn't a preacher but he would be the godly man and father she needed him to be. They would more than survive out here in this wild frontier. They would thrive and build a life and a family together.

Johan tossed his ax toward the shed and pulled his hat off the hook by the door. He headed for his stable where Ginger stood waiting for him.

"Where you going, boy?" Frans called after him. "What about all this?"

Johan mounted his horse and spun her around. He called back to his uncle, "It doesn't mean a thing if I don't have her. I need to go to town."

"Good man, Johan! There's some Finnish *sisu* for you," Frans said. "I'm going home to bed. Stay at the Emerson's tonight, if you like. I'll check on things here in the morning for you."

Johan dismounted at the Emerson's front gate and tied off Ginger. He strode to the front door, peeking in the dining room window as he went. No company tonight as far as he could see. Things were looking hopeful.

Just then, the front door opened and Reverend Malcolm stepped out, patting his clergy hat down on his head. He glanced up in time to avoid bumping into Johan.

"Mr. Nevala," Daniel said, extending his hand and shaking Johan's. "In need of a home-cooked meal, I see." He laughed. Johan did not. Calling over his shoulder, Daniel said, "If you hurry, Bonnie is just clearing the table. You might catch her before it's too late."

"Emily?" Johan asked, absentmindedly.

"No," Daniel said, stopping abruptly and turning around. "I said *Bonnie*. You might catch Bonnie before it's too late. Mrs. Davenport has retired for the evening. We spent a wonderful day together building a stained-glass window. She loved learning how to do it. Looks like we'll be spending quite a bit of time together to finish it. How fortunate I am to have a hobby that interests her so much." He shrugged his shoulders and patted Johan on the back. "Well, good evening to you. It's been a while since we've seen you. I'm sure the Lutheran minister has missed seeing you as well."

Johan only answered with a grunt and touched his hat out of respect before turning to the front door. He rapped on it lightly and entered. He slid his boots off and was hanging up his coat when Emily came out of the kitchen to gather more plates. She didn't see him so he took the opportunity to check her over. She looked strong and healthy but tired. Her dress and apron betrayed her growing tummy underneath. She was darling. When she turned around again, she didn't even look pregnant from behind. He stepped further out of the shadow by the front door. When she came in again, she gasped.

"Johan! You startled me," she said, putting her hand over her heart. "Come in and sit down." She motioned to his normal chair. "We, uh, didn't expect you tonight so we started clearing things. Just sit there and I'll be back with a plate in a moment." She turned to go back in the kitchen but paused and turned around. "It's good to see you," she said smiling, then retreated to the kitchen.

"Is that my wayward one out there?" Bonnie called from the kitchen.

Johan called back, grinning. "Bonnie, I'm starving out there in the woods. I need potatoes quick!"

Emily came back in a plate of mashed potatoes, gravy, squash and stew meat. "This is Henry's deer. He was pretty proud of it last week. You should have seen him." Emily set it in front of him and put her hand on her hip.

"Can you sit with me while I eat, Emily?" Johan asked, pulling out the chair beside him.

"I'll just go get some coffee and Bonnie," Emily said, turning. Johan caught her arm first.

"I'd like to talk to you alone first, if I may," he asked quietly. He waited for her to sit down before proceeding. "I heard that you sold your property the other day. Is that right?"

"Yes," Emily said, sitting straight with her hands clasped in front of her on the table. "Yes, I did sell it. Mr. Boelling made me a good offer and I felt that I should take it. I'll need the cash to take care of the baby and cover my expenses here at the Emerson's or to buy passage home."

"Or to buy a parcel of land from me," Johan added, his tone serious.

"I think we both know that's not feasible," Emily said, avoiding his eyes. "I was on my feet all day today and I'm so sore I can hardly walk. How would I build a house for myself? Honestly!" Emily picked at her fingernails nervously.

"I could build one for you," Johan said, setting down his utensils and turning to her. "I could help you with whatever you want to do, Em."

"You can't even finish your house for you and your--" Emily stopped short and regained her composure. She glanced over her shoulder at the kitchen. "Belongings."

"My belongings?" Johan sat back in his seat and smirked. "I'm making good headway on it."

"We haven't seen you for weeks, Johan. I won't make you do that for me and my baby. You'll kill yourself working that hard out there." She looked him over with pity. "You've lost weight. Are you eating?"

"I could ask you the same thing," Johan teased, snorting back a laugh.

Emily's jaw dropped at his joke. She slugged him in the arm and shoved herself to her feet, preparing to leave. Johan stood quickly and put his hands on her arms to still her.

"You get your hands off me," Emily whispered, struggling and frustrated. "How dare you tease me when I'm concerned about you. Forget it! You can just die out there for all I care."

Johan's smile faded and he pulled her closer to him. He slid his hands up to her shoulders without taking his eyes off of her face. She was trembling with anger and hiccupped back a sob. "I told you that you needed one of these often," he said, pulling her into his arms, kissing her firmly on the lips. He held her there for a moment and pulled back.

"How dare you kiss me like that under the Emerson's roof!" Emily stammered, shocked.

"You're beautiful when you're angry, Em," Johan said, smirking. "I've missed you."

"You've missed me? Or you've missed having someone to kiss? Let me be clear, Mr. Nevala," she said, pointing her finger into his chest. "I'm not waiting around here for you to kiss whenever you like. You are no gentleman," Emily fumed. "I am a lady and you should treat me as such. You're no better than those sailors with their crude remarks. They would *never* do what you just did."

"Oh yes, they would," Johan said, his smile long gone. "They've just never had the chance." He dropped the volume in his voice to a whisper. "How dare you compare me to one of those immoral sailors, Em. You should know by now that I love you."

"How can you say that to me?" Emily put her hands on her hips. "I know what you're up to. Just keeping all your options open, are you? Don't touch me again, Johan Nevala or I'll-"

"You'll what?" Johan's face flushed with anger. "You'll leave? You'll have me thrown in jail? What, Em?"

"I don't know what I'll do, but you won't like it," Emily said, flinging her braid over her shoulder and storming into the kitchen.

Bonnie came stumbling out with a bowl of apple cobbler in her hands. "Young man, if you hurt that girl, you'll have Mr. Emerson and all his boys to answer to. When they're through with you then I'll take over. You don't want that."

Johan dropped his head into his hand. He shook it in disbelief at how horrible the evening turned. Instead of gaining ground with Emily, he just dug a pit but didn't know why. He hoped it had nothing to do with the Reverend.

CHAPTER TWENTY

"You can't teach anyone gillnetting, you have to do that by experience."

– Gunnar Hermanson

Standing at the docks, with the wind whipping around them from the river, Uncle Frans patted Johan on the back. "All right, boy," he said. "I'll be looking for you tomorrow night. Good luck acquiring what you need for the house. Remember, Portland isn't as bad as Astoria, but trust no one. Keep that money against your skin. It's not even safe in your boot."

Johan smiled in appreciation to his uncle. "Why do I feel like this could be a complete waste of money and time?" He grimaced and looked out over the river. "I could come back with the stove and the pump and it could all be for naught. She might leave anyway."

"Now, now, boy," Uncle Frans said, shaking his head. "You can't afford to think that way." He smiled at Johan.

"I can't afford to make any mistakes," Johan said. "This could cost me everything I have saved and in the end I'm stuck with a fine, empty house."

"If you're that concerned about being alone," Uncle Frans said, "I'll come live with you." He chuckled while Johan shook his head. "She didn't slap you after you kissed her. She must not hate you altogether." Johan shot him a pained look. "Don't worry, Johan. You're a good man. You'll win her heart in the end, wait and see."

"Last call to board!" Captain John C. Ainsworth called from the Lot Whitcomb steamship, headed to Portland.

Johan slung his duffle over his shoulder and walked down the gang plank onto the steamship. Once on board, he turned and waved to his uncle. He clenched his fist at his side. His hard-earned money was strapped around his stomach with a tight piece of cloth. No one would rob him of his future. The only one that could take it from him was a little, pregnant woman with long, dark hair and blue eyes.

Dearest Emily,

Waiting to see you is so difficult, especially in your condition. How we hate to miss this time with you! We hope you are feeling well and progressing fine. We have enclosed Ronald's documentation of his assets invested with the American Fur Company. They are not worth much now as that industry has waned but you can probably sell your stocks to someone in Astoria if you need more money.

Enclosed is Fifty Dollars to sustain you while you survive out there. It pains us to think of the squalor you must have to endure until you return home. Living among people who are not your equals must be so tedious. Remain strong and you will be back in acceptable society soon.

We've taken the liberty of fielding a few eligible husbands for you. Do you remember Elliot MacTavish from down the street? It seems that he has finished law school and is making a name for himself in New York City. We find his family and connections suitable for you. As this would be your second husband, we can't be sure he would have you and the child. But if you want us to pursue this, we would gladly speak to his parents about a possible union.

Please write soon and inform us of your health and success in closing your late husband's affairs in Astoria. The sooner you are back under our roof, the better. We will help you get on with your life and become reestablished back where you belong.

Be strong and write soon,
Daddy and Mother

Emily read the letter over and over. Her heart pounded in anger. *Elliot MacTavish!* How could they choose Elliot MacTavish for her? Did they know nothing of his carousing reputation? She would rather remain in Astoria as an old widow than return to a union with such a man!

Emily sat in her white nightgown, drying her hair by the window, overlooking the river. Henry made the window extra wide to take in as much of the view as possible. *Dear Henry!* He was such a sweet boy to her. It broke her heart that he wouldn't even consider any other young lady as long as she was around. Poor naïve boy. The addition he built for her was such an endearing gesture of his affection but they could never be. Surely the Lord would bring him a suitable wife in time.

Henry's mention of mail-order brides continued to vex Emily. But how different was her parents' manipulation of her future? Instead of her coming to the West coast for a husband, they were sending her back to the East coast for one. *Ironic.*

A crystal vase with wildflowers stood at the edge of her side table begging for her attention. Daniel picked them for her yesterday on their walk home after working on the stained-glass window. He walked more closely to her side of late, tucking her hand protectively under his arm and holding it with his other hand. The thought made Emily smile. He was as gentlemanly as any man in New York. He seemed to enjoy her company and invited her over at least three times a week to work on the window together. Their conversation was easy and interesting but it lacked something. It felt one-sided like he was always educating her. She was the student and he was the teacher. Creating the stained-glass was becoming an important part of Emily's life. It gave her a goal besides just reaching full-term in her pregnancy. It served as a distraction from her worries about the future. Maybe she could talk to Daniel about her parents' letter and get his advice on it.

Johan came to mind. Emily's heart fluttered at the thought of him. She felt remorse over their last conversation. It certainly didn't end well and her harsh words rose unbidden in Emily's thoughts as she tried to fall asleep at night. The next time she saw him, she would make it a point to apologize. Why couldn't she remain even-keeled around that man? There was no problem with Daniel. But with Johan, she felt off-balanced, never knowing what he might do. It was exciting and unnerving being around him. If he remained true to his heavy work schedule on the farm, she wasn't due to see him for another three weeks at least.

A storm cloud blew in over the bar. The sideways slant of October rain hit the river. Emily's spirit felt as dark as those clouds.

Suddenly, lightning struck the water, splitting the sky in two. Emily jumped with alarm. The fishing boats on the river pulled up anchor and their nets. They began rowing hard for the shore. Emily was relieved that Johan wasn't out there in these conditions.

Lord, keep those sailors safe.

The clear ring of a ship's bell rang through the air as it crossed the bar. It served as a warning to fishermen who might not be aware of its entry due to the roar of the ocean and the howling of the wind near the bar. The ringing continued and continued which struck Emily as unusual. She pulled on her burgundy dress and adjusted the waistband again to fit her belly. Huffing to gain a deep breath, she ran over the window again to see what the ruckus was all about.

She gasped. The huge ship plowed through the bar, rocking precariously back and forth on the shoals. Directly in its path was a lone fishing boat still anchored. Its sailors raced back and forth on the row-sail, drenched by the rain and crashing waves. The ship was bearing down on them at an alarming speed.

"Bonnie!" Emily cried, racing out of her room to the kitchen next door. "Bonnie! Look out the window!" Emily pointed to the boat out in the middle of the river.

Bonnie wiped her hands on her apron and peered out the window. She squinted her eyes and brushed her hair back off of her face. "Oh Lord," Bonnie prayed. "Oh Lord! They're going to crash. Why don't they cut their lines?"

"Can't they just pull up anchor?" Emily gasped in disbelief at the catastrophe happening right before her eyes.

Shouts bellowed below their kitchen window as sailors raced toward the docks. They were pointing to the steam ship.

"Cut your lines!"

"They don't have a knife! They don't have a knife!"

"Oh Lord, have mercy. Have mercy," Bonnie wailed, wringing her hands. Her eyes settled on a large kitchen knife laying on the chopping block.

The bells from the steam ship clanged over and over and the distance between them and the row-sail narrowed at an alarming rate. Twenty feet. Ten feet. Five feet.

Bonnie cried out and grabbed Emily's arm tight as the steam ship drove right down on top of the row-sail, splintering it in half. The women screamed with horror. "No!" They both ran for the front door, grabbing their shawls off of the hooks as they went. They gripped each other's hands as they ran down the boardwalk toward the docks. A crowd gathered ahead of them. A mixture of sailors, prostitutes, and fish mongerers leaned against the rail leading down to the boats below.

A wave crashed against the rock retaining wall, soaking the onlookers.

Emily and Bonnie gasped as the water sprayed over them. Their hair hung down their backs, dripping from the rain and waves. Shouts from the crowd met them.

"Who was that?"

"Who's going out there to see if there are survivors?"

The name Veith came up over and over throughout the crowd. Bonnie and Emily pressed in closer to pick up any news of the sailors. Gus and Charles Veith pushed their way through the crowd toward them.

"Bonnie!" he cried. "Have you seen the boys?" The panic on his face made Emily's heart threaten to stop.

"No, Gus!" Bonnie called back to him. "I thought Spurgeon and Luther were with you? Where's Henry?"

Emily scanned the boats below them. She looked for the Finnish flag painted on the bow of Johan's boat. Henry would be safe if Johan's boat was among these ones tied up to the docks. Back and forth she looked. No flag. It wasn't here. She ran around the crowd to get a better look. Surely she was mistaken. She reached the other end of the docks and put her hands on her hips to draw in some deep breaths. A sharp pain hit her lower belly and she grimaced. She pressed her hand to the spot and felt a little foot push back. Straightening, she made herself look at each boat again. It had to be here.

"Charles Veith's son..."

"...someone in the boat with him."

"No knife on board...couldn't cut the nets."

"Seen this before...so unfortunate. Poor lads!"

Emily gripped the rail by the docks and pressed her hand hard to her abdomen. The pain wasn't letting up. Two small rowboats were halfway to the wreck but had to wait until the steam ship passed by before they could look for survivors. *Lord, let the sailors be alive.* She felt suddenly grateful that Johan couldn't possibly have been on that boat. He was home at his farm, safe.

Above the shouts and murmuring of the crowd, Emily heard Bonnie wail. Emily pressed her hand to her mouth in dismay. Now she remembered. Henry was to fish with Hugh Veith today. It was Henry and Hugh Veith who were in that boat. Sobs bubbled up from Emily's gut and she pushed her way back through the crowd, desperate to know the truth. Sailors and prostitutes stepped out of her way as she pushed to get back to Gus and Bonnie.

When she saw them, her heart ached. Bonnie sat in a pile on the boardwalk, beating the ground. Gus hunched down beside her. His red hair matched his red, swollen face wracked with pain and sorrow.

Emily froze and shook her head. "No, no, no," she whispered. She looked out to the rowboats. She forced her feet to walk over to the rail and watch them pull in two bodies from the river. Her fingernails dug into the wooden rail. Her mind flashed back to the horrible night that she was pulled from the river in pitch darkness. *Maybe there is hope. She had survived, hadn't she? Henry was much stronger than she was.* But the sickening truth could not be avoided any longer. She strained to see out to the middle of the vast river. The bodies didn't move even after the sailors bent them over to expel water from their lungs. They hung limp over the seats in the row boat.

Cries from the sailors on board the steam ship echoed across the water. Curses returned from the sailors on the docks. The men of Astoria shook their fists at the crew of the steam ship. The painted ladies in the crowd huddled together for warmth and scurried back to their cribs in the nearby boardinghouses.

Emily let the rain fall on her face, soaking her hair and clothing. She was in too much shock to care. She turned to Bonnie and Gus and gingerly lowered herself down beside them on the boardwalk. *Poor Gus.* He was bawling unashamedly.

"That was my boy, Bonnie," he cried, wiping his nose on his sleeve. "That was my boy out there. My Henry. That was *my* Matthew Henry."

Bonnie wailed. Her body shook as she poured out her grief.

Emily glanced up to see Frederika Veith running down the boardwalk towards them. Her eyes held fear and her cheeks were flushed from running. "Charles," she called out to her husband. Her strong German accent clipped her words, giving them extra force. "What has happened? What is going on?"

"Awww, Frederika," Charles said, dumbfounded. He still stood looking out over the river at the rowboat carrying his son back in. He pointed limply in his shock. "Hugh had accident, Frederika."

His wife ran to his side and looked out at the rowboats returning to the docks. "Hugh? Not Hugh!" She was angry now. "Hugh said he help you with the boats today. That is not Hugh!"

"Yes, Frederika," Charles said, grabbing her hand. "Henry and Hugh fish today. Steam ship come over the bar…" He couldn't continue. Frederika cried out in German, throwing her hands in the air. She pulled Charles to the docks where the sailors were just arriving to tie up the boats.

Bonnie and Gus helped each other to their feet, arms clasped around each other. They staggered over to where the Veiths stood at the top of the ladder. The first sailor came up with Hugh slung over his shoulder. Frederika gasped and clamped her hand over her mouth. She and Charles stood like two pillars of stone as the other sailors took him from the rescuer's arms. Everyone shook their heads in disbelief.

The next sailor came up the ladder and Gus pulled Bonnie forward. The poor rescuer barely reached the top wrung of the ladder when Gus and Bonnie dragged Henry from his shoulder and laid him down on the boardwalk between them. They touched his neck and cheeks, feeling for a pulse or warmth. There was none. Bonnie laid her head on his cold, wet chest and wrapped her arms around her son.

"Lord, help him, please." she begged.

Gus wiped his son's soaked hair off of his forehead and closed his eyes. He held one hand over Henry's eyes and covered his face with his other hand in grief.

"Get him a blanket!" Bonnie cried, sitting up suddenly. "He's cold. He needs a blanket." She sobbed, holding her son's hand. "Momma's so sorry, Henry. Come back to us, please. Please. Please." She tried warming his hands with her own.

Gus put his hands over hers. "Bonnie, honey. He's gone. Henry's gone."

Just then Spurgeon raced up to his parents, slipping on the wet boardwalk. Luther was on his heels. "Pa! What's happening?" The boys jumped backward in disbelief at what they saw. They took a knee beside their brother and raked their fingers through their hair. "What happened?" they said between tears. "How did this happen?"

Emily sat in the pouring rain a few feet away from them. Unable to move. Unable to process this tragedy. *How did her Ronald die? Was he flung into the ocean like these poor souls? Was he stuck on board with no escape as she had just witnessed? Horrible. It was just horrible.* His death was just a bad dream that remained a mystery until today. Now it was clear what he faced in his last moments. She shuddered with cold and trembled with anguish.

"Emily, dear," a voice said behind her.

Before she could turn to see who spoke to her, she felt strong arms pull her to her feet. She turned to see Daniel. His hair was soaked. He forgot his hat. She looked at his face and couldn't think of what to say. She felt numb. She turned to look at Gus and Bonnie and Henry. Daniel followed her gaze and gasped.

"Gus! Bonnie!" he cried, letting Emily go and running over to their side. "What on earth happened?"

"Steamship." That was all Gus could say.

"He forgot the kitchen knife," Bonnie muttered. "I saw it on the counter. I told him over and over to just keep it in the boat. Sailors always need one just in case you gotta get free from those blasted nets. But no, he didn't want to keep it in the boat. He thought someone would steal it. He didn't want to lose my kitchen knife." She laid her had back down on his chest. "Oh, my Henry…"

"Let me assist you in getting him home, Mr. Emerson," Daniel said. "Spurgeon, Luther, give me a hand." The boys snapped out of their stupor and each grabbed one of their brother's legs. Daniel carefully picked him up under his arms and walked backwards toward the Emerson's.

Emily helped Bonnie to her feet. Their dresses were stained with mud and muck from the boardwalk. They stumbled toward home. Bonnie stopped suddenly and looked behind her. "Frederika," she mumbled to Emily. "She needs help."

Emily squeezed Bonnie's arm and staggered over to Frederika. She took the woman's arm and Frederika looked back at her with empty eyes. All the light and fire had gone out of them. Emily bit her lip and pulled the woman toward home. A few sailors picked up Hugh and helped Charles get him home.

The families took their dead home and closed their doors. They drew their blinds and removed the candles from the windows. It was a gloomy day and it would be a long night ahead.

CHAPTER TWENTY-ONE

"The past is at least secure"
- Daniel Webster

Emily lay in bed that night, chilled to the bone. Her nerves were raw. Sorrow filled every room as the Emersons grieved. Neighbors came by with food for the family. Emily took it upon herself to answer the door each time and see that things were put away properly.

Bonnie sat in her rocker in Henry's room, rocking back and forth, back and forth. His lifeless body lay on his bed, covered with a white sheet up to his chest. Gus and Bonnie changed their son out of his wet sailing clothes and put him in his nicest church clothes. Bonnie combed his unkempt hair for him, mumbling to herself what a good boy he was to her.

Emily's eyes burned from the constant stream of tears welling up in them. This was not how things were supposed to go at all. All the grief from losing her young husband came back in wave after wave. *Could she ever be sure of anything?* She had already lost so much: her husband, their savings, their property.

A firm kick under her ribs served as a reminder. The little life inside her was her only comfort on the long, cold nights in Astoria. He, if it was a he, seemed to sense her distress or sadness and chose to kick or move at just the right times. Love filled her for the tiny person she had yet to meet. Emily protectively placed her hands on her swollen belly and prayed for safety over her precious child. With only two months to go, she grew more and more attached to her baby. *How must Bonnie be feeling tonight losing one of her babies?* Emily could not begin to fathom that kind of grief.

*   *   *

Johan paced the floor of the Occidental Hotel in Portland. He chose the smallest, most reasonably priced room to save his money for the more important purchases the next day. The small fireplace was comforting and the room was pleasant enough with a floral brocade wallpaper and firm, brass bed. The oil lamps hanging on the walls cast a soft glow over the room but his spirit was troubled.

His trip on the steam boat downriver was uneventful despite the pouring down rain and intermittent lightning and thunder. He kept to himself most of the trip, enjoying the scenery along the river. His mind would drift off to Emily when he saw wildlife on the shore or bald eagles above them. Maybe, someday, he could take her to Portland and they could enjoy these things together.

Soft snickering across the aisle from him reminded him that he was being watched by a pair of teenage sisters in expensive dresses. The smile on his lips straightened out and he turned to look out the window. He didn't want or desire their attention. It was best to keep to himself and get his business done.

A nagging premonition kept tugging at him the whole day and now into the evening. Something wasn't right. He could feel it. He prayed his worry had nothing to do with Emily. He hoped it was his anxiousness of being in a big city alone.

I'll be up early. Buy the stove first, the pump next and still catch the afternoon ferry. Johan looked out his third story window to the street below. His stomach grumbled in protest when he saw a few restaurants offering steak dinners. "Nope," he reminded himself. "I'll not waste my hard-earned money on those things. Emily is having a baby and we'll need every last cent I've got." He emptied his duffle onto his bed and sorted through it until he found the brown bread his uncle sent with him. He unwrapped a cotton cloth with some hard cheese in it. Taking his knife, he sliced off a few pieces while plopping into an armchair beside the fireplace. He pushed off his boots and tried to calm his mind and stomach with his simple repast.

*   *   *

"There ya go, Mr. Nevala," said the Lot Whitcomb's crewmember. "We've got your stove tied down on the bottom level. That's a real beauty! You paid a pretty penny for that there, didn't ya?"

Johan ignored the question and peeked into the cargo hold. "Where is the pump?" he asked.

The crewman pointed to the opposite corner. "Over there, sir. If you are satisfied, then we'll board and get this tub moving up river."

A call from the upper deck shouted, "Next stop, Eminence, then on to Astoria. Please board now. Stow your belongings." He pulled the cord on a large brass bell on the beam above him and the clanging rang down the pier.

Johan marched up the ramp and settled into a window seat for the trip home. Apprehension filled him and he wiped his sweaty palms on his pants. Uncle Frans would meet him at the docks when he arrived to get his supplies home in the wagon. But something felt wrong and he couldn't shake it.

The boat began to shake as the steam built up and the engines started pumping. The final passengers made their way on board, filling up the indoor seating area. A few children and parents walked on the outside deck to watch the boat pull away from shore.

Johan leaned back in his chair beside the window and pulled down his sailing cap over his eyes. He put his hand on the cash tied around his stomach, making sure it was secure then he fell asleep.

He woke with a start. Sitting up straight in his seat, he pulled his cap back and surveyed his surroundings. He was still on the sidewheeler. No wonder he felt disoriented. He had slept fitfully for the past few hours. Nightmares plagued him. He couldn't remember details but he felt the nagging urgency to get home.

A businessman walked by and Johan reached out to him. "Excuse me, sir," Johan said. "May I trouble you for the time?"

"Certainly," the man said, pulling out his pocket watch on a chain. "It's almost five o'clock. We're nearing Eminence and should arrive in Astoria just after eight tonight."

"Thank you," Johan said, touching his cap out of respect. Three or four more hours to go. He groaned. Checking in at the Emerson's tonight would be out of the question. Seeing Emily would have to wait until another time. Johan hung his head and rested it in his hands on his knees. He needed to think this through. The stove would be set this week. The well would be dug next week. He had the roof on and walls sealed but the house lacked furniture that Emily would need. *Why didn't he buy her a nice rocking chair in Portland?*

He pictured her before the broad fireplace in the middle of the dining room. He split the oak mantle himself. The thick slice of wood nearly broke his back as he hauled it in and held it to the wall while his uncle nailed its supports in place. But it was worth every ounce of effort if Emily would like it.

He built their table out of pine with matching chairs. He only made two for now. Once Emily's baby was big enough, he would make more. Then there would be their children coming along in the next few years. Johan leaned his head back against the wall, imagining a table full of children that shared his Finnish looks and Emily's soft, beautiful complexion. He grinned. Remembering where he was, he quickly wiped the smile from his face. He could afford to take another nap; it would be a long night moving the equipment home. His uncle would need him to be rested. Johan pulled his cap over his eyes again.

Hmmmmmm. He pictured Emily at the Skipanon River on his birthday. How hard it was to not pull her into his arms and kiss her soundly. That kiss on her forehead was an afterthought. It pained him to tell her goodbye but if he didn't leave then, he wouldn't be able to. Something changed that day. Johan couldn't put his finger on it. Emily closed herself off to him.

Their last meeting at the Emerson's concerned him. She scolded him for treating her as an "option." Why could she not see that he loved her? She wasn't a second priority to him, she was the only priority. Her welfare and care was his utmost concern every moment of the day. It hounded his thoughts while he worked. Her taste and style filled his dreams as he put the house together – hopefully for the both of them.

What kind of stove would she want? Where should the bedrooms be? He would take extra care with the room they would share someday. Bonnie mentioned that Emily liked to sit by the window while her hair dried. He built her a window seat in their bedroom with the forest opening up to her through a large, leaded glass window. He could see her there now. Curled up in a long, white muslin nightgown with a lace collar, tucking her feet up under her on soft, velvet pillows.

She needed a crib for the baby. As far as Johan knew, Henry had missed that detail in trying to meet her every need. A swinging crib with a sturdy base was what she needed. One that she could rock while laying in bed to put the baby back to sleep. Johan's heart ached with longing. As much as he wanted her, he wanted what was best for her. Going home to New York might be the best thing for the baby. Being raised with money, a respectable education and wealthy benefactors would certainly have its rewards. But being raised by a young, ambitious father who knew the value of family was equally as important. Hopefully Emily had the sense to see that.

One more week and he would approach her again. He would ask her for her hand and take her to his farm to see what he had been working on so hard. If she refused him, then he didn't know what he would do. His dreams didn't extend beyond that point. That unknown was as dangerous as the plunge into the river the night he saved her. He would avoid thinking too far ahead.

CHAPTER TWENTY-TWO

"What befalls the earth, befalls all the sons of the earth. This we know: the earth does not belong to man, man belongs to the earth. All things are connected like the blood that united us all. Man does not weave this web of life. He is merely a strand of it. Whatever he does to the web, he does to himself."
- Chief Seattle (1786-1866)

The Lot Whitcomb chugged up the river nearing Astoria. Johan joined the parents and restless children on the outside deck near the paddle wheel. They were turning the last bend on the Columbia River before seeing the night lights of Astoria. The paddles rolled around and around and the spray from them soaked Johan's coat. He moved his bag to his other shoulder to block himself from it.

The first lights came into view. They turned the bend. The city was lit up much brighter than Johan ever remembered. Perhaps he had been out on the farm and not realized how lively the night life of Astoria had become.

"Fire!" someone shouted.

"The city is on fire! Look there!"

A woman shrieked in fear. "The docks are burning!"

Johan ran around the group of people and struggled to get a better view. Over their heads, he could see an inferno blazing along the waterfront. One of the saloons, possibly the Monitor, was completely consumed with flames. Johan tried to see the extent of the damage. It appeared that only the one saloon and a nearby brothel were affected so far. In front of the flames, he could see a bucket brigade lined up from the docks to the disaster site. Unless it rained, there would be no stopping this raging fire. It would leap from building to building as they were situated too closely together.

Fortunately, the Emerson's house was far enough away down Bond Street. It would remain untouched. The Emersons and Emily were safe. He would have to help get this fire stopped though. Offloading his supplies would have to wait.

He was among the first of the passengers to disembark from the Lot Whitcomb when it docked downriver from its normal mooring. Johan raced up the boardwalk to Uncle Frans.

"It's about time you got here, boy," Uncle Frans teased. "The whole city is going to go up in smoke before morning. It's been a horrific two days around here. Seems God decided to judge this wicked city all at once."

Johan slowed his pace for his uncle to catch up. "What do you mean?" he asked.

Frans held onto Johan's arm and held him still while he tried to catch his breath. He straightened and Johan saw the sadness in his uncle's eyes.

"What happened, Uncle?" he demanded. "Emily?"

"Emily is fine, boy." Uncle Frans said. "It's Henry. He drowned out on the river yesterday."

"No!" Johan turned away from his uncle, trying to understand. His hands shot to his head in disbelief. *Henry was in his boat. It was a solid vessel. There shouldn't have been any issues.* "He drowned? How did that happen?"

"A steamship got them," Uncle Frans said, gently. "Both boys died – the Veith boy and Henry."

"My row-sail was a trustworthy vessel," Johan said, still not understanding.

"A steamship smashed your boat. You don't own a boat anymore." Uncle Frans said, pulling on Johan's arm. "I'm so sorry but right now we need to help get this fire out."

Johan shook his head in disbelief. All those feelings of worry that he kept dismissing should have been unfounded. Now the nightmare was real. Astoria was on fire. People were screaming and carrying furniture and injured people out into the streets.

"We need a fire break!"

"Jump in the fire brigade, men!"

Volunteers from the Lot Whitcomb jumped into the line and passed bucket after bucket to those closest to the flames.

"We need a miracle," cried Uncle Johan. "We'll never get this fire out this way."

"Out of all the nights for it not to rain, why tonight?" Johan called back.

"Pray, boy," Uncle Frans shouted.

"I am, Uncle, I am," Johan passed another bucket full of river water toward the flames and juggled passing an empty one back to the river. *Lord, we need a reprieve. We need rain. Please have mercy on us, though we don't deserve it.* Johan thought of Henry and groaned with grief. *Father, help the Emersons.*

Hour after hour, the fire engulfed the Monitor and the Bonita Brothel next to it. Only the Wigwam Saloon and the boardinghouses stood between the fire and the Emersons on the other side of the mill pond. They soaked the side of the Wigwam with water hoping to keep the flames from attacking it next.

"Let's knock that wall inward!" one man yelled.

"Yeah! Collapse the building in on itself. It will save the Wigwam."

"Let the Wigwam burn," Frans called to Johan, who nodded in agreement.

"How did the fire begin?" Johan asked the sailor next to him.

"No one knows for sure," the sailor yelled back above the crackling of the flames. "Someone thinks there was a scuffle in one of the upstairs rooms and a candle got tipped over. Not sure, though."

Johan just shook his head and continued passing the buckets until his arms ached. He stepped out of the line to check on their progress. Near the flames, he noticed a familiar figure in a white shirt and black pants. Reverend Malcolm hauled the next bucket and passed it on. At that same moment, he stepped back and made eye contact with Johan. He nodded once in greeting and stepped back into line in time to pass the next bucket.

Men with axes braved the flames, breaking down the walls of the brothel to keep the fire from spreading. Soon the crackling of timbers warned the men to run. The wall landed in the middle of the building, shooting sparks into the midnight sky. Chucks of burning wood fell out onto the boardwalk. Men from the fire brigade quickly kicked them into the river to save the wooden boardwalk.

Within an hour, the two buildings were a pile of smoldering rubble. The brigade disbanded, exhausted from their efforts. A cheer rose from the crowd and men, of all classes, dragged their feet homeward.

Johan turned to Uncle Frans.

Frans laughed when he saw Johan's face. "You're covered in soot, boy," he said.

"You don't look much better," Johan teased. "I wonder if Mrs. Kuntas will let us clean up at her sauna."

"We better hurry," Frans whispered. "It won't be long and everyone will get the same idea." He started toward Kuntas' Boardinghouse, then stopped suddenly. "What about your stuff on the paddlewheel?"

"They don't leave until tomorrow morning at eight," Johan sighed. "Let's get cleaned up, see if we can get some food and stay in town tonight."

"If you're paying, I'm game," Uncle Frans said, wheezing from the smoke he inhaled. He doubled over in a coughing fit.

"Come on, Uncle, we'll get you some food in you to straighten you out," Johan urged. He grabbed his uncle's arm and pulled it over his shoulders. He half-carried him to Kuntas'.

After a bath and a shave, Johan stepped outside of the boardinghouse. They wouldn't stay with the Emersons tonight and be a burden while they were grieving. Before he left town in the morning, though, he would stop by and pay his respects. Johan had so much adrenaline running through his veins from the fire tonight, he knew he wouldn't be able to sleep right away. Kuntas' was right across the mill pond from the Emerson's. He might as well walk around it and pray for a while until he settled down. Uncle was already in bed.

Johan strolled down Bond Street with only the stars and moon shining to light his way. He stopped next to the pond, shoving his hands into his pockets to keep warm. The reflection of the stars and moon shone back at him on the water. He turned to continue walking when he saw someone coming toward him. It was hard to tell who it was. He stood still and stared as it looked like an apparition after such an eerie night with the fire. He doesn't trust his eyes or nerves after such a trying evening.

A soft voice called out, "Is it you?"

Johan's heart almost jumped up into his throat. *Emily.* He cleared his throat and called back. "Yes, Em. It's me. Wait there. I'll come to you." He jogged over to her in the dark, barely able to see his steps in front of him. His breath made a fog in the air in front of him as the night turned chilly just before the dawn. He reached her and couldn't take his eyes off of her.

"What brings you out here at this hour?" Johan asked, desperately wanting to take her in his arms. He thrust his hands deep into the pockets of his coat to control himself.

She took a step closer to him but he could barely see her face. She was shivering with cold but her forehead was sweaty. "I haven't been able to sleep with the fire. I have been watching it for hours to make sure it didn't come any closer." She hung her head and pulled her thick shawl more tightly around her shoulders. "I couldn't sleep anyway. Did you know that Henry--"

Johan pulled his hands from his pockets and raked them through his damp hair. "Uncle Frans told me tonight as soon as I got back into town."

Emily shot a quick glance up to his face. "Back into town? Where were you?"

"I had to go to Portland for...some things," Johan said, avoiding her eyes.

"It's been such a long two days," Emily sniffled, putting her fist to her mouth. "When I didn't see you, I thought ..." She buried her face into his wool coat.

Johan stroked her hair to comfort her. This felt like a dream. *Why was she here right now?* In the middle of the night? He glanced around to make sure they were alone and safe. "What can I do to help the Emersons? What do *you* need?"

Emily pulled back from him and wiped her eyes on the corner of her shawl. She shook violently with cold.

"Come here," Johan unbuttoned his coat and pulled her into his warmth. After she nestled in, he said, "Now, what can I do?"

"You can forget building me a house on your property," Emily said. "I don't think I can leave Astoria now. Bonnie is as close to me as my own family. It would crush her if I left in a few months." Emily sobbed. "With Henry dying, she would be devastated if I ever moved out."

Johan blinked in disbelief at Emily's words. "Forget building you a house?" he asked. *How did she know?*

Emily looked up at him. "You know, selling me the parcel of land?"

Understanding registered with Johan and he sighed in relief. She was speaking out her grief and emotion. Time would take care of the Emersons. If he knew Bonnie, she wouldn't hang on to Emily if it meant their happiness was at stake.

Johan kissed the top of Emily's head with the softest of kisses. Something stirred in him and one kiss was not enough. He kissed her temple gently. To his surprise, she didn't pull away. Her eyes shone, reflecting the stars above them. He tilted her face upward with one finger and laid a soft kiss on her cheek, then one on the other. She was feverishly hot and trembled.

"My parents keep writing me letters," she mumbled. "They want me to marry Elliott. How can they even think that I would consider that? Don't they know me at all?" She slumped in his arms, her knees weak. "Ronald died at sea…Henry drowned in the river…" She shook with cold. She pressed her white knuckles against her temples. "My head aches…"

He had to get her inside. Never mind how her eyes captivated him right now in the moonlight. There would be all the time in the world for kisses and holding each other but this was not the time or the place for it any longer. He had to get her safely to her bed.

Johan swung her up into his arms and carried her gingerly, unable to see well in the dark. His boots crunched the twigs from the walnut trees under his feet. Johan reached the front door handle and tiptoed inside. Setting Emily down on the bench, he took her heavy shawl from her shoulders and realized what a thin nightgown she had on. She must have been freezing out there. He led her to her room and opened her door. She padded in silently, crawled into her bed, and pulled up the covers. As much as Johan wanted one more kiss before he left, he willed his feet to stay at the threshold of her room. He would never be accused of impropriety on her account.

"Good night, love," Johan whispered to her in the dark.

Emily coughed and shivered under her covers, "Good night, Ronald," she whispered back and turned over.

Ronald? Her late husband's name? What was this? Johan felt like he'd been kicked in the stomach and all the air went out of him. Exhaustion overcame him and closed her door quietly. He tiptoed out of the house, making sure everything was secure.

He trudged back to Kuntas'. *What just happened here?* In one moment, by the pond, he was in heaven. The next, Emily had him turned all topsy-turvy. He needed sleep. Maybe this would look better in the morning...but he doubted that.

CHAPTER TWENTY-THREE

*"Sit in reverie and watch the changing color of the waves
that break upon the idle seashore of the mind."*
-Henry Wadsworth Longfellow (1807-1882)

Johan stopped by the Emerson's in the morning, afraid
of what he might face. He shouldn't have worried. Bonnie met
him at the door with a warm embrace. "Wait here, Johan," she
said. She disappeared up the stairs to Henry's room and
returned a moment later, holding something in her hands.
"He would have wanted you to have this." Bonnie handed
him Henry's Bible and touched the top of it with one of her
hands. "This was one of his most prized possessions," she
said. "I heard your uncle say that you forgot to bring your
Bible over from Finland. Reading this will teach you English
better anyway. It will be a double blessing." Bonnie smiled
and Johan embraced her, unable to speak.

He cleared his throat as tears stung his eyes. "Thank
you, Bonnie," he said. "I'm sorry I can't stay longer but I have
some business to attend to. Please give my regards to Gus and
Spurgeon and Luther."

"Henry's funeral will be next Saturday," Bonnie said,
wiping away a tear. "He's already in the ground at the
primitive cemetery. We had to do the burial right away." Her
voice caught with emotion. "I hope you can come."

"Of course, Bonnie" he said. "I wouldn't miss it for
anything." Johan turned to leave when Bonnie stopped him
again.

"You know, Johan," said Bonnie, thoughtfully. "I'm
making Reezy-Peezy tomorrow night. The boys could use
some joy in their lives right now. Could I ask a huge favor and
have you come to dinner tomorrow night with Uncle Frans?"
Bonnie held onto Johan's arm until he answered.

"Anything you need, Bonnie," he said, with a smile.
"Have you seen Emily this morning?"

"She hasn't been well since Henry's death." Bonnie glanced toward her room. "I'm concerned about her emotional state. She hasn't been sleeping well. She was sleepwalking the night Henry died and I found her in the kitchen. Her coloring has been off. I've asked Sikkus to come by today and see her. She has hardly eaten since the accident. I think it brought back nightmares of her shipwreck."

"I'll be here tomorrow night," said Johan, resolutely.

Johan hurried to Kuntas' and fetched his uncle. They drove their wagon down to the dock where the Lot Whitcomb was anchored. The crew was anxious to get their cargo offloaded so the men were on their way home in less time than expected.

"That's one nice stove, boy," Uncle Frans said, looking over his shoulder as they rode along. "Kind of a shame that she can't cook better, huh?"

Johan chuckled. He remembered their late night rendezvous and resolved that if she never could cook, they'd get by on love alone. He smiled.

"Now what's that all about?" Uncle Frans said, studying him. "You know something I don't know."

"Maybe," Johan said, smiling.

The next morning, the men set the stove, cut holes for the chimney and began building a box for kindling. It was a productive day. Johan was eager to get cleaned up and head to the Emerson's to see if his fears were unfounded regarding Emily. It was amazing how not seeing her everyday made him feel like he was missing a piece of himself. He prayed all day for Emily's health and that Sikkus didn't find anything that concerned her with the baby.

"Let's go," Johan urged his uncle.

"In a bit of a hurry, are we?" Uncle Frans teased. "Alright then, I'm coming. I like rice and beans as much as the next guy even if Bonnie gives it a funny name. What does she call it?"

"Reezy Peezy," Johan said, flicking the reins on Ginger.
"Why do these Americans have to call things such weird names?" Frans called after him from his own horse.
"How do you think 'rieska' and 'kala soppa' sound to them?" Johan said back.
"Ok, I'll give you that," Frans laughed.

They tied off their horses at the front gate and walked up to the Emerson's. Bonnie had the door open before they could even knock. She smiled warmly. "I remember a night, not too long ago, when you came to my door for the first time, Johan Nevala." She hugged Johan and patted Uncle Frans on the shoulder. "Come in, come in. I hope you're hungry."

Johan stepped into the dining room and everyone was seated for supper but Emily's place was empty. Johan looked at Bonnie with concern.

"She's not well, today, Johan." Bonnie set the big bowl of rice and beans on the table. "Sikkus couldn't make out what was wrong. Seems that her blood is not right...or something. I'll feed her after we've eaten. She's not hungry yet."

Johan reached over and patted Gus' arm. "Good to see you, Gus. How are you doing?" Johan held his eye. Both men teared up suddenly.

Gus looked down at his plate and coughed. "Well, boy, I got a 'hitch in my get-up' but I'm gonna be fine one of these days."

Bonnie filled their plates. The men jumped into their usual camaraderie of fishing talk, trying to avoid the pain of Henry's absence. Johan avoided looking at the empty places at the table. First Henry. Now Emily. Bonnie was the gracious hostess but kept retreating to the kitchen. She came back with blotchy cheeks from fresh tears. Gus reached over and patted her hand occasionally, his face red.

"Bonnie, may I check in on Emily?" Johan leaned over and whispered. He couldn't wait any longer. He had to see her.

Bonnie glanced over to Gus for his approval and he nodded once at Johan.

"Excuse me," Johan said, scooting his chair away from the table. He walked down the hallway to Emily's room built on the back of the house. Less than twenty-four hours before, he stood at this doorway. *What would he find tonight?* He cracked her door open and peeked inside. Everything was dark. The curtains were closed. The room felt oppressive and he didn't like it. He marched across the room and yanked the curtains open. Light from the hallway crept in through the door. The soft light from the moon and stars came through her window. *That's better.*

He pulled the wicker chair to her bedside. She was asleep or so it appeared. He sat down and took her hand in his. It was cold. Concern filled Johan and he reached up to feel her cheek. It felt warm so he took in the breath he was holding.

"Emily, I'm here, love," he said. "Can you hear me?"

No response.

Her chest rose and fell evenly. That brought Johan a measure of comfort at least.

Pray. He could pray. Johan bowed his hand as he held her hand. He prayed for Emily to fully recover. Suddenly, he was worried about the baby. *Was her health failing because something was wrong with her baby?* He looked toward the door. No one was coming. He began to pray for the baby. Tentatively, he rested his hand in the middle of her abdomen. Emily didn't move.

A memory crept its way into his mind. He remembered his mother singing to him when he was sick. It was a Finnish lullaby: "Nuku nuku nurmilintu." If this baby was to be his child one day, why not care for him as though he were his now? He began to hum the song from his childhood. The Finnish words rolled off his tongue and strangely brought him the same comfort he felt when he heard it as a child. Just holding her hand and being near her was all he wanted.

After some time, a shadow fell across the room. Bonnie stood in the doorway with her hands on her hips. She held a tray of food and a glass of milk. "I suppose you want to feed her, too, Casanova?" Bonnie said, smiling.

Johan snatched his hand away and Bonnie chuckled. "Oh, dear boy," she said. "I'm not a naive, old woman. I know how you feel about her."

Johan blushed even in the dark. "I'm so sorry about Henry, Bonnie. I know that he cared for Emily too. You must have had some hope…" He couldn't continue.

"Emily is a daughter to me now," Bonnie said, setting her tray of food down on the small table beside the bed. "I don't mean to sound selfish but is it wrong that I hope she won't go home?" Bonnie took Emily's other hand in her own. "She's the daughter I never had. And you are like a son to me, Johan, you know that. There's nothing I would love more than to see you two together."

Johan felt his throat constrict with emotion. His own dear mother would never see his wife or children but Bonnie, Gus and Uncle Frans would. He thanked the Lord everyday that He gave him the courage to get on that Finnish fishing boat bound for Astoria. *Where would he be now if he hadn't?*

"It's late, Johan," Bonnie whispered. "Do you and your uncle want to stay the night or are you heading home?"

"I need to go," Johan said, regretting every word. "But we will see you Saturday. In the meantime, please take good care of her, Bonnie."

Bonnie put her hand over Johan's. "You know that I will."

TWENTY-FOUR

"Love is the only thing that we can carry with us when we go,
and it makes the end so easy."
- Louisa May Alcott (1832-1888)

October 1853

"That fishing in the channel is good but it's not worth a man's life. You got to have that kitchen knife just in case one of those massive steamers comes in over the bar."

"The Veith boy had a sense for gillnetting. Such a shame. Seems he was born to it. Died by it, too. Poor fellow."

Gus and Bonnie huddled beside the grave for Henry. Charles and Frederika stood across from them at Hugh's grave. Reverend Malcolm was at the head of the graves behind their white wooden crosses, his hands folded in front of him. When the crowd assembled, he cleared his throat and began.

"Dearly beloved, we have gathered here today to honor the memory of Hugh James Veith and Matthew Henry Emerson of Astoria. We gather to edify their families with our presence and solitude in this difficult time. We grieve the loss of these admirable young men to the river last weekend. Let's remember the words of our Lord when He said..."

The service was done well. Reverend Malcolm stood beside the Emersons and the Veiths as they bid farewell to those who attended. Emily lingered by Henry's grave. Johan stood across from her and kept his eyes on her. Her face was pale and her eyes lacked luster. Dark rings hung under them from the fever.

Reverend Malcolm kept glancing over at Emily between visitors. He finally excused himself and strode determinedly to Emily's side. "Emily," Daniel said, glancing over at Johan. "Are you well? May I walk you home?" He took her arm and she absentmindedly turned to leave with him.

Johan followed them with his eyes and desperation filled his soul. This was not how he pictured today ending; Emily on Reverend Malcolm's arm. Anger filled him mixed with desperation. Suddenly, he wanted a drink. He never felt the desire to go in one of Astoria's saloons but tonight he might make an exception. He was worn out through and through. Forget trying to win her when she didn't want to be won.

He marched over to Ginger and mounted in one leap.

"Johan!" Frans called after him, but he was down the road before his uncle could stop him.

Johan pulled hard on the reins and directed his horse toward John Steers Tap Room. He could get good and drunk if he wanted in that simple, woodchip-floored saloon. He wouldn't have the distraction of prostitutes. He rode down Bond Street past the Emerson's. Daniel and Emily arrived at the front steps. She turned and waved at Johan as he rode by. Her hand hung limply in mid-air when he flew by them without slowing.

Johan sped down the street past Sixth, then Tenth. John Steers Tap Room stood across from the main docks, making it easily accessible to tired sailors coming off the river. Johan had seen it a thousand times and never once considered going in. He pulled hard on the reins and stilled his horse. He swung his leg over his saddle and tied her to the hitching post in front of the bar. Johan stood there, fists resting on the post, weighing the consequences of his decision. If he went in, it could begin a downward spiral in his life that he had seen happen to countless others in Astoria. Where would it end? Hours spent at the counter, trying to drink away his sorrows. It would lead to an unending pit. His hard-earned money would be swallowed up in corruption. Johan hung his head and slammed his fist into the post.

"It's just not worth it," he muttered to himself.

"Oh I think it might be," came a sinister voice from behind him.

Johan felt a piercing pain in the back of his head and then his world faded to black.

*   *   *

A sharp knock came at the Emerson's door. Gus padded over in his wool stockings to answer it.

"Mr. Bell?" Gus said in surprise. "Come to pay your respects, friend? Come in, come in."

George Bell filled the doorway with his massive frame. He turned and looked over his shoulder. "Gus, I do extend my sincere condolences," he said, "but I'm here on another matter, friend." He pointed over his shoulder. "That Johan Nevala's horse there?"

Gus peeked past his friend's massive frame to see. Sure enough, there stood Ginger with a gash in her front right shoulder, nibbling at a tuft of grass in their yard. She favored her wounded leg and settled on the other three.

"Yeah, that's her," Gus said, confused. "Did she throw Johan? Where is he?"

"I was hoping you knew," George said. "Found her at the other end of town by my sliming house. Somethin' didn't seem right. Thought I better see if someone tried horse-napping her. Looks like she put up a fight, no matter what happened. Someone had a knife."

Gus called up the stairs to his boys. "Spurgeon! Luther! Come 'ere, boys. Looks like we have a little game of Hide 'n Seek happening tonight."

Bonnie and Emily stepped out of the kitchen. Emily sank into one of the dining room chairs and wiped her brow.

Bonnie spoke up first, "Gus, what is this all about?"

George tilted his work cap. "Just came by to see about Mr. Nevala. Seems he and his horse got separated somehow."

"Johan?" Emily said, starting to stand up again.

"Just rest, honey," Bonnie said, resting her hand on Emily's shoulder. "The men will take care of this."

"I don't know if this helps," George whispered to Gus. "But there have been some suspicious looking sailors from the Finnish fishing ship anchored in the river. I've heard of guys getting shanghaied before."

Gus glanced over at the women whose faces blanched white. He turned back to George, just as his boys came down the stairs. "Any man who tried tying Johan up and dragging him out to sea has got another thing coming. First of all, the boy don't drink...at all. He wouldn't be caught dead in a hurdy-gurdy house. His reputation is too important to him." Gus nodded over at Emily. "Some things are too valuable to mess up in his book. Know what I mean?"

George nodded and hung his head. "I'm not accusing anyone of anything. It was just a possibility. Good luck finding him. Is Frans around to help?"

"Frans headed back to the farm thinking that Johan went that way." Gus sighed, wiping his face with his hand. "George, can you help us look for him tonight?"

"That I'll do, friend," George said. "I'll wait for you out here by his horse."

Gus closed the door and pulled on his boots and oil slicker. "Bonnie, come here, please," Gus whispered. "Don't alarm Emily but Johan has gone missing. She doesn't need this right now. We don't need this right now, for that matter, but apparently the good Lord thinks we've got the shoulders to handle it." Gus bowed his head and Bonnie took him in her arms. "If he comes here, light all the candles in the upstairs windows. That way we'll know he's safe."

"Godspeed, Gus," Bonnie said, hugging him tightly. "Just bring my boys home to me...all of them, you hear?"

Emily sat up straight in her chair and patted the table. "Bonnie, please tell me what's happening. I know I haven't been myself this week but I need to know whatever it is that you don't want to tell me."

Bonnie sat down, across the table from Emily, in Henry's old chair. She looked at the chair that Johan normally sat in next to Emily.

"Not Johan, too," Emily gasped.

CHAPTER TWENTY-FIVE

"Sailors must be slaves no more" – Mayor Henry Lane of Portland
(1855-1917)

Johan woke to complete darkness. An acrid, burlap sap covered his face, stifling his breathing. When he tried to remove it, he realized that his hands were bound behind his back. Panic gripped his chest. He was lying on a mattress of some kind. He struggled to get his hands free.

"You stay put there, sailor," someone whispered next to him in Finnish. "We'll let you loose, but not yet. No one on board has a wish to die today. We don't want trouble."

Johan's mind spun. *On board? What does that mean?* The man speaking to him was Finnish. He had seen the Finnish fishing boat at the docks. Uncle Frans warned him to steer clear of the waterfront in case they recognized him. Now he wished that he had listened. He closed his eyes and felt the sway of the ship on the river. The ocean's roar filled his ears and the smell of salt water and tackle filled his senses. He recognized the smell from his voyage over from Finland. After three years, he was right back where he started from. Johan felt a heaviness like lead fill his spirit. He would lose his land, his home, his family. He thought of Emily. His future.

"Check at Kuntas'," Gus hollered above the tempest to his boys.

Luther and Spurgeon ran down Bond Street and rapped on Kuntas' door, inquiring after Johan's whereabouts.

George and Gus trudged through the streets to Karhuvaara's Boardinghouse. Gus pounded on their front door. Mrs. Karhuvaara opened it, startled.

"Mr. Emerson, how can help you?" she said, in her halted English.

Gus, out of breath, wheezed, "Have you seen or heard anything of Johan Nevala?"

"Johan? No. Have not seen since funeral earlier," she said. "Not look good, though. You know? Face not look good. Is he ill?"

"He's missing," Gus said. "Please keep your ears open for any news."

Mrs. Karhuvaara nodded hard in agreement and closed her door.

"Gus, this isn't good," George said, as they continued down Bond Street. "I've only heard of one other sailor getting crimped and we never saw him again."

"Crimped?" Gus stopped and turned to George. "You mean killed?"

"No, crimped," George said. "Shanghaied."

"Johan is too well known around here. Who would dare to kidnap him?" Gus shook his head at the ridiculous idea. "Who could handle him? That would be like taking a bear on board a ship. Not a good idea."

George grimaced. "They would not try to take him consciously. Perhaps if he were drunk--"

"Stop right there," Gus ordered. "That boy has never been drunk once since I've known him. There's got to be a logical explanation for this."

"Gus, listen to me," George said. The men stopped under the coal oil light on the docks, pulling their oil skins closer to the faces. "I'm down on the docks. I hear what goes on around here. My Finnish workers have been gossiping about that fishing boat needing more crew members. No one wanted to go from the cannery. They make more working for me than on board a ship. When a crew gets desperate enough, they'll fill their crew list however they can. Boys are jumping ship at every Pacific dock to get off those boats."

Gus knew George spoke the truth. Wasn't that how Johan came to them in the first place? He shook his head in dismay and looked down the dock to where the Finnish ship should have been anchored. It was gone.

"When did the Finnish ship weigh anchor?" Gus asked, spinning around, looking out to the bar.

"The tide turned around three this afternoon," George grumbled. "My guess is that they are past the shoals by now."

Luther and Spurgeon came running down the boardwalk to their father. "Dad," they cried. "Mrs. Kuntas overheard some of her renters say that their Boarding Master needed a few more crew members before they could leave. At dinner last night, she heard them whispering about 'getting paid by the body,' if they could fill the ship's roster." Luther put his hands on his knees and drew in a sharp breath.

"They can't just take him," Gus argued. "There are rights! He's a landowner in the United States now!"

George put his hand on Gus' shoulder. "They'll forge his signature, Gus. They'll make it look legit. There's nothing we can do until his tenure is up. Most likely he'll find his way back here in a year or two, if we are lucky."

"Pa, no!" Spurgeon cried. He leaned over the rail, searching the bar for the fishing ship. "We've got to do something!" Spurgeon and Luther took off running down the boardwalk to their row-sail.

"Boys!" Gus called after them. They stopped running reluctantly and turned. Gus marched toward them. "We are going to do something. But not out there tonight. First we're going to check all the businesses in town and make sure he's not here."

"All the businesses?" Luther looked at his brother in disbelief. "Uh, Pa, you don't mean--"

"I mean *all* the businesses," Gus roared. "We're gonna find out whose holding the blood money for that boy and someone is gonna pay." Gus' red hair shone like fire in the oil light and his angry face matched it.

"Lord have mercy on the soul who has to deal with him," George mumbled. "Let's get going. This could be a long night."

Luther and Spurgeon tromped into their home, peeling off their wet oil skins and boots at the door. Bonnie and Emily looked up from the table, expectantly.

"Any news?" Bonnie asked, with her hand on her chest.

"Not yet, Ma," Luther mumbled. "We have an idea of what might have happened. Mr. Bell and Pa are checking into any further leads."

"Right now? It's dark. It's late," Bonnie argued. "Who would be up at this hour?"

Spurgeon cleared his throat and shook his head in the negative. But Luther spilled, "They are checking the bars and saloons and...other places to make sure Johan isn't ...misplaced." The boys looked at each other and grimaced at bearing the news with Emily sitting there.

Emily gasped, startled and knocked over her tea cup. She put her hand over her mouth and looked to Bonnie.

"Now, now," Bonnie said. "I don't believe it's as it sounds. They just want to make sure there's been no mischief, right?" She directed her question to Spurgeon who quickly nodded.

"Bonnie, Johan didn't look well today," Emily whispered. "I think he took Henry's funeral very hard." Emily righted her spilled tea cup and began mopping up the tea with her apron. She put her hand to her brow and wiped off the cold sweat forming.

"You don't look very well, either, Missy," Bonnie said, concerned. "When Daniel brought you home, I was worried you might not make the walk."

Emily shooed Bonnie with her hand. "Bonnie, don't worry about me right now. How can we help Johan?" Emily stood to her feet. She rested her hands on the edge of the table to keep her balance. Suddenly, she cried out in pain. She collapsed on the floor pulling the lace tablecloth over as she went. Her tea cup fell to the floor and shattered to pieces. Emily gripped her sides and curled over.

Spurgeon and Luther were at her side instantly. "Em!" they cried. "Ma, do something!"

"Let's get her to bed," Bonnie ordered. "Careful now, boys."

The boys lifted Emily and carried her gingerly down the hallway to her room. Bonnie hovered behind them and got Emily situated in her bed. Emily's face lost all color and when Bonnie put hand to her brow, it was cold and clammy. "Oh dear," she mumbled. She turned and whispered to Spurgeon and Luther, "Run to Sikkus' house and bring her quickly. Stay together. There's all sorts of mischief out there tonight. I think Emily is going to have this baby early."

*   *   *

Someone ripped off the burlap sack, scratching Johan's face. He tried springing to his feet to fight but they had tied his hands to the bed rail.

"You don't think we are that foolish, do you?" the Finnish sailor teased. "We're not letting you loose until tomorrow when we are good and far from shore. Nice to have you back, *Johan Nevala*."

Johan felt the air go out of his lungs. He stood face to face with the Boarding Master for the fishing ship he signed on with in Liminka. He hung his head in defeat.

"First you will pay with your rightful punishment for jumping ship," the man growled. "I believe that's twenty lashes strapped to the mast of the ship. You look younger and stronger than I remember. We might make it thirty just to break you." Some men behind the Boarding Master laughed in mockery. "Then you will pay with your first three month's wages."

Johan's head snapped up in defiance. He glared at the man but said nothing.

"We will get the work out of you that we should have received three years ago." The Boarding Master sneered and hit Johan hard across the face with the back of his hand.

"And you wonder why I jumped ship in the first place," Johan mumbled.

"What's that, sailor?" the man bellered. "You have something you wish to say to me?" He punched Johan in the gut.

"You will pay for this," Johan wheezed out. His side ached with piercing pain. He had a broken rib for sure. He tried straightening himself to breathe better.

"No, boy, that's where you're wrong," the Boarding Master muttered. "You are the only one who will be paying for anything."

George and Gus walked up to the Columbia Bar and paused before entering. Gus turned to his friend. "If my wife knew I was about to go in here, I would have hell to pay."

George shook his head and put his hand on Gus' shoulder, urging him forward.

"George Bell," the owner called from behind the bar. "You brought a drinkin' buddy tonight, I see. Why, that's Mr. Emerson! You don't say! Never thought I'd see you darken my door. This is a real treat." The snappy, little bartender could barely see above the counter. His bald head and round spectacles made him look anything but intimidating. He walked down the counter, collecting his tips and shoving them into his apron pockets.

"Well, I ain't here for nothin' that you got," growled Gus. "I need to know if you have seen my boy, Johan."

The bartender squinted his eyes and looked around to make sure no one else was listening. "Yeah, I saw him," he smiled, crookedly, resembling an over-sized rat with his beady eyes and pointy nose. "Who could miss him? He came barreling through town on that horse of his. Tied up over by the Tap Room--"

"How dare you--" Gus lunged forward, almost reaching the bartender from the other side of the counter.

"Gus!" George grabbed his arm and held him back. "Let him finish."

The bartender gulped hard and straightened his bow tie. "I don't know if you deserve to hear the information I have…"

"Now come on, Silas," George pleaded with the little man. "We gotta find this kid. What do you know?"

Gus and George leaned forward while the bartender loosened his collar. "It all happened so fast. But that Finnish boy, Johan, tied up his horse in front of the Tap Room. I don't know if he went in or not but next thing I know, he's unconscious and getting carried down the street by some buddies."

"Buddies?" Gus bellered. "What buddies?"

"Hold your voice down there, Emerson," the bartender sneered. "You're disturbing my paying customers." He looked around and smiled at the sailors now watching them. "Back to your business, boys. Nothing to see here."

He leaned in toward Gus and George, wiping the counter absentmindedly. "You know, his Finnish buddies. The fellas from the ship. They're all Finnish, right? I figured they were just grabbing some drinks together…for old times' sake."

Gus and George looked at each other. George slapped the counter. "You better give me a shot, Silas. This is bad news."

Johan sat on the foul mattress with his hands tied behind him. His shoulders ached as he was unable to stretch out his arms for almost a full day now. His muscles burned but not as hot as the anger that threatened to drive him crazy. *How dare they shanghai me?* He would get off this stinking tub again if it cost him his life. He would not go back to Finland. He would not be caught on this boat crossing oceans while Emily had her baby and thought him dead and gone. Throwing himself overboard and swimming for shore was his only hope.

"Time for your punishment, sailor," a fellow shipmate muttered, entering the reeking, dam cell he sat in. "Get up. Take it like a man." He sneered and revealed a whole section of missing teeth.

"What punishment?" Johan said, barely audible. He was so angry he didn't trust himself to not go ballistic on the sailor.

"The punishment for all deserters," the sailor continued, now joined by a comrade. They began to untie Johan's hands from the bed frame. "You know what you signed on for back in Finland. You were to sail and serve this ship for three years. You barely did four months. That's not right, is it? Faking your own death and disappearing may have worked for a few years but we've looked for you in every port between here and San Francisco. We figured you would show up at some point. Fool!"

"Thirty lashes," the other sailor grumbled. "Fair enough. Just enough lashes to scar you for life but not enough to kill you."

"You won't be jumping ship anytime soon, I'm thinking," the first sailor mocked.
"You won't be able to swim in salt water after your back is laid open like a salmon filet."

Johan hung his head. He had known the punishment for getting caught. He probably had this coming. Things were going too well to last. Nevertheless, he would face this like a man. When it was over, there wouldn't be a man on board this ship who would be able to hold him.

Gus stumbled into his house. Bonnie tiptoed down the hall to meet him, wringing her hands.

"Any word, Gus?" she asked.

Gus hung his slicker on his peg and sat down on the bench to pull off his boots. "He's done for, Bonnie. They got him back. Seems Johan got crimped and taken back to Finland."

"Crimped?" Bonnie shrieked. "Not Johan! How will we ever get him back, Gus? How far out to sea is he?"

"The boat left with the tide," Gus rubbed his forehead, thinking. "They must be a day's journey out to sea by now."

"We could still reach him," Bonnie said, excitedly. "You know that any number of the sailors would help us, if we ask them. First thing in the morning, Gus, we'll go after him. We'll get Frans and the Veiths--"

"Bonnie!" Gus said, holding up his hand to still her. "I know this is hard for you but this is very dangerous. We would be in the wrong to try to take him back."

Understanding crossed Bonnie's face. Tears welled up in her eyes. Gus saw the sorrow on her face in the candlelight. He stood and took her in his arms.

"Do we give up?" Bonnie cried. "He's one of our own now."

They stood holding each other for a moment. Suddenly, Gus pulled back. "No!" His face burned red with anger. "We don't give up. We've lost Henry. Emily needs Johan now. We can't lose him too. We have to at least try. First light, I'll head down to the docks with the boys and get a crew together. Veith has an ocean-going vessel he was ready to put up for sale. We can take that. It's fast and sleek. I think we can catch them. I'm sure of it."

"Gus Emerson, I love you!" Bonnie said, kissing his cheek firmly. "I'm going to get you boys some food together. It will be by the door in the morning. Meanwhile, Sikkus and I have a very unhappy mother back there who is undergoing the beginning of labor."

Gus looked past Bonnie down the hallway. He put a hand to his heart. "I don't think we can handle much more," he said.

"Oh yes, we can," Bonnie said, resolutely, already marching to the kitchen. "We're all they've got. We better do our best!"

CHAPTER TWENTY-SIX

"Freedom is the last, best hope of earth."
-Abraham Lincoln (1809-1865)

Johan's muscles ached. He strained against the cords that tied him to the mast. Rain began pelting his face in the early morning hour.

"He loves this boat so much, he's clinging to it," the Boarding Master mocked. "He can't bear to be separated from it."

Johan pushed himself to his full height with his legs. Somehow he had managed to sleep a few hours with his hands shackled around the ship's main mast since midnight.

"Sound the bell," the Boarding Master ordered. It clanged loud enough for the whole ship to hear. "Assemble all the sailors. This morning we are going to give a lesson I don't want any of the crew to miss." He snarled, curling one lip up over his teeth. "This will teach everyone to quit jumping off the *Hai!*"

Once the crew was assembled, the Boarding Master continued his torture. "Cut his shirt off of him," he ordered. "Loose his shackles and hook his hands above him."

A nearby sailor took a knife from his waist and slit the back of Johan's shirt. It hung in two pieces off of his shoulders. His bronzed skin from the summer's work lay exposed to the rain and cold.

Another sailor unlocked the shackles around the mast only to take both of Johan's hands and lock them together again in front of him.

"Hands above your head," he growled. Johan lifted them and he hooked them above his head. "Pull back on the hook," he ordered. The hook on the rope pulled Johan's arms taut. His sinews stretched to the point of ripping before they secured the rope. Johan tried to draw in a breath and stood on his tip toes.

"Alright, pretty boy," the Boarding Master sneered. "My first mate will read your punishment and it will begin at once."

A stocky Finn stepped forward and Johan caught his eye before he began. A flicker of remorse crossed the man's visage before he cleared his throat. "Johan Nevala of Liminka, Finland. You are hereby held responsible for and punishable for the lost wages due to the *Hai* for jumping ship two and a half years shy of completing your tenure. You will receive no more than and no less than thirty lashes with a knout for your crime."

An outcry from the crew members erupted.

"Thirty lashes!"

"The punishment for jumping ship is twenty lashes!"

"This is unjust!"

Johan turned his head toward the stone-faced sailor holding the leather whip. It had been soaked in milk and hardened in the sun. He cracked it once in the air for effect and the sailors silenced.

"You think this is unjust!" the Boarding Master bellowed. "Perhaps you'd like to be next. You will see what happens to the man who crosses the Master of this ship."

The stocky first mate cleared his throat and called out. "You may begin the lashing." He stepped clear of the mast and the length of the whip.

Johan hung his head, breathed a quick prayer for strength and steeled his resolve. He would take this punishment with dignity. He would not beg for mercy as he had seen others do before. The same *sisu* that caused him to rise from the road in Liminka would lift him off the bloody deck when this was over. He clenched his teeth.

"*Yksi!*"

Johan gasped at the sting of the leather ripping his skin open.

"*Kaksi!*"

Red and yellow flashed across his vision. He had not expected this much pain so soon.

"*Kolme!*"

He tried to draw in a breath.

"*Nelja!*"

"*Viisi!*"

Drops of blood began to drip down Johan's back and land on the deck at his bare feet. It mixed with the rain water running across the boards. Johan's vision blurred from the pain and the water splashed into his eyes.

On and on the counting continued. Not a sound was heard on the deck of the *Hai* but the crack of the whip and an occasional grunt that would escape from Johan's lips.

"*Kymmenen!*"

Ten. He had only had ten lashes and already he knew that his back would never be the same. Muscles burned and tendons severed as the whip tore through them again and again. His arms trembled in the shackles and shook violently.

Murmurs from the crew grew louder and louder.

"Silence, you dogs!" The Boarding Master marched around the mast, daring anyone to stand up for Johan's defense. He was met with steely glares but not one word.

"*Viisitoista!*"

Johan clenched his teeth to keep himself from crying out in anguish. He held his eyes shut tight to block out everything around him. The whip flung across his back again and his eyes shot open with the pain. He took in the faces of the crew. Instead of self-righteous smirks, he saw compassion on their faces. Frowns replaced the sneers from the beginning of the lashing.

Johan's body began to shake from the torture. The loss of blood made him dizzy and lightheaded. His mind couldn't maintain concentration. *Lord, help me.* He blinked his eyes hard to focus but they would not. His legs trembled underneath him. The shackles cut into his wrists as he hung more and more from them, unable to hold himself up.

"Kaksikymmenta!"

Twenty. Johan gasped for air and a sob threatened to escape. He didn't know if he could go on. Black dots filled his vision. He gulped in air before the next stroke hit his back. He clenched his jaw and looked up to the heavens. Huge drops of rain came falling down, stinging the raw flesh on his back. Heat and flashes of cold shot through him and sweat broke out on his brow. He gasped for air again.

"Kaksikymmenta viis!"

Twenty-five.

Now the crew was in an uproar.

"It is enough!"

"This is unjust! You must stop!"

"Twenty lashes is the right punishment. You cannot keep going!"

The cries from the crew grew so loud that the captain of the ship emerged from his quarters.

The knout kept tearing into Johan's back in spite of the outcry on the deck. Johan's legs doubled underneath him and his shoulders hung slack in the shackles. His eyes rolled back in his head and everything faded into the background. He could still hear the distant cries of the men around him. But the pain was gone. *Am I dying? Is this what it feels like? No more pain. No more suffering.* He would be with his father and mother soon with the Lord. Incredible peace overwhelmed him.

No Johan, you're not done yet. You need to raise Seth first.

Seth? Suddenly, Johan regained the will to live and he let out a breath of air.

*   *   *

Emily screamed. She sucked in a quick breath and tried to hold it. The pain threatened to drive her out of her mind. With each contraction, she felt she couldn't go on but she had to.

"For your son, Miss Em. Do it for your son," Sikkus said, urging her on. "That's it. That's it. You see, Miss Bonnie. We almost there. Just bit more now. Don't give up."

Bonnie applied another cool cloth to Emily's brow.

Sikkus motioned to Bonnie for the warm oil. "This will help. Make easier."

"Please, Lord," Emily prayed between breaths. "Help my baby." She thought she would faint from pushing. It seemed to go on and on. Only the encouragement from Sikkus and Bonnie kept her going.

"You do good, Miss Em," Sikkus whispered, focusing on her task. "We close now." She reached up and laid her hand on Emily's stomach. "Rest. Take deep breath. Shhhhhhh."

Emily obeyed and closed her eyes. *Soon she would hold her baby.* Her life would never be the same. She must be strong. She must be brave. Just a little while longer. The contraction began to spread over her stomach again and involuntarily her muscles pushed.

"Now, Miss Em," Sikkus urged, the excitement in her voice was contagious.

Emily's arms shook with adrenaline and effort. In one miraculous moment, all her efforts from the past five hours were summed up with one final push. Deliverance from all her pain. It was over.

Sikkus laughed and held up a small but perfect baby boy. His eyes were closed and his mouth gasped for air. Sikkus held him over to Bonnie. "Grandma! Give him good slap," she ordered.

Bonnie didn't hesitate. She spanked the little man on his behind. He gasped for air, letting out a healthy cry. Bonnie and Emily broke down, sobbing and laughing all at once. Sikkus just smiled with pride.

"He's beautiful, Em," Bonnie sobbed. Sikkus handed the baby to Bonnie who wrapped him a clean soft towel. Sikkus cut the cord and quickly rubbed the baby down with a fine sea salt to ward off any infection.

Emily leaned back on her pillow, soaked in sweat, exhausted. She could not take her eyes off the tiny bundle in Bonnie's arms. All the pain was gone. Complete and utter joy flooded her as Bonnie laid her son in her waiting arms.

"Hello, little one," she whispered, through her tears. A giggle escaped and her body shook with spasms of adrenaline as she held him.

Bonnie knelt down beside the bed and placed her hand under the baby to steady him. "Congratulations, Emily. You've brought a healthy, strong son into the world. Praise the Lord."

Sikkus moved silently around, cleaning and arranging and fussing. She moved over the mortar and pestle and worked on a fusion for Emily. She ground away, casting a sideways glance every now and then to check on the mother and baby.

"Color good," she mumbled.

Bonnie looked over to her friend and smiled. She rose to her feet and crossed over to Sikkus. "What would we have done without you, dear?" Bonnie hugged Sikkus' shoulders, who continued to work.

"We not done yet," Sikkus beamed back at her. "Ready?"

Bonnie furrowed her eyebrows in confusion. Sikkus just smiled.

"I'm so hungry," Emily exclaimed, laughing.

"See?" Sikkus chuckled. "She need some steak and potato and cake! Time to feed momma and baby."

Bonnie laughed, understanding. She came back to Emily's side.

Emily nestled her baby and gave him a kiss on the cheek. "Seth Henry Davenport," Emily cooed.

Bonnie gasped. "You don't mean..."

"Yes," Emily said, resolutely. "Seth is the name that Adam and Eve, in the Bible, gave their son to have a new start. I am making a new start in Astoria. Ronald would have liked Henry. I want to honor Henry's memory and love for us. Lord willing, Seth will have a stepfather who will raise him to be a godly young man like your son, Bonnie."

"We are working to get him home right now," Bonnie said absentmindedly, looking out the window at the dawn stretching across the sky.

CHAPTER TWENTY-SEVEN

*"Hope is the expectation that something outside of ourselves,
something or someone external, is going to come to our rescue and
we'll live happily ever after."*
- Dr. Robert Anthony

Gus, Spurgeon and Luther crept down the hallway to Emily's room at first light. Gus gently knocked on the door which Bonnie promptly opened.

"How's our girl?" he asked, deep lines etched in his forehead.

"You mean 'how's our new boy'?" Bonnie beamed. "Emily is fine. She's resting now. *Seth* is wide awake, it seems." She retreated into the room and reappeared with a tiny bundle in her arms. Gus, Luther and Spurgeon crowded around to see his face.

"He's so little," Spurgeon whispered.

"Hi nephew," Luther cooed, touching his tiny fist. "Just wait until we can take you fishing and boating and--"

"How 'bout we just let him get some sleep first," Bonnie said, snuggling the baby closer. "Isn't he wonderful?"

"And Emily?" Spurgeon asked, suddenly concerned.

"She's going to be fine," Bonnie whispered, careful not to wake her. "Sikkus and I will take care of her. You go get Johan home." Bonnie's face grew serious. "Emily doesn't know anything yet. Let's keep it that way. We need her to be calm and rested."

"We're off," Gus ordered his boys. He took one last long look at the baby and grinned at Bonnie. "God is good." He whispered, stifling a sob and wiping his nose on his sleeve.

"Let's go crack some heads," he muttered, stumbling out of the house into the early morning chill.

*   *   *

"But Charles," Gus argued, "if we don't use the new boat, we can't get Johan back."

Charles shook his head once in the negative. "It not tested yet, Gus. Not safe."

"Oh bother!" Gus threw his hands up in the air. "We are wasting precious time, Veith. You know as well as I do that this boat is sea-worthy. We only build the best."

"It already sold," Charles growled. "Not even my boat to let you use!"

"We will test it for the new owner then," Gus said, with a twinkle in his eye. "Huh? Huh?" He nudged Mr. Veith in the ribs and watched his resolve crack. Time to make the final blow. "This is for Johan. He's like my son. What if that was Hugh out there?"

Charles' head snapped to attention. His eyebrows furrowed.

"You would do whatever it took to get him back, wouldn't you?" Gus said, tenderly. "Let's go get our Johan. He's one of us. We can't let him go without trying."

Charles Veith clenched his German jaw.

The deal was done.

Gus slapped his hands together. "Board the ship, boys. We're wasting daylight!"

A make-shift crew from Bond and Taylor Streets clambered down the ladder to Gus and Veith's newest boat. They whistled their approval at the fine piece of workmanship.

"Maiden voyage, huh?"

"That's right, boys."

"Let's try her out. Get those sails open. Man the oars." Gus bellowed.

Charles Veith ran a hand down the rail of his ship and stood next to Gus. "We do this for Hugh and Henry."

"For Henry and Hugh!" the men echoed.

*   *   *

Johan lay face-down on a bed frame with no mattress on it. A blanket lay over the wooden slats to provide some cushion. His face hung through the slats for the mattress so he could breathe easily without turning his neck. He could only focus on breathing in and out and not moving. His friend, Veli, sat beside him placing bandages with ointment over his open wounds.

"You weren't supposed to come back to the *Hai*," Veli said quietly. "Brother, you almost died."

Johan faded back to sleep, exhausted.

*   *   *

Gus and Charles took turns at the helm as they crossed the bar. The sail caught the wind and pulled them out to sea. They smiled at each other. Their boat was light and fast. It flew across the waves like a sea bird.

Luther stood at the bow with eyes fixed on the horizon.

"First sign of that Finnish ship," Gus called out, "let us know."

The crew was wound up as tight as a sailor's knot. Tension filled the air.

"There could be serious danger ahead. The *Hai* isn't just going to let Johan go without a fight," one sailor whispered near Gus.

"Each of us has thrown in what bartering money we can spare. Hopefully it's enough to buy a soul," his mate answered.

"We must pray," Charles whispered to Gus, holding the rutter.

Gus nodded once in agreement. "You keep her straight. I'll bow my head." Veith nodded. "Father in heaven, we ask for Your divine help. We are not worthy. We are humble men in need of Your aid. Guide our ship to Johan. Allow him to come home in Your mercy. Keep us from all harm. Amen."

"Amen," Veith echoed and coughed.

"There!" Luther cried, pointing. "Do you see that spot on the horizon? Do you think it's the *Hai*?"

"Let's go see," Gus ordered. "To your posts, men!"

They neared the *Hai* unobserved. The Finnish ship didn't appear to have weaponry visible but Gus and George's crew proceeded with caution anyway.

"You have that Colt 45?" Gus asked the sailor closest to him.

"Yep," the sailor patted the handle of the firearm tucked into his waistband.

"You know how to use that, if needed?" Gus asked, raising an eyebrow.

"Yep," the man answered, spitting out some chew juice over the side.

"Ok then," Gus said, taking a deep breath. He turned to Uncle Frans. "We're ready when you are."

Frans cleared his throat and called up to the *Hai* in Finnish. "*Hei!*"

A sailor peeked over the rail above them and waved. "Astoria?" he called down.

Frans nodded and said in Finnish. "We've come for Johan Nevala. We've come to take him home." He spoke sternly, trying to keep his anger at bay.

The Finnish sailor waved and disappeared. He returned with another sailor.

"*Hei!*" the next sailor called. "Family of Johan Nevala?"

Uncle Frans cried, "*Kylla!*"

"One moment," the sailor called back in halted English. "I am Veli, Johan's friend from Liminka. I bring him to you."

"Veli! *Kylla!*" Frans called back, remembering Johan tell about his friend, Veli, who helped him jump ship in Astoria.

Gus nudged the sailor with the gun. "Stay on your guard," he warned, apprehensive at how easily this was going. The sailor nodded, keeping his eyes above them.

What seemed like forever passed. Gus' crew grew restless as they waited.

"We should climb the side of this ship and just go get him ourselves."

"It would be faster."

"Finnish work ethic – my eye! They are moving as slow as molasses," one sailor whined until he turned to see Frans' fierce glare. "Never mind."

Just then, a handful of sailors marched down the deck of the ship.

"Steady," Gus warned, as the sailor drew his gun. "Steady."

The sailors held a large bundle wrapped in a sheet between them.

"Is he dead?"

"They killed him!"

Veli popped his head over the edge to face the Colt 45 aimed at him. He pulled back again quickly. "Johan not dead!"

He peeked back over with his hands in the air, surrendering. "I am Veli, friend of Johan. He not dead. Please. We give him to you."

The men fastened Johan to a plank with ropes at each end to lower him over the side.

"Careful now," Gus cried as they lifted Johan's limp body over the side on the plank. One false move and he would plummet thirty feet into the sea. "Smoley Hokes," he mumbled, biting his nail. "Get ready to catch him, men."

The Finnish sailors slowly lowered him inch by inch, foot by foot until he reached the waiting fingertips of the sailors from Astoria. They pulled him into their boat and gasped at what they saw.

Johan lay facedown on the plank with his head turned. He was unconscious. The blood from his back soaked through the thin sheet he was wrapped in. His skin looked like a slaughtered animal much less a man.

A collective cry of rage rose from them. They shook their fists in the air at the Finnish sailors.

Veli held his hands up again in surrender and cried out. "Uncle! Uncle!"

Frans quieted the crew on his boat to hear. His clenched fists were on his hips and he trembled with rage. "Veli! What happened?"

Veli held up his hand and looked down the ship's deck. "Captain coming. Please wait. He explain." Veli spoke in halted English. "Please wait."

The captain of the *Hai,* leaned over the rail and held up his hand. He spoke in broken English. "Men of Astoria, we, the crew of the *Hai,* most respectfully sorry for over-punishment of Johan Nevala. He took scourging like a man but Boarding Master of *Hai* violated law. Administered ten lashes too many. Thirty not twenty as I ordered. Because of this, Johan is free from all contract even though jump ship before. I release him and give sincere regrets for fault is mine."

Gus, Frans and the crew looked from Johan to the captain above them. Anger raged inside of them but the compromise was fair and they would take it.

Frans answered in Finnish and no one dared to ask for a translation of it. The captain saluted him and he turned to Gus. "Let's get him home." He sank down onto the deck beside his nephew, surveying the open wounds. Infection had not settled in yet. Someone had taken meticulous care of him. Frans looked back up to the deck of the *Hai* and Veli peered down at him. He gave one final wave. Frans choked back the tears. At least the Lord had given him one faithful brother aboard.

Gus called out the orders everyone was waiting for. "Get this tub turned about and head home!"

CHAPTER TWENTY-EIGHT

"Most folks are as happy as they make up their minds to be."
-Abraham Lincoln (1809-1865)

Dearest Emily,

We have not heard from you for a while. We pray that all is well with you and the baby. This fall has been very busy for us, preparing for your return. Per our last letter, we are sorry to announce that Elliott MacTavish has recently gotten married. Don't fret, though. There are many eligible bachelors who might be willing to take on a stepchild.

It is odd that you have not returned our letters to confirm your arrival. We so hoped it would be before Christmas so we could celebrate the holidays with you. There are parties planned which you will be obliged to attend with us, of course. A benefit for the hospital on Christmas Eve is one, in particular, which we simply cannot miss. Your presence will add a certain excitement to the evening. You could tell a few appropriate tales of the Wild West and raise much needed funds for the hospital, while entertaining on our behalf.

How good it will be to have you back! We redecorated your old room for you. Until you are remarried and can move out, we are sure you will find it suitable. You will appreciate the expensive French tapestries we bought for you. I'm sure you have missed the finer things in life. Comfort is coming soon. Be a strong girl and come home as soon as possible.

> *Yours fondly,*
> *Daddy and Mother*

Emily blanched at the ridiculousness of the letter. French drapes? Remarriage? Hospital benefits? She cared for none of those things. All Emily wanted in the world, she now held in her two hands. Seth's sweet, round face was outlined in a velvety quilt Bonnie made for him. She could not and would not raise him in her parent's world. It was a foreign land to her now. Much the same as Astoria felt when she first arrived here.

Small wildflower bouquets and presents filled her room. Emily let her eyes drift from each gift to the next. Daniel's miniature stained-glass window was a replica of the full-size one they completed for the church. It hung on a nail above her window so the light could pass through it. It was beautiful.

Frederika Veith brought Emily a bouquet of her prize mums, the first of the season. Sikkus brought the baby a tiny pair of moccasins. They were darling and showed hours of painstaking stitching and beading. Emily felt truly blessed.

Strangely, Gus, the boys, Johan and Frans had not been in to see her and the baby.

By the third day, Emily began to worry.

Bonnie entered the room and opened the curtains. "Good morning, my dears."

Emily sat up in bed and baby Seth lay peaceful and content at her side. She rubbed the sleep from her eyes and yawned. "I had a few good hours of sleep last night," she muttered.

Bonnie smiled and carried over fresh diapers for Seth to Emily's bedside table. "Is our little man ready for a bath yet? Hmmmm?" Bonnie reached for him and Emily smiled her approval.

Seth squirmed in Bonnie's arms as he woke up. He let out a pitiful wail and tried to eat Bonnie's finger.

"I think he might need you first," Bonnie chuckled, handing him back to Emily.

Emily smiled and looked around. "Bonnie? Why haven't I seen the boys?"

Bonnie's smile faded. She cleared her throat before speaking. "Something has happened."

Emily gulped hard and held Seth closer. "What happened? Where are they?"

Bonnie smiled weakly and reached for Emily's hand. "There, there, don't worry now. The worst is over." Bonnie looked out the window, searching for the right words. "The night you went into labor, Johan went missing. We didn't tell you because we didn't want you to worry. The men only just arrived home with him early this morning. Johan should be fine."

"Johan?" Emily's face blanched. "Where did he go? Why did he leave?"

"He didn't have a choice," Bonnie said, careful to not alarm Emily. "He was taken by some sailors from his old ship."

"Where did they take him?"

"Out to sea."

"Out to sea?" Emily held Seth close.

"They found him and punished him for jumping ship three years ago."

"How did they punish him?"

"That's not important now, dear. What's important is that he is home now. In fact, he is upstairs in Henry's old room."

"May I go see him?"

"That's not such a good idea." Bonnie straightened Emily's covers. "Let's give him a bit more time."

Emily caught Bonnie's hand and held it. She looked her in the eye. "What happened? I can handle it."

Bonnie sat on the edge of the bed and put her hands in her lap. "They nearly killed him, Em. The legal punishment for jumping ship is twenty lashes. They gave Johan thirty."

"On his back?"

"The whip wrapped around his neck in some places. The scars will run deep." Bonnie's eyes filled with tears. "As if that boy hasn't been through enough already. I've asked Sikkus to make a poultice to help it heal faster."

"You always allude to all that Johan has gone through," Emily said, quietly, snuggling Seth close. "What happened in Finland? I know that he was going to be married before he came. Her name was Emilia."

"This is not for me to tell," Bonnie began, looking out the window. "But Frans told me shortly after Johan arrived, that his fiancé was killed by the Russians."

Emily gasped. "How horrible! And his family? Where are they?"

"All gone," Bonnie whispered. "Frans is all he has left…and you."

"Me?" Emily asked, her throat tightening.

"You must know how he feels about you, dear."

"Yes, he has told me," Emily turned Seth to feed him. She hesitated before continuing. "He has asked me to marry him before. A few months ago."

"Months ago?" Bonnie chuckled. "He didn't waste much time, did he?"

"Then he has been gone so much lately," Emily said, looking away. "It seems he has turned his affections elsewhere."

Bonnie frowned. "There's no one else for Johan but you, dear. Who could you possibly be talking about?"

"Henry told me about the bride from back east," Emily whispered, avoiding Bonnie's eyes. "At the Skipanon picnic?"

"That's *you*," Bonnie said, frowning. "You're the only bride from back east that I know of."

"Why did he go to Portland then?" Emily asked, her heart pounding.

"I don't know. I guess you'll have to ask him." Bonnie said, standing to her feet. She wiped her hands on the front of her apron. "Sounds like you do need to talk to him...and soon. I'll let you know how he fares in a little while."

CHAPTER TWENTY-NINE

"Come again when you can't stay so long..."
- Walter Sickert

Bonnie poked her head in the door, "Reverend Malcolm to see you, dear."

"Again?" Emily whispered, frowning. "Tell him I'll be a minute."

"I'll have him wait in the parlor."

Emily dragged herself out from under her warm quilt, careful not to bump Seth and wake him. She stood before her wash basin and looked in her mirror. Dark circles hung under her eyes. Waking up every few hours throughout the night was rough. She glanced back over at Seth. He brought a smile to her face. He was worth it all.

Splashing water on her face, Emily quickly cleaned up. She pulled her long braid over one shoulder and combed it out with her abalone comb. Splitting her hair down the middle and twisted it up the back, she pinned it at the base of her neck. Stepping into her wool skirt, she prayed that her waistline had shrunk enough to wear it again. To her surprise, it fit. Now her jacket was another deal all together. There would be no fitting into the tailored jacket until she was done nursing. Dismayed and clutching her thin lace blouse, Emily called for Bonnie.

Bonnie slipped into Emily's room. "What is it, dear?"

Emily held up her blouse and jacket and shrugged. "What am I going to wear?" Her chin trembled. "I haven't had to step outside my bedroom this week. I never thought about my clothes not fitting."

"Now, don't cry," Bonnie said, stifling a giggle. "We are in a predicament, aren't we?" The giggle escaped. "Silly man! What is he doing visiting at this hour anyway?"

Emily clamped her hand over her mouth to hide her own giggles. "Bonnie, this is ridiculous! What can I wear?"

"Just a minute!" Bonnie slipped out of the room again. She returned with a frilly apron. "Put on your blouse and we'll put this over it to hide...you know."

Emily laughed. "Seth is fed. He woke me up about an hour ago. He should be fine while I visit with the Reverend. But would you check on him?"

"Of course," Bonnie said. "But just in case, I'll take him with me." She wrapped Seth up tightly in his blankets and held him close as Emily left the room.

Emily straightened the apron frills to cover herself as best she could. Walking into the parlor, she found Daniel standing in front of the fire place, admiring an old grandfather clock. His back was to her. He wore his Sunday best which surprised her.

"Good morning, Daniel," Emily said, clasping her hands in front of her.

Daniel crossed the room to her. "You look well. How are you feeling?" He smiled warmly, taking one of her hands in both of his. "Are you getting enough sleep? Where is your little man?"

Emily glanced over her shoulder. "Bonnie has him. She is amazing. She can do all her chores while holding him. I don't know how she does it."

"Experience is a great teacher." He smiled at Emily and motioned for her sit beside him on the horsehair couch. Their knees touched, sitting so close together.

Emily felt a pit in her stomach. Daniel was fidgety and tense.

"Are you enjoying the stained glass I made you?" Daniel asked, suddenly.

"It's lovely. Thank you," Emily said, clasping her hands in her lap. She hooked one of her ankles behind the other and tried to relax.

Daniel reached over for her hand and held it tight. "I can't hold my peace any longer," he said, breathlessly. "Emily, I cherish every moment I've had with you since you arrived here in Astoria. Working beside you on the stained-glass window was really a test to see if we were compatible. I have found you to be a pleasant and amiable mate for my soul. I want to be joined with you in holy matrimony." At these words, Daniel slipped to one knee in front of her.

"Emily Grace Davenport," he choked out. "Would you do me the honor of becoming my wife?"

Heat filled Emily's face. She put one hand to her chest and tried to breathe. What to say? She couldn't think of any words. She couldn't make this decision right now. Reason told her that it was coming. It wasn't a huge surprise but she was shocked nonetheless.

"Daniel," Emily began, not sure how to continue. "I need some time…"

"You can have all the time you need," he said, eagerly. "There's no rush. Your life has changed so much in this past year. I know this must come as a shock. But surely you must know how I admire you. I hope I have made that clear at least."

"Yes, thank you," Emily said, trying to withdraw her hand. He wasn't releasing it. "Before I make any big decisions, I need to contact my parents--"

"I wrote to them, Emily," Daniel said, clearing his throat. "There is a right way to go about these things. I wrote to them two months ago when I was sure that you were the one for me."

Emily's face went white. "You wrote to my parents? Before speaking to me? Before knowing my answer? Daniel, I-- I don't know what to say."

"Say yes!" he said, leaning forward. "I haven't received their reply yet. But I couldn't wait any longer to speak to you."

All the freedom that Emily gained since coming to Astoria felt like it was being sucked out of her. She tried to breathe but couldn't. She tried to pull her hand away from Daniel and he reluctantly let go. Emily felt her chest tightening. She needed space. Crossing the room, she stood by the fireplace and leaned on the mantle, drawing in a deep breath.

"Won't it be wonderful, darling," Daniel said, standing to his feet also. He walked over to her, placing his hands on her shoulders.

"No," Emily whispered.

"I'm sorry," Daniel said, leaning in closer to her.

Emily felt anger and confusion. She shirked his hands off of her shoulders and spun away from him. A knot in her stomach threatened to fill her whole chest. "Daniel," she said, purposely not looking at him. She focused on a flower on the rug beneath them. "I know it's proper to ask my parents for my hand. But you should have spoken to me first. I'm not a new bride. I'm a mother and a widow. This isn't New York society out here. We don't need to do things the same."

Daniel cleared his throat and hooked his thumb in his pant's pocket as he also leaned against the mantle.

Emily dared to meet his eye. He was strikingly handsome. His cheeks were flushed and he held his lips tight together with his jaw clenched. He was meticulous in his appearance and carried himself with respect and pride. He was a good pastor. He had a good heart. Her parents would definitely approve the match between them. But could she?

Emily drew in a deep breath and smoothed her apron nervously. "I don't think I'm what you want, Daniel," she said gently. "You will make a wonderful husband and father someday. But I don't know if I am the right one for you."

He met her eyes. "I don't take any decision lightly, Emily. When I ask you to marry me, I mean it with all of my heart. I don't just *want* you to become my wife like I think that it would improve my existence here. I *need* you like I need the air I breathe. When I am not with you, I think about you. I dream about you and our life together…with Seth. I believe that I can give you a safe and loving home. I want to protect you and give you a good life, even here in Astoria. We are cut from the same cloth in society. We could travel the world. We can settle wherever we like. We are a good match."

Emily looked away from him. Daniel was so much like Ronald, it would be comfortable to marry him. She knew what to expect. If she wanted a life like she had with Ronald, this was her chance. But deep in her heart, she knew that she wanted more. There *had* to be more for her and her son.

"I love you," Daniel said, stepping forward and slipping both his hands around her waist.

She lifted her face to look at him. He was searching her eyes for an answer.

"Tell me that you'll be my wife," he said, with a hopeful smile at the corner of his mouth. "If you can't tell me now, then at least let me show you how I feel about you." He pulled her to him and kissed her softly and pulled away again.

It was sweet kiss. Emily closed her eyes and prayed for wisdom. This was safe. This was comfortable. Seth would have what he needed – the right upbringing, respect in society, the right education. *Lord, help me.* She could live without Johan, couldn't she? Unbidden, her mind flashed back to the kiss Johan gave her on Coxcomb Hill.

You need one of these everyday, from me.

Then she knew. She couldn't marry Daniel. Not now. Not ever. Her heart wouldn't let her. Even if it meant losing everything, she would not toy with him.

Opening her eyes, Daniel stood so close, it gave her pause. He did love her. Even though she did care for him; she had to let him go gently. "Daniel," she said. "You are a wonderful man. I appreciate your kindness to me and your friendship. But--"

"You won't marry me," he whispered. "You won't marry me because there is someone else."

"I'm not right for you," Emily said.

"That is where you are wrong," Daniel said, setting his jaw. "We are perfect together. You can't see it now because of this other person between us. You will see it eventually. So I will wait for you."

"Please don't say that," Emily begged. "I won't ask that of you."

"This is what true love is, Emily," he said. "It waits. It doesn't seek its own. It is patient and kind. You'll see that what I offer is what you need. I'll be here."

With that, he leaned over and kissed Emily on the cheek, pausing afterward. Her heart pounded as she waited for him to kiss her lips again, but he didn't. He spun on his heel and let himself out of the house.

What have I done? Emily knew she would hear about this from her parents.

CHAPTER THIRTY

"Love is patient, love is kind, it is not proud, it is not rude, it is not self-seeking..."
I Corinthians 13:4-5

"I've got to get out of this house," Emily said, straightening her bed. "I feel like a caged animal."

Bonnie chuckled in the doorway. "The cabin fever of motherhood is setting in," she said, giggling. "Don't worry. This is nothing that a quick walk won't fix. Bundle up Seth and come to market with me."

Emily obeyed and wrapped Seth like Sikkus showed her. She tied him into the wooden carrier Sikkus gave her on her last visit. Strapping it to her front, Seth felt secure and tight against her. It also left her hands free to carry supplies home. She smiled, pleased with herself.

Emily stepped out into the dining room where Gus, Bonnie and the boys sat for breakfast. "I'm ready," she said, beaming.

"Oh no, you're not," Bonnie chided. "You've got to eat first or you'll be no good in an hour."

"Bonnie, really..."

"Trust me and at least take an apple and some of this bread. You'll be ravenous in a short time without keeping up on your meals. I can't believe you are already down to your normal size." Bonnie said, checking her over. "Pretty soon, there won't be much left of you."

Gus laughed and slapped the table top. "That boy is eating you out of house and home already!"

Spurgeon and Luther grinned and stuffed their eggs and cinnamon rolls into their mouths.

"This is what I have to look forward to, is it?" Emily asked, pointing to the boys. She laughed. "Ok Bonnie, I'll take that food. I've got to keep one step ahead of this little man. Next thing you know, he'll be grabbing all the food before I can get to it!"

Bonnie flung her scarf over her shoulder and grabbed her basket from the floor. "We'll be back in an hour. Check on Johan, Spurgeon, and change those poultices, will you?"

"Yes ma'am," Spurgeon called back before the door closed.

"Bonnie," Emily said quietly, straightening the baby board on her front. "How is Johan? I haven't seen him yet. He hasn't left his room, has he?"

"He can't be outside yet, dear. Infection." Bonnie said, keeping her eyes ahead of her. "Watch that loose board there," she warned. "Ugh! These planks come up sometimes and they can make you sprawl headlong quicker than anything."

Emily focused her eyes downward on the foot-wide planks making up the boardwalk. She stepped around the edges that bowed upward. With both hands, she had to lift the hem of her wool skirt out of the mud seeping through the boards. The stench of the cannery wafted to them on the breeze. Emily gagged and turned her face away.

"Still bothers you, does it?" Bonnie chuckled.

"I don't believe that is a smell one can ever get used to. I don't care what Gus says!" Emily put her hand over her nose in protest to the acrid smell. Another breeze whipped around them, clearing the air. Now just the rotting moss of the pilings and rocks filled the air. "Much better," Emily said, smiling.

Sea gulls cried above them. Bonnie kept her eye on them as well as the road. "One time Gus wasn't paying attention when we first moved here," Bonnie puffed, waddling along. "A sea gull flew right and pooped on his bald head. I laughed so hard, I cried! He just stood there fuming and sputtering like an old steam engine about to explode!" Bonnie's cheeks were flushed from their walk. "Hold on, dear. You walk too fast. Let's rest for just a moment."

"You two have done well here," Emily said, leaning against the rail, overlooking the river.

Bonnie swung her basket up onto the railing as well. "Yes, and no," she said, sadly. "A mother never wants her children to go before her." Bonnie looked over at Seth nestled tightly against Emily. "I wish I could have kept Henry safe like that. But I couldn't. That's part of life as well. Saying goodbye." Bonnie teared up and her chin quivered.

Emily looped her arm through Bonnie's. The salty air from the ocean blew past them. Cormorants swam in front of them, diving for fish.

"Will we be saying goodbye again soon?" Bonnie said, turning to Emily now. "What have you decided to do, dear? I know that your parents have made it possible for you to return home, if you chose to."

"I have the money now, Bonnie," Emily said. "I could leave Astoria any time." Emily patted down the soft wool cap on Seth's head then looked up again. "But I don't want to." She smiled and hugged Bonnie's arm tight.

Bonnie's eyes flooded with tears. "Will you stay then? Do you want to continue living with Gus and I? We can help you raise the baby, if you need."

"I've had a few offers to help me raise my baby," Emily said, wincing. "Am I awful for refusing Daniel's hand in marriage?"

"Oh my!" Bonnie said, turning to Emily. "Is that what he was up to? We all saw it coming. He finally got up the nerve, did he? But you refused..."

"Am I wicked for doing so, Bonnie?" Emily asked, her eyes pleading. "He's a wonderful man but..."

"But..." Bonnie raised her eyebrows, waiting for Emily to continue.

"He's not..." Emily kicked her boot against the bottom of the rail. "He's so kind and compassionate. He's a wonderful pastor."

"But, he's not..." Bonnie repeated, crossing her arms over her ample bosom.

Emily gulped hard. "He's just not Johan, is he?"

Bonnie clapped her hands together. "That's what I wanted to hear! So you'll stay in Astoria and marry Johan, will ya?"

"I hope to," Emily said. "If he'll have me...and Seth."

"Then you need to tell him so," Bonnie said in a whisper. "He needs some encouragement to get better. When we get back, you go up and see him."

Emily nodded, tears filling her eyes. Seth's little chin began trembling and he let out a wail. It made Emily laugh. "Seems we all need a little comfort right now."

"Well, Mr. Emerson needs a little more than comfort right now," Bonnie muttered. "He wants some good lamb chops from the butcher and more potatoes. I bet Johan could be cheered up with some smooth, buttery taters as well! There's only a few other things besides taters that can fix a man right up!"

Bonnie opened Henry's door with the dinner tray. Emily followed tentatively, not sure what state Johan might be in. She had not seen him since the funeral. She was so ill until the baby was born, she couldn't remember anything else. Seth snuggled against her chest with his head tucked up under her chin.

Bonnie set the tray on a small table next to the bed and checked to see if Johan was awake.

"Bonnie," Johan murmured. "Could I have some water, please?"

Emily waited outside the door until Bonnie told her to enter. But she could hear the pain in his voice. He was worse off than she realized. What was she thinking? He almost died. How could he possibly be ready to marry and care for a child any time soon? Her throat constricted at her selfishness. She wanted to be taken care of. She never thought of what she could do for him until this moment. She clutched Seth closer to her heart.

Bonnie opened the door slightly, still hiding Johan from view. "Now, dear, please brace yourself." Bonnie whispered. "I'm sure you've never seen these kinds of wounds before."

Emily nodded and swallowed hard. She followed Bonnie into the candlelit room. Johan lay on the bed, chest down, keeping his back exposed so it could heal. Emily gasped at the sight of it. After a week, the stripes torn into his flesh and muscle were still raw. The shallow lashes had started closing but the skin was thin and delicate. Ghastly, deep red and purple gashes criss-crossed his back where his tanned skin once covered him. Emily gagged and ran back out into the hallway to compose herself.

Seth began whimpering.

Emily's own tears fell. Johan knew this was a possible consequence for seeking freedom. It was horrible. Worse than she could have imagined. She drew in a ragged breath and stifled her sobs. She sank down the wall to the floorboards and cradled Seth until Bonnie came out.

"Here, dear," Bonnie said, reaching for Seth. "Let me take him for you. When you are ready, go in. I told him you are here to see him." Bonnie tucked Seth into her arms. "It was the first time I've seen him smile this week."

Emily shook her head, whispering, "How can I help him? I don't know what to do."

Bonnie kissed Seth on the forehead. "It's just like learning to be a mother. You learn one thing each day. Take this one day at a time."

Emily nodded and stood to her feet. She squared her shoulders and tiptoed inside. The warmth of the candlelight gave the room a reverent feeling like church on Christmas Eve. Emily stood at the end of the bed and steadied herself holding onto the brass rail. Her mind could not take in the gruesome sight before her. She held her breath. *Oh Lord, what can I say? Use me somehow. I don't know what to do.*

Johan groaned softly. "Bonnie? Could I have more water please?"

Emily hurried over to his water pitcher and glass, refilling it. She turned and knelt beside the bed so that her face was close to his.

His eyes were closed and his lips were chapped and dry. A soft beard framed his chin with blond curls against his tan skin.

"Here is water, Johan."

His eyes shot open. He struggled to focus them to see her. "Em?" he whispered, his voice raspy.

"Yes, Johan. I'm here." She held the cup to his lips with a towel under his cheek.

He drank as much as he could but started coughing. His face winced with pain until the coughing spasm ceased.

"I'm so sorry," Emily said, not sure how to help him. She reached out to touch him but drew her hand back, fearful of hurting him.

He took in a breath and opened his eyes again. Such strength shone out from them that Emily struggled to hold his gaze. "Em," he said. "You are well?" He tried to look her over but could only see her face.

"Yes, Johan," she said, smiling. "I'm very well. I have a healthy, baby boy."

Johan closed his eyes and a smile tugged at the corner of his mouth. "Seth," he whispered.

"Yes," Emily said, surprised. "Bonnie told you then."

"No," he said.

"Gus did? The boys?"

Johan opened his eyes again. "I could eat something. I smell mashed potatoes."

Startled, Emily pulled the plate closer and scooped some mashed potatoes onto the spoon.

"Here you are," Emily said, trying to hold the spoon steady for him. "As you can taste, I didn't cook these."

Johan smiled weakly. "She's such a good cook," he mumbled. "You have to learn how to make these, Em." He took another bite.

Emily ventured to look at his back again.

"This is not how I wanted you to see me," he whispered.

Emily felt the heat rise in her cheeks. He needed to know how she felt. She reached out and touched his beard between her fingers. "I love you, Johan." She followed the outline of his cheek with her fingertip.

He never took his eyes off of her. "You're sure?"

Emily nodded and kissed him on his lower cheek. "Are you still hungry?"

Johan smiled, "Yes, I have to get my strength back. This could take a while though."

His smirk made Emily's heart flip. She didn't care if it took the rest of their lives. There was nowhere she'd rather be than by his side.

Just then the door cracked open, Bonnie popped her head inside. "I've got another hungry man here," she teased. Seth announced his presence with a hungry wail.

Johan's eyes lit up. "Bring him in, Bonnie." He tried turning his body to see the baby, but couldn't.

Emily put her hand over his. "Hold still, we'll bring him to you."

Bonnie handed Seth, crying and all, into Emily's arms. She turned him so that Johan could see his red, little face. Johan took Seth's tiny fist in his own strong hand. Seth's fingers curled around Johan's ring finger and tried pulling the finger toward his mouth.

They all laughed.

"I will be back soon," Emily said, quietly.

"Bring Seth back with you, Em," Johan said, never taking his eyes off the boy.

"Of course," Emily said, standing to her feet. She turned to Bonnie. "I'll feed my little boy if you feed this big one. He's not anywhere close to being full yet."

The girls giggled at Johan's frown.

"Just keep in mind that I won't be in this bed much longer..." he growled.

CHAPTER THIRTY-ONE

"The sound of music that the boats made while mooring by pulleys on the docks. That's something you never forget...Boat, sky, water, net, fisherman – all become one – work as one out there. The jingle of the weights and floats is music to the fisherman's ear..."

Saturday, October 1853

"Monday through Friday, the men fish," Mrs. Veith said. "But Saturday, we mend the nets." The cool air of Gus and Charles Veith's shop chilled Emily but she chose to ignore it. Sawdust covered the floor, making a soft bed for Seth to sleep on.

"Ok, teach me more," Emily said, studying Frederika's movements as she mended. "When we are done today, I want to understand Johan's world at least a little bit better."

Sikkus looked up from her basket-weaving. Her hand held a bone awl used to pull the reeds in and out of the stick base. "You learn this next then, Miss Em," she said, grinning. "Then my poor finger get rest." She grinned showing all her perfect, white teeth.

"I want to learn everything," Emily said, distracted.

"Nets first, girl," Frederika snapped. "Can't move on til learn something well."

"Pardon me, you are right, Mrs. Veith," Emily said, respectfully. "Please continue." She studied as Frederika's fingers untangled a snare in the net. She tugged this way and that until the netting stretched out again. There was a hole in the middle of the netting. "Now to mend." She grabbed her large bone needle and thick linen to mend the tear. When she pulled the linen string the vibration on the spool made the windows sing.

Emily smiled at the rhythm and beauty of each of the women's work. Sikkus on her mat on the floor weaving baskets for Emily's new home. Frederika mending Johan's nets so he could get back to work. Bonnie stitched and mended his clothing as his suit from the funeral was soiled and torn by the Finnish sailors. All these women took it upon themselves to get Johan back to work as soon as he was ready.

Meanwhile, Charles and Gus and their younger sons were building Johan a new row-sail outside the shop on the docks. Johan had no idea that he would be back in business and set up better than ever even after being shanghaied.

Bonnie mended Johan's dress pants while she rambled. "Emily, here's what you need to know about fishermen. There are a few things that bring good luck for a fisherman. Number one: fish bite best before a storm. Two: cans or anything else must be stored with labels right-side up, to keep the boat from capsizing. If they are upside down, it can also throw off the compass."

Emily giggled. "Bonnie, that is ridiculous! They don't really believe that stuff." Her giggle stuck in her throat when she saw the straight faces staring back at her.

"The boys don't ever take off the hatch cover until the first fish is landed. Next: never cook pea soup on board a fishing boat, it brings stormy weather. Never whistle on board, it calls up the wind. It's bad luck to leave for a fishing trip on a Friday."

"Alright then," Emily said, tilting her head. "Gus and Johan really follow those superstitions?"

Bonnie looked over to Frederika with a solemn expression. They both burst into laughter. "Of course not! You know us better than that!"

"Do any of the sailors believe in those?" Emily asked, wide-eyed.

Frederika set her net in her lap. "Yah, they do. They don't have the Lord to keep them safe so they come up with all sorts of foolishness out there."

"It's the Graveyard of the Pacific," Bonnie mumbled, her chin tucked to her chest, sewing. "We've lost many a boy out on that bar."

"Isn't there anything we can do to make it more safe?" Emily asked, picking up Seth and holding him tight.

"You can't control the weather, dear." Bonnie flipped the pants inside out to check her work. "Only the Lord has control of that. It rains and storms here more than not. But the springtime is beautiful. Isn't it, Frederika?"

"My flowers come into bloom," Frederika said, wistfully. "Summer, my roses return. It reminds me of my garden in Germany. Warmer, simpler days."

"Will you teach me how to garden?" Emily asked Frederika.

The hard, German woman melted at the request. "Yah. Yah, I will. It's goot thing to learn. This spring, you spend few days with me. We learn to garden...bring the baby. I hold, you work." Her stern face broke into a broad smile. "Now let me see your net. Hold up please."

Emily obeyed, holding up the small section of net she mended. She bit her bottom lip, ready for disapproval.

"Yah, it's goot." Frederika said. "Keep going. We do fourteen feet section. Yah?"

Bonnie and Sikkus shared a knowing smile. A compliment from Frederika was few and far between.

"My boys are out hunting today," Bonnie said, licking her lips. "If they get anything, you must all come over tonight for venison."

Sikkus looked up from her work and smiled. "I need to check on Johan. He eating well? How are wounds? Infection?"

"He's doing well," Bonnie and Emily both spoke up at the same time. They caught each other's eye and laughed.

Emily dropped her head and let Bonnie talk. Who was she to speak about Johan yet? They weren't officially engaged yet.

"The deeper stripes are beginning to close up," Bonnie said, wincing at the thought of the deep cuts in his back. "The bruising has gone down. Now it's just the redness of the skin that concerns me."

"No fluid seeping?" Sikkus asked, her eyes on her work.

"No," Bonnie said quickly. "I don't believe it's become infected. Thank the Lord."

Sikkus patted her satchel on the floor next to her. "I bring him something. Friend give me sage from far away tribe. It help heal cuts. Also have purple coneflower and arnica for bruising."

Emily's mouth dropped open. "How will I ever learn all this?"

"Johan's place not too far from me," Sikkus reminded her, "I help you be ready."

Frederika looked from Sikkus to Emily to Bonnie. Her bushy eyebrows furrowed with concern. "Emily will be at Johan's place?" She pursed her lips with disapproval.

Bonnie laughed. "They will be married, Frederika." She looked to Emily for permission. Emily nodded. "There is an agreement between them." Bonnie raised one eyebrow, waiting for Frederika to understand.

Frederika pulled hard on the net in her hands. "Goot! That's goot!" She glanced over at Emily. "He goot choice, that Johan. Hard worker." She nodded once, then mumbled. "Not German, but Finnish is pretty goot."

Emily giggled at the incredulous expressions from Sikkus and Bonnie.

"My boy take you out on Monday," Frederika said to Emily. "I go with and watch baby for you."

"Excuse me?" Emily gasped.

"We need to try out nets." Frederika held up her work. "You go with Heinrich to the beach with Johan's horse. He show you how to pull nets in with horse. Yah? Boat not ready yet."

Emily looked to Bonnie. Bonnie nodded and added, "It's steelhead season. If Johan doesn't get his share, it will be a long winter. We will all have to do our part to get him through the next few months."

Sikkus patted her stomach. "Steelhead good. No smell too bad, Miss Em."

Emily held Seth up in front of her. "Well son, looks like the men will have their way and teach you to fish already." Seth cooed while his blanket and diaper slipped off of him. He peed all over Emily's front.

"We need teach you how do better diaper," Sikkus laughed. "That next!"

CHAPTER THIRTY-TWO

November, 1853

Torrents of rain poured down on Emily, Heinrich and Frederika on the sand bar east of Astoria. Their wagon stood under a large oak where Bonnie held baby Seth. Heinrich pulled his hat lower over his face to keep the water from splashing in his eyes.   Emily's wool skirt hung heavy and limp from her waist. Johan's oil skin coat covered the rest of her, but her hem dripped with water. Her boots were caked with sand.

"I think I wore a hole through my right boot," she called to Frederika. "My toes are freezing!"

Frederika looked up from pulling the nets apart and grimaced. "Mine too. Lots work to do in winter in front of fire, yah?"

Emily shot a glance over to Seth. She hated to be parted from him for even an hour but the work had to be done. If the Veiths were willing to help Johan, of course, she could, too. No matter what the cost, Johan's part of the fall catch had to be covered, even just partially.

Heinrich straightened the nets and called to his mother and Emily. "We are ready. I've tied off one end of the net to this stump. Now I'll throw it out into the current. See the fish jumping? We'll catch some of those for sure." He grinned through the sheets of rain.

"Goot. Cast away," Frederika called. She stepped back from the net and put her hands on her hips. Heinrich tossed the gillnet out into the current. The bobbers held them above the surface and the leadline sank to the bottom of the river. Instantly, the line attached to the stump went taut, almost to the point of breaking. The strain of the current pulled hard against it.

"Good knot, yah?" Frederika motioned to Emily. "He tie good knot. Don't lose net."

Emily noted the double fisherman's knot. "I need to learn how to make knots like that," she called to Heinrich.

"Not hard," he called back, sputtering from the rain. "Look Emily!" Already the steelhead littered the net. One tried to jump free but tangled itself worse near the top.

Emily clapped her hands with delight. "Will we sell these for Johan? Or smoke them for the winter?"

Heinrich looked to his mother. She nodded back to him. "What do you think is best?" he asked Emily.

"I- I don't know." Emily looked out to the catch collecting right before her eyes. "What would Johan want? Probably to sell most of them and smoke a dozen or so?"

Frederika nodded her approval. "We ask him tonight. I think that what he say." She glanced over Emily's shoulder to Bonnie. "Look like baby need food, too." She smiled just briefly and pulled her bonnet lower.

Emily tromped through the sand of Tongue Point to the waiting wagon. "Is he staying dry?" She called to Bonnie. "Is he warm enough? This rain is horrible," she cried, shivering.

"Welcome to winter in Astoria!" Bonnie grinned. "Seth is fine. He's just trying to eat my scarf."

Emily giggled, pulling herself up onto the seat of the wagon. "He's so little to be out here. I worry that he'll catch cold."

"A little fresh air is fine," Bonnie said, keeping his head covered. "It's that wind that we need to be careful of. We don't want an ear ache or no one will get any sleep tonight." She smiled sadly. "I remember an ear ache that Henry got as a baby. He howled all night long until his ears popped and drained. Terrible stuff. It's almost worse for the mother when you don't know how to help them. You want to take their pain for them…but you can't." Bonnie lifted one end of her scarf to the corner of her eye. She took in a deep breath and stood up in the wagon. "Watch how we pull in that net now. You haven't seen anything like it!" She grinned and called out to Heinrich. "We 'bout full yet, ya think?"

"Yes, ma'am!" he called back. "Grab Ginger and get the ice box ready!"

Bonnie stepped out of the wagon and wobbled over to the ice box. She dragged one end of the wooden crate closer to the water's edge and opened the top. She glanced back at Emily and grinned.

Emily fed the baby and watched the scene before her. Heinrich tied a rope to Ginger without untying the other line. Then after Ginger was secure to the net line, he untied the stump line. The weight of the catch pulled Ginger back a few steps and her hooves sunk into the sand.

Emily gasped with worry.

Heinrich gave the horse a slap on the rump. "Hya!" Ginger's muscles strained against the weight pulling her backward. With Heinrich's constant encouragement, she slowly dragged the nets from the river onto the sand.

Emily watched in amazement how the nets held the fish even dragging them over the sand. She started counting the catch of huge steelhead fighting to be free. They flipped and flopped over the sand and each other. One broke loose and flipped itself toward the water. Frederika scooped one hand under it and tossed it higher onto the beach.

"Bravo!" Bonnie cried, clapping her hands.

Frederika curtsied and the women laughed, wiping the rain out of their eyes.

"Hya!" Heinrich urged Ginger up the hill until the nets cleared the water by ten feet at least. The mass of fish made the beach look alive. Every inch of it jumped and bounced.

Emily giggled at the sight before her. Two middle-aged women kicked fish back into the net and Heinrich ran back and forth, trying not to lose any fish. Seth pulled away from her and looked up at her face. His eyes were wide and confused. Then he smiled the sweetest smile Emily had ever seen. "Oh Seth," she laughed. "If you could only see this!" He went back to eating while Emily watched them haul each fish out of the net. Heinrich tossed the larger fish into one wooden crate with blocks of ice in the bottom. The smaller fish went into a second crate.

"You watching this, Em?" Bonnie called. "You're up next!"

Emily giggled and waved back. She could do this. She would touch those slimy fish if it meant helping Johan. Whatever it took to get him back on his feet, she would do. After all, this was her future at stake as well as his.

From the looks of the catch, they would do just fine together.

*   *   *

Dearest Emily,

Please be seated before you read this. We just received notice from a sea captain, who arrived in New York, that Ronald is alive! Captain Dawson is his name and he can attest to the truth of your husband's survival because he rescued Ronald himself. It seems that he jumped ship just before the Sophia sank below the surface. The Captain's fishing vessel rescued a handful of survivors, including Ronald.

Captain Dawson did not want to risk crossing the Columbia River Bar to deliver the survivors so he headed south to San Francisco. Ronald has been recuperating there at the local hospital for months. The staff sent word that he was alive to us because Ronald was not lucid enough to give an address in Astoria to reach you. The doctor wrote that Ronald planned to head north by horse as soon as he could find a guide. Needless to say, my dear, your husband might arrive at any time before or after you receive this letter. How we rejoice that you are both alive and can return to New York with the baby!

We also received a letter from a certain Reverend Malcolm of Astoria. We presume that you know him. He has asked for your hand in marriage. While this offer could have been considered even a month ago, obviously, it is null and void now that your husband has been found alive. Please send word to the Reverend that you are still married.

Enclosed is another Three Hundred Dollars to cover any of Ronald's lingering expenses. It should also cover both your boat fare to come home. We will expect to see you shortly after the New Year, darling.

Our prayers are with you,
Daddy and Mother

CHAPTER THIRTY-THREE

*"I know your works. See, I have set before you an open door, and
no one can shut it; for you have a little strength, have kept my
word, and have not denied my name."*
Rev 3:8

November 1853

Emily sank into the horsehair couch, clutching the letter
to her chest. Seth lay beside her, sucking his thumb, blissfully
unaware how much his life just changed. His father was alive.
He would be raised with money and education and prestige.
All of which Emily had resigned herself to live without.

Ronald is alive.

What would everyone say? What would Johan think?
She told Johan she loved him. She *did* love him. Her heart
pounded in her chest. How could she love two men? She
couldn't. Her covenant could not be broken with Ronald and
he could arrive at a moment's notice. He must never know
that Emily had ever thought to pursue a life without him.

Pressure filled Emily's chest. Air escaped her lungs and
she felt light-headed. She tried to breathe but couldn't. She
gripped the wooden arm of the couch; her nails digging into
the wood. She pictured herself living up on the hill with
Ronald in a house like Reverend Malcolm's. Forget fishing
and working alongside her husband, she would sit at home
like the other society ladies sewing, drinking tea and
entertaining in her microscopically, small world. Anxiety
filled Emily's heart, what if Ronald chose to live like the other
high society men? Living at home with her while frequenting
the Taylor Street brothels?

Emily gasped for air and tried to reason with herself. In
their short marriage, he had never been anything but attentive
to her. Why should that change? But she sold their land. She
had friends here now. What if he chose to take them back to
New York after their horrific arrival on the West coast?

Emily's eyes drew in every detail of the Emerson's home. *Her* home now. The crackling fireplace with their grandfather clock in the corner. The rocking chair across from her where Bonnie would sit and talk for hours in the evenings. The dining room with enough chairs for the Emersons, Emily and a guest or two. Her bedroom that Henry built with love and detail, just for her. Luther and Spurgeon were more than her friends, they were her brothers now.

Johan. He was still laid up in Henry's room upstairs. *How would he handle this?* Emily's heart raced in her chest. Just last night, she held Seth in front of him so he could see him. Though Seth wasn't his son, he took to him as though he were. This would devastate him.

Emily's eyes drifted to the staircase leading upstairs. To her surprise, someone was coming down slowly. One foot appeared, then another. Johan's wool socks.

Johan gripped the rail and descended carefully. He couldn't stay in bed any longer. The thought of Emily sitting downstairs alone when he could be with her was motivation enough. But one slip on these stairs and his wounds would reopen. He reached the bottom step and glanced up to see Emily watching him.

"Look at you two," he said, with a warm smile filling his face. He couldn't wait to marry Emily and take her home with the baby. Then they could sit before *his* fire.

Johan glanced toward Seth on the couch. His little arms lay extended and relaxed next to his head. *Not a care in the world.* Emily rose slowly as not to wake the baby. She crossed over to Johan and took his arm to help him take his last step down.

Unbidden tears filled her eyes as soon as she stood before him.

"Hey now," he whispered. "What's wrong? More baby emotions?" He grinned.

Emily could not even offer him a smile. She would not meet his eyes. "My husband is alive, Johan," she blurted out, putting her fist to her mouth to suppress a sob.

"What?" Johan's smile melted from his lips. His mind raced with confusion. "How do you know? How is this possible?" He gripped the banister to steady himself.

Emily looked over her shoulder at the letter scrunched up on the couch. "My parents..." A sob escaped her throat. "My parents just wrote..."

Johan's eyes darted from her face to the letter beside Seth. "Where has he been? New York?"

Emily clasped her hands together in front of her. "It seems that a captain rescued him after the shipwreck and took him to San Francisco. He was very sick and was in the hospital all this time." Her face was red from crying. She pulled a hankie from her sleeve to dab her runny nose. "I just found out, Johan. I don't know what to say." She finally looked into his eyes, searching for an answer to their dilemma.

Johan's eyes settled on the little bundle on the couch. He smiled sadly. "He will have his own father to raise him," Johan whispered slowly. "That is good, Em." He smiled at just one corner of his mouth. "My father died when I was young, I missed him my whole life."

"Johan," Emily said, sobbing. "Is that all you can say?" She buried her face in her hands.

"What else *can* I say?" Johan whispered, his voice strained. Heat and frustration filled him. His chest tightened and his heart ached. "Your husband is alive. You are a married woman." He tried to stand up straighter but the healing skin on his back pulled. He grimaced from the pain. "Thank the Lord we found out now and not..."

Emily's eyes shot up to meet his. Obviously, she had not considered that scenario. "Johan, I'm so sorry--"

He held his hand up. "There is nothing to be sorry for," he said. "The Lord was merciful and spared his life. I can't be upset at that." Johan put his hand on his chest. His breaths came short and quick. He smiled bravely. "Em, look at me."

Emily lifted her tear-filled eyes to his, her gaze faltering.

"I'm blessed to have known you. You gave me hope for a better future here. I won't be bitter about that."

Her chin trembled. "I'm so sorry. I didn't know…"

Seth woke up, startled at being alone, and began whimpering. Emily spun around and was at his side in an instant. She wrapped him tight in his blanket and lifted him to her shoulder.

Johan eased himself across the hallway to where they stood. "I can walk now," he said, placing his strong hand on Seth's tiny head. "It's time that I headed home."

"Johan, you don't need to go because of me," Emily begged. "You are not well yet. You must stay here and let Bonnie and Sikkus care for you. I can go elsewhere until…maybe Kuntas' boardinghouse…"

Johan shook his head. "How would that be? I rescue you, then I lose you to the sailors at Kuntas'. That is not an option and you know it. I'll be going today. Uncle Frans is coming this afternoon to fill me in on the property. He can take me home then."

"Johan," Emily cried, burying her face in Seth's blanket. "I'm so sorry…"

Johan's arms ached to hold her one last time but he couldn't trust himself to let go. He forced himself to go back upstairs. He paused at the bottom step. "The house is done," he mumbled. "*Your* house is finished. The timing is ironic, isn't it?" He hung his head, dreading to leave them.

He had to leave before her husband arrived. Johan shot a glance over his shoulder. Emily snuggled Seth tight and her shoulders shook with her tears. He couldn't bear to see her reunited with her husband. Jealousy and covetousness were definitely sins and he had to flee as far from them as possible.

* * *

"Right down Bond Street. Keep going 'til you see the tall walnut trees. That's the Emerson's place down there," the sailor spit some chew onto the ground near Ronald's feet.

"Thank you, kind sir," he replied, swinging back up into his saddle. The reprieve from riding in from Portland was welcomed. He was so close and relieved to finish his journey. Emily was waiting. He didn't know if she would be expecting him or not. The anticipation of the seven hundred fifty mile trek was nearly driving him insane. His breathing grew labored and he coughed hard to clear his lungs.

"You alright, Mr. Davenport?" his guide asked him. "Looks like your wife is only a few blocks away. We'll get you settled, sir, and I'm going to find a stiff drink, among other things." The guide was eyeing a pair of women in frilly dresses passing them. Their made-up faces alone were the only advertising the exhausted man needed.

"First things first," Ronald chided. "Finish your job, then you'll be paid handsomely. What you do with yourself next is between you and your Maker."

"Suit yourself," the guide mumbled. "Let's hurry. I ain't had a good drink since the waterfront in Portland. My canteen has been dry since Eminence. That ain't good."

Ronald rolled his eyes. He was glad to be rid of the jaded traveling companion. A married man can only listen to so much filth before he can't take it anymore. Thank the Lord he was almost reunited with his bride!

* * *

A sharp knock at the door came at dinnertime. The Emersons and Emily were all seated at the table when it came.

Emily gripped the edges of her seat and shot a glance over to Bonnie. The look in Bonnie's eyes was a mixture of sympathy and hope.

"Here we are, then," she muttered. "Can't hold off the future when it comes knockin' now, can we?" She pushed herself to her feet and waddled over to the door.

Luther and Spurgeon's faces went white and they stared at Emily from across the table. She smiled bravely back at them but felt nervous and nauseous.

"Good evening, may I help you?" Bonnie asked the visitor.

Ronald's unmistakable east coast accent drifted into the room. "Good evening, madam. Please pardon my intrusion. My name is Ronald Davenport and I wondered if my…"

Emily slipped out of her seat and stepped in behind Bonnie. She and Ronald's eyes met and he burst through the door. He caught Emily is his arms and buried his face in her neck. "You survived," he cried. "I thought you might have, but I didn't know."

Bonnie closed the door and stepped around the couple in her entryway.

Ronald held Emily by the shoulders. "You look wonderful! Just look at you! Surviving in this frontier town for months. You are healthy and strong and--"

"A mother," Emily said, quietly.

Ronald's face registered shock and awe. "You are a mother?" He looked around them, confused. "You had a baby?"

"*You* have a baby, Ronald," she whispered. "I was pregnant when the ship went down."

"Oh Emily," he gasped, pulling her into his arms tightly. "We have a baby! Where is she?"

"*He* is sleeping in my room," Emily said. "Would you like to see him now?"

"Of course," he beamed. "I have a son! I never could have dreamed." Ronald's breathing grew raspy and he tried to clear his throat.

"First," Emily said, turning him to the Emersons, "Ronald, this is the Emerson family. This is Gus and his wife, Bonnie. Their two sons, Spurgeon and Luther."

"Fine boys," Ronald said. "So nice to meet you, Mr. and Mrs. Emerson. How can I ever thank you enough for caring for my wife." At the word *wife*, Ronald turned to Emily and grinned.

"It was our joy," Bonnie said, quietly. "Nice to meet you as well, Mr. Davenport. Finally."

"Yes," Ronald said. "Finally." He looked back at Emily and smiled.

"Come, let me show you Seth." She took his hand and started to lead him down the hallway.

"Seth? His name is Seth?" Ronald paused. "This is like a dream. I have a son named Seth. I like that name, dear. It's a good name." He continued down the hall muttering *Seth Davenport* over and over to himself.

They entered Emily's room where Seth lay sleeping in between two pillows in the middle of the bed. A single candle lit up the room. Its warm light cast a soft glow over them.

Ronald strode over to the bedside and dropped to his knees in wonder. "Just look at him. That's my son," he whispered. "I'm a dead man come alive again, Emily." He looked up at her with tears in his eyes. "You are alive." He gulped hard and reached for her. Then he looked back to the baby sound asleep before him. "I have a child." Ronald took Emily's hand and pulled her down beside him. "I thought my life was over on board that sinking ship last April."

Emily nodded once, unable to speak.

"You were gone from our cabin. The last lifeboat was released without any sign of you. I tried calling to you from the deck to make sure you were on one. I couldn't see you. I couldn't hear anything but the roar of the fire."

"How did you survive?" Emily whispered.

Ronald turned back to her, half his face darkened in the shadows. "I don't know how I survived really. Even though I was still breathing, clinging to the rail of the ship, I felt dead inside. You were gone. I felt that I had failed you in bringing you out here to this treacherous place. The guilt ate me up. The terror you must have felt. You had no money, no connections. I couldn't possibly see how you could make it here alone. But look at you." His dark brown eyes shone with such warmth and love for her, it made it hard for Emily to breathe.

She swallowed hard. "But how did you make it off the ship? The waves were so high. It was so dark."

Ronald looked across the room as if trying to remember. "Another gentleman and I swore to stay together. Some chap from New Jersey. We vowed to jump ship at the last minute and survive on anything that floated, so we did. The ship went down. It pulled us below the surface for a moment then we submerged and grabbed onto a set of luggage that was floating. God bless some wealthy woman and her expansive trousseau. That's how we survived. Sitting on top of a floating piece of luggage until the next morning when a fishing ship came right across our path. We were saved before we even began starving! You'll be glad to know, dear, that I never had to resort to cannibalism."

"That's wonderful, dear," Emily said, absentmindedly. "How did you come to be here in Astoria?"

"I took ill on board the ship. Seems that I was unconscious for most of the voyage back to San Franny." Ronald reached over and took Seth's tiny hand in his own. "The captain got me to a hospital where they cared for me until the pneumonia passed."

"Pneumonia?"

"Yes, it seems that it wanted to take up residence in my excellent well-bred lungs and refuses to leave," Ronald said, placing one hand over his chest. He coughed once. It was shallow and raspy.

"But you are here," Emily whispered. "However did you get here from San Francisco?"

"Well, I wasn't about to get back on board a ship willingly," Ronald teased.

"I understand," Emily said, grimacing.

"I hired a guide to take me by horseback through the Southern Oregon pass. Fortunate for us, the weather was beautiful and the path was clear. We made good time but it was already almost the middle of October. We reached the northern Oregon territory by the beginning of November and here we are."

"Ronald," Emily said, furrowing her eyebrows. "It was April when we wrecked. It's past Thanksgiving. Why were you gone so long? My parents must have received your note three months ago." She shook her head, not understanding.

Ronald whispered, his breathing shallow. "I thought you were dead. I had no will to live. The pneumonia set in and I let it. There were a few nights that I could feel death at the foot of my bed. If I would have given up, I would not be here. But something in me couldn't believe that you were gone. I fought the sickness hard. There is some kind of infection in my lungs still. But now that we're together, I know that everything will be fine."

"Infection, Ronald?" Emily gasped. "What kind of infection?"

"It won't heal," Ronald said, quietly. He kept his eyes on Seth. "It steals my strength and my breath. I do well for a few days and have to rest for a few. That's why it took so long to get up north. Traveling goes slow when you take breaks like that."

"But here you are," Emily said, amazed. This tenacity in her husband was surprising to her. "I'm proud of you, Ronald. Thank you for coming."

Ronald's face softened. He took Emily's hand in his and kissed it. He held her gaze and studied her face in the candlelight. "You are more beautiful than when I last saw you." Leaning in, he cupped her chin in his hand, and placed a soft, sweet kiss on her lips. "How I missed you."

"I missed you, too." Emily said, truly meaning it. "I thought you were dead, Ronald. I grieved for you for a long time. Please bear with me as I try to adjust to seeing you again."

"I understand," Ronald said, looking down at their clasped hands. "You didn't seem very surprised. Your parents must have contacted you in time." He smiled.

"Just in time," Emily said, exhaling sharply. "Just in time."

CHAPTER THIRTY-FOUR

"Do not be afraid of sudden terror, nor of trouble from the wicked when it comes; for the Lord will be your confidence, and will keep your foot from being caught."

Proverbs 3:25

December 1853

Johan and Frans pulled the wagon into the field next to Johan's home. Careful to not bump his back as he climbed down, Johan swung his legs over and slipped off the bench.

"Got that, boy?" Frans called from the other side.

Johan put his hands in his pockets and stared at his home. Beautiful hand-hewn beams, criss-crossed at the corners. Two wooden rockers sat on the front porch. Frans must have made those. Johan looked over at him. Frans looked away and shoved his hands into his pockets as well.

"Well, I thought you and..." he began, not wanting to finish his thought.

"They're very nice, Uncle," Johan said, sincerely. "Thank you."

"Come see what else Spurgeon, Luther and I finished up for you," Frans said, urging him forward.

Johan's feet felt planted in the ground he stood on. He didn't want to see the finished home. Three bedrooms. A pantry. A new pump for the kitchen. It was all for Emily and the baby. He didn't want them all to himself.

Johan glanced over at the shed to the right of the wagon. He would, more than likely, sleep in there tonight. This house was ready for a bride to move in, not a depressed bachelor.

"I'm telling you, boy," Frans said. "If you won't live in here, I will. Now come on."

Johan tried to smile but it hurt too much. He dragged one foot in front of the other, careful not to lift them too high. The motion would pull on his back muscles and they weren't ready to be stretched yet.

Frans opened the front door. "Now see here," he pointed. "Isn't that beautiful?" To the left was the stone fireplace and heavy oak mantle. In the center of the room was the pine table and chairs just waiting for a couple to sit on them.

Frans jumped forward and pulled a baby's high chair off to the side. "I'm sorry, Johan," he mumbled. "I forgot that the boys and I finished that. I'll take it out to the shed for you."

Johan put his hand on his uncle's wrist. "No, Uncle, leave it here. Just leave it where it is." He turned to the right. The pump was set up with a large wooden sink carved out to catch the water. A broad, pine cutting-board counter stood on four sturdy legs. Johan's few pots and pans hung from thick, steel nails on the wall. Sikkus' baskets sat under the cutting block, full of linens, dried herbs and sewing supplies.

Johan put his hand over his mouth. Evidence of his friends' generosity and care was everywhere he looked. They covered him and the prospect of his future bride to the final detail. He felt ill at the thought of living here without her.

"I don't know if I can do it," he mumbled.

Frans closed the slim pantry door. "How's that?"

"I don't know if I can stay here, Uncle."

"You don't know if you *can*...or you don't know if you *will*?" Frans rested his hands on the top of the cutting block. "You are my only family, Johan. If you go, I go." He glanced around the home they built together. "This is just a home. It's nothing without family. I understand that."

Johan dragged his feet slowly across to the fireplace. On the other side of the wall was the master bedroom. He couldn't bear to see it finished. The small room next to it was supposed to be for Seth. Close enough for Emily to get to him; big enough for him to grow up in and share with future brothers.

Johan wiped his hand over his face and took a deep breath. "One day at a time. That's how I'll do this. I'll get through today. Then I'll get through tomorrow. I've lost everything before. I think I can do it again."

"Well, you're not completely alone. I'm here this time." Frans said. "And we'll more than get through this time, Johan. We have *sisu*..."

"Yes," Johan said, "Yes, we do."

CHAPTER THIRTY-FIVE

"There is a time for everything, a season for every activity under heaven. A time to be born and a time to die..." Ecclesiastes 3:1-2

December 1853

"That was a lovely service, Reverend Malcolm," Ronald said, shaking Daniel's hand after the service. "Emily showed me the stained glass window you worked on together. It's exquisite. Thank you for taking the time to teach her."

Rev. Malcolm glanced from Emily to Ronald. "It was my pleasure and honor, Mr. Davenport." He cleared his throat. His face flushed and he avoided Emily's eyes.

Emily slipped passed Ronald out the door, snuggling Seth close against the cold. "Others are waiting, dear. Let's be going."

Ronald put his arm around her and held the blanket up against Seth. "Shall I hold him, darling?" He coughed as he stepped down the first step. He grabbed the hand rail, almost losing his footing. A deeper coughing spasm took over. He turned away from Emily and the baby, coughing into the sleeve of his coat. Gripping the rail, he tried to expel the fluid from his lungs but his breathing grew labored in between coughs.

"Your lips are turning blue, Ronald," Emily gasped.

He kept coughing and sucking in air to no avail.

"Please," Emily begged, quietly at first, to an older couple leaving the church. "Could you help my husband get back inside? I'm concerned that the cold air has set off his cough."

The older gentleman tried to urge Ronald back toward the church. Ronald gripped the rail, gasping for air.

"Please," Emily cried out, "Anyone, help us, please!"

Reverend Malcolm was at her side. "Emily, what is happening?" He reached under Ronald's side to lift him. Ronald shot him a look of desperation and grabbed his throat, mouthing that he couldn't breathe. Ronald's lips were a pale blue now and his coloring was white and blotchy. His skin was clammy with perspiration on his brow.

"Ronald! Let them help you, please!" Emily pleaded, holding Seth close as he began to whimper.

Just then, Bonnie, Gus and the boys came outside. "Emily! Ronald!" Bonnie cried, hustling over to Emily's side. "Get him inside quickly." Gus, Luther and Spurgeon grabbed Ronald by the legs while Daniel carried him under the shoulders. They hurried him up the stairs and laid him down on the pew in the back row. Ronald was still gripping his throat, choking for air. His eyes grew wide, looking around wildly for Emily.

Bonnie took the crying baby from Emily's arms and she ran to Ronald's side. "I'm here, Ronald," she whispered. "I'm here. Breathe, please breathe." Their hands were clasped tight, interlocking their fingers. Ronald's eyes held Emily's until they rolled back into his head.

Emily shrieked. "Ronald!" She pumped his chest, willing air to fill his lungs. "Ronald! Can you hear me? Breathe!" She put her ear to his mouth to listen.

Gus put his two forefingers on Ronald's neck under his chin and waited.

Emily looked up to him for any hope. Gus shook his head slowly and ran a hand over his beard in dismay. Emily shook her head and looked from Gus to Bonnie to Daniel. "No…" she said, leaning over Ronald again. "No! This can't be happening." She took Ronald's face in her hands, searching for any sign of life.

Bonnie turned away from Ronald with the baby.

Gus whispered to his boys, "He's gone. There's nothing we can do."

Emily looked to them for direction. "This isn't happening," she murmured. "I don't understand. He can't be dead. He just got here!"

Ronald really was dead now. He was very sick. She knew that. The evidence of his illness became more and more obvious in the past three days but Emily chose to ignore it. The long naps, the coughing fits. He had only lived this long to see her again. She knew that now.

Emily ran her thumb over his blue lips. She closed his eyes gently and sank onto the hardwood floor with one hand cradling Ronald's cheek. She laid her head on his chest.

"This isn't happening," she murmured. "Lord, help me. Lord, help me. This isn't happening."

A sharp cry from Seth snapped Emily to attention. "Give him to me," she said, quietly to Bonnie.

"Are you sure you're alright, dear?" Bonnie said, tentatively putting the child in Emily's hands.

"Yes, Bonnie." Emily held Seth against her chest, pressing his head to her shoulder. The baby instantly relaxed and sighed. She rocked Seth absentmindedly. Emily kept her eyes on Ronald's lifeless face. "Why did the Lord bring him back here just to die?" Now she turned to Daniel. "Why, Daniel?"

Daniel put his hand over his mouth and shook his head in disbelief. He whispered, "There is nothing that can be said, Emily. I'm so sorry. May the Lord receive him into his kingdom." He put his hand gently on Emily's shoulder, held it there for a moment, and stepped out the front doors.

Spurgeon knelt next to Emily and put his arm around her. "I'm sorry, Miss Em." He put one hand on Seth. "I'm sorry your baby won't have his daddy." He sniffed and wiped his nose on his sleeve.

Luther was next. He leaned over the pew and wiped his tears on his shoulder. "I'm real sorry too, Em. It just don't make sense."

"We're here, honey," Bonnie whispered. "We'll do this together just like when…" Bonnie's voice caught. "When Henry died, you were there for us. Now we will see you through this."

Gus put his hand on her shoulder and squeezed lightly then stepped outside with Reverend Malcolm. They whispered between themselves while the family sat in shock and grief. After some time, when the building grew chilled and Emily began to shake, Daniel stepped back inside.

"We need to get you home, Emily. The baby needs you and you must rest." He helped her stand to her feet. Seth slept in her arms but he would awake fussy and hungry from missing a feeding.

Emily's body ached all over. It was like a poison released in her veins. She felt nauseous and chilled. Her joints ached and throbbed. Black spots filled her vision.

"Watch her there," Bonnie warned, jumping to her feet. "She's not well. Spurgeon, steady her."

Spurgeon was at Emily's side in an instant and Bonnie took the baby from her arms.

Gus stood by Emily's other side. "We'll take care of Ronald, Emily. You and the baby need to go home in the wagon with Bonnie." Emily just nodded once, weakly, and allowed Spurgeon to half carry her out to the wagon.

She felt like she was in a nightmare. Everything was happening in slow motion but she couldn't wake up from the terror of it all. She looked around her. Nothing was making sense. She shuddered and almost fell off the wagon seat before Spurgeon swung up beside her and put his arm around her waist. *Lord, help me. I can't do this again.* Her head felt heavy and she leaned into Spurgeon's shoulder for support. *Not again.*

*   *   *

Dear Daddy and Mother,

Ronald did surprise us with his arrival last week. How overjoyed he was to see his son! He didn't even know he had one. We had three days together, trying to rebuild our lives and make sense of our future here. Ronald's sickness from the shipwreck plagued him day and night. It appears that pneumonia stayed in his lungs, making his breathing difficult. At church last Sunday, Ronald went home to be with the Lord.

It was so sudden that I could not write until now. I have lost my husband twice now in one year and can hardly bear it. It seems cruel for him to be allowed to live just to die when we are finally reunited. At least Seth will have seen his father, though he will never remember him. We have laid his body to rest in the primitive cemetery up on the hill near Henry's.

The weather is turning so cold and dismal that I hesitate to come home by boat until spring. The thought of Seth on board a dirty ship in the freezing, vicious ocean makes me physically ill. I cannot make a trip that dangerous with him until the weather is warmer. How I wish there were a railroad available across the United States instead! Perhaps we will join a guide heading east to pick up more people in Missouri on a wagon train. Ronald came north with a guide. Maybe that man can take Seth and I home. There is nothing left for us here.

The Emersons are as dear to me as family. I believe that they would let me stay with them as long as needed with Seth. I can care for him on my own now, cooking and cleaning. I long for a family of my own, though. I long for the safety of my own home where Seth can grow up with a father. As much as I love this wild, free place, I cannot stay here any longer. There is too much pain and I cannot bear it. Life is just a vapor and gone so quickly here.

Please send Aaron to come fetch me in the spring. I dread taking the trip home alone. Have a Merry Christmas together and know that my love is with you.

Always your daughter,
Emily

*　　　*　　　*

"He did what?" Johan threw the hammer he was holding to the ground and leaned one hand against the outside wall of his shed. "That's...unbelievable."

Frans tilted his hat up so the rain would pour off the back. "It's sad but true. Her husband is gone. He died at church last week. Seems that his lungs were bad. Some sort of infection set in that he couldn't shake. With our weather here, they went from bad to worse."

Johan's mind reeled. *Emily's husband was gone. Seth was fatherless again.* His heart ached for the little family that he had grown to love as his own. He began picking up his tools and chucking them into his shed.

"What are you doing, boy?" Frans asked, grabbing a shovel and putting it away.

"I'm going," Johan said, quietly.

"Where are you going?"

"I've got to see her. I need to see Seth."

Frans ran a hand over his face. "She may not be ready...it's only been a week."

"No, Uncle," Johan said, "She will never be ready but does that mean that I stay here and never try? I've wanted to crawl out of my own skin all week trying to picture my life without her and I can't. I can't do it."

Frans put his hand on Johan's shoulder.

"Every time I pound in a nail, or haul in a catch...it's for her. It's for our future together. I still see her and Seth in my future. I can't change that. She needs to know that I'm still here...waiting."

Frans walked over to Ginger's stall and began saddling her up. She looked up from her grain and whinnied.

Johan raked his fingers through his hair. "I'll be right back. I must go change, then I will leave."

Frans continued working, nodding once.

Johan ran, in spite of the pain shooting up his back, through the soft, December rain, splashing mud as he went. He stepped inside his new home and shucked off his boots. His hands were trembling with excitement. He tore off his wet shirt, wincing from the burning wounds on his back. He shucked off his work pants, leaving on his long underwear. *Better change to get dry. I can't afford to get sick too. There's too much at stake.*

Crossing the pine floor to his bedroom, he thought about seeing Emily again. He drew in a deep breath and walked over to a small table holding a pitcher and basin on it. The oval plate glass mirror hung on the wall a little low for him but just right for Emily's height. Looking back at him was a full-bearded pioneer with long blond hair. It wouldn't do.

Johan poured some water into the basin and soaked his face. He wished he had time for a full bath but it was already getting late in the day. If he was lucky, he might make it in time for Sunday supper.

He lathered up some shaving cream in another small bowl and took the razor in his hands. Had he really looked in this same mirror this morning, unable to get cleaned up for church? Shame on him. Here he was cleaning up, hoping to win Emily back. He hung his head.

Lord, I don't deserve Your mercy, but please help me. Forgive my callused heart and make me a faithful man. I know I can be the man that Emily needs. I know I can be a good father to Seth. Give me a chance.

He looked back in the mirror at his lathered face and went to work. His blond whiskers fell into the basin below him. After a few minutes, Johan grabbed a towel and wiped his face clean. A smooth-faced youth looked back at him. He felt like ten years had been lifted off of him.

He yanked his good Sunday shirt out of the top dresser drawer. Pulling it on gingerly and buttoning it up, he felt hope begin to fill him. His heart pounded. He had to try to win her back. He couldn't just let her go. Pulling on his Sunday pants and dry wool socks, he stepped out of his bedroom as Frans came inside.

"Well," he said, grinning. "You clean up well. Ready?"

Johan pulled out a chair from the table and sat down to put his boots on. Looking up, he said, "I'll never be ready. But I'm ready to try."

"Course you are," Frans said, smiling. "Take some of this salted deer jerky for Gus and the boys. I'll wrap some up for you."

"Thanks Uncle," Johan said, tying up his boots. He pulled his suspenders over his broad shoulders, winced and thought the better of it. He took them down again and sued a belt instead. Yanking on his overcoat, he grabbed his hat from the peg by the door and patted it down on his head. Running a hand over his face, he drew in a deep breath.

Frans stepped over to Johan from the kitchen and handed him a small bundle tied up in twine. "Here you are then, ready as you'll ever be."

"Do you want to come?" Johan said, meeting his uncle's eye. He felt guilty for not asking sooner.

Frans shook his head. "I've got the farm here for ya. Stay in town and fish tomorrow for the both of us. I'll finish patching that leak on the shed for you. Now you better get going. It's getting dark out there."

Tucking the meat into his coat, Johan turned to leave. He held his hand on the door latch and turned. "Thank you, Uncle," he said, pulling Frans into a hug. "Thank you for all you've done for me."

"There, that's enough," Frans said, clapping Johan gently on the arm. "You're losing daylight. I'll see you tomorrow night. Godspeed to you."

Johan stepped out into the rain where Ginger waited for him, tied on the door post. He loosed her reins and swung up into the saddle. He waved one last time at Frans standing in the doorway. His future opened up for him again and he was riding to meet it.

CHAPTER THIRTY-SIX

"Controversial proposals, once accepted, soon become hallowed."
Dean Acheson – American Statemen, diplomat, lawyer (1893-1971)

December 1853

"Johan!" Bonnie cried, opening the front door.

He barely had Ginger tied up and the gate open before she was waving him in. It was a good sign. He didn't want to intrude on their privacy.

"We have missed you," Bonnie whispered, taking his hand in hers. "It's been a long week. I take it that you know what happened last Sunday."

Johan nodded once and hung his head. He felt guilty knowing his true intentions toward Emily. Now that she was free, he wanted to marry her. He would not come out and say that tonight, however. He was here to pay his respects; that was all.

"I came to pay my respects, Bonnie," he said quietly.

"She will be grateful to see you," Bonnie whispered back. "She has never said as much but her eyes are quick to check the window when someone passes by. She's been waiting for you, I think." Bonnie stood close to Johan while he pulled off his boots. She sat on the bench next to him. "The Reverend has been by a few times this week…every evening, in fact."

Johan shot a glance up to Bonnie, anxious.

"Not to worry," Bonnie giggled. "His attentions are not as welcome as he would like to think they are. He's a good man but…he's not you."

Johan kept his eyes on the floor. "Am I too late?"

"No, she'll come around," Bonnie said, looking over her shoulder to the kitchen.

"I mean," Johan said, glancing up at her and grinning. "For dinner?"

"You!" Bonnie hissed at him and slapped his arm. "I should have known. I've got your taters ready. Come sit down, if you like. Your spot is open."

Johan wondered where Ronald Davenport had been seated at the Emerson's table. It was best not to think about it. It did no good. He walked into the dining room and stood behind his chair.

Bonnie rang her dinner bell from the kitchen and the heavy footsteps upstairs thudded down the hallway. Spurgeon and Luther slid into the dining room in their wool stockings. "Johan!" They grabbed his hand and almost slapped him on the back but stilled their hands just in time.

Johan winced, awaiting pain on his tender wounds.

"Sorry, Johan," Luther said. "We forgot about your uh--"

"Thank you for remembering in time," Johan said, grinning.

Just then, Emily came into the dining room with Seth in her arms. She wore a simple black, wool dress with a white lace collar. Her face was as white as the lace and under her eyes were dark rings. Her eyes lacked their luster. Seth's cheeks were pink and beginning to get chubby. But even the baby was quiet and still.

Emily stopped short when she saw Johan across the table from her. "Johan," she whispered, tearing up. "When did you get here?"

He smiled and took his time looking her over. "I just arrived," he said. "How are you doing, Emily?"

Emily hugged Seth closer and pursed her lips to keep them from trembling. Johan quickly moved around the table and pulled out her chair to distract her.

"Here you are," he said, motioning for her to sit. She slipped into her chair and he helped push her in.

Bonnie entered with a roast duck, mashed potatoes, steamy, yellow squash and a tray of her dill pickles.

"Bless you, dear woman," Gus said, patting her hand as she took her seat. "Father in heaven, thank you for this bountiful meal. Bless it to our bodies for our nourishment that we may do your work. Thank you for Your Son who binds up the brokenhearted and gives us new strength to keep going. Amen."

Johan and Emily sat in the parlor after the meal. He sat in Bonnie's rocker and Emily took the couch opposite him with Seth beside her. *How should he address her? Mrs. Davenport? Emily?* Better to not say much tonight, he reminded himself. He tried to keep his eyes on the fire but they kept drifting back to her and the baby.

"I didn't make it church this morning," Emily said. "Perhaps you could tell me what your pastor spoke on. I could use some spiritual encouragement." She tried to smile but failed miserably when her chin quivered.

Johan hung his head. *She caught him.* "I didn't attend church this morning, either." He glanced up at her quickly. "I guess you could say I didn't feel up to it as well."

Emily's eyes met his and tears pooled at the bottom of them. "You're not turning into a heathen, are you, Johan?" A weak smile tugged at the edge of her mouth but she didn't laugh. She looked at the fire instead. "What would we do without the Lord?" The question didn't seem directed to him in particular.

Johan leaned back in the rocker. He pushed it back and forth slowly, deep in thought. Without the Lord, he would have died in Liminka. Without the Lord, he would have never had the courage to start a new life in the Oregon Territory. Without the Lord, he would have become a depraved, bitter man in Astoria. He never would have been in the right place to help a poor widow get her life back together after a ship wreck. Here she was asking him for spiritual encouragement but she gave it to him. "Hmmmmm," he sighed.

"What?" Emily said, turning her gaze back to him.

He looked up at her slowly and continued rocking. He looked over at Seth lost in peaceful sleep. "You have a good future ahead, Em."

"I hope so," she said, straightening her back and smoothing out the wrinkles on the front of her heavy skirt. "I have written to my parents concerning Ronald. They needed to know." She pressed her fingers to her mouth and took in a deep breath. "I've asked them to send my brother Aaron out here in the spring."

"To visit?" Johan was intrigued, leaning forward. He thought he would like Emily's brother if they ever got a chance to meet.

Emily met Johan's gaze head on. "To accompany me home."

"Home?" Johan gasped, planting his elbows on his knees.

"Ronald took care of our business issues the Friday before he passed. He was so animated about getting our affairs in order that I couldn't convince him to rest. It was like he knew…"

Johan rolled back and held the rocker still again. His elbows rested on the arms of it and his chin sat on his hands. He couldn't speak, he was so shocked. *She was leaving?* After what seemed a lifetime, he got up the courage to ask. "Why must you go?"

Emily seemed taken back by his directness. Her face grew flushed for the first time that night. It suited her. "I can't presume to live with the Emersons forever," she whispered so that Gus and Bonnie wouldn't hear her from the kitchen. "I guess I was reminded of what having my own family would feel like for the brief time while Ronald was here." She ran her fingers over Seth's soft hair. "I must consider Seth's future, not my own now."

Johan leaned forward again. "What do you want, Emily?" The intensity of his gaze took her back.

"Why…" she began, looking around from the fire to the old clock.

Everything in Johan wanted to fall on his knees before her and beg her to stay. He willed himself to remain in his seat. He could not convince her to stay. She would resent him later for it. No, she had to *want* to stay. She had to say, of her own accord, that she wanted him in her life. He could not decide that for her.

He hung his head, avoiding her eyes. "What do you want, Emily?" He focused on the fire instead.

"I don't know anymore, Johan," she whispered, tears streaming down her cheeks. "Do you?"

"Yes."

"And what is that?"

"I asked you first."

Emily shot her gaze to the fire as well. "I can't…"

He looked at her now. "You can't what?"

"I can't say what's in my heart. The timing is wrong. No one would understand…"

Johan scooted to the edge of his chair. "What would people not understand?"

"That…that…"

"Say it, Em."

"That I *love* you," she blurted out, cupping her hand over her mouth. She let out a sob and stifled more threatening to come out.

Johan was at her side, kneeling on the floor before her. He wrapped his arms around her waist and pulled her to him. She held her face in her hands, unable to look at him.

"People will say it's wrong, Johan. It's too soon. I have to leave," Emily sobbed. She gasped and looked at Johan. "It's not that I didn't love my husband."

Johan nodded once, understanding. He said, slowly, "You just allowed yourself the chance to love again. I know what you mean."

Emily searched Johan's face and remembered Emilia. "Yes, you do understand, don't you? But what if you had her back? Right now? What would you do? What would I do? What is right?"

Johan hushed her and wiped her hair away from her face. "We can't play this game of wondering what might have been. We only have today, right now. There's no guarantee of tomorrow. But how we choose to live is up to us."

Emily drew in a deep breath.

"I want you to be my wife," Johan whispered, taking her face in his hands. "I want to grow old with you. I want to help you raise Seth. What do you want, Emily?" Heat rose in his neck. Every muscle strained as he waited. Desolation or jubilation was his lot with just a simple answer.

"Yes."

"Yes?"

"Yes." Emily's cheeks flushed and her eyes glimmered in the firelight. "I want nothing more than to grow old with you too, Johan." She turned to Seth. "There is no father I want for Seth more than you."

"Em," he whispered, allowing the joy welling up in him to overwhelm his heart. "You have made me so happy." He took her face in his strong, callused hands. She leaned toward him and waited. He kissed her as he had on the hill over Astoria months before. He pulled her to him and enveloped her in his arms.

A gasp from the other side of the room startled them. Johan and Emily shot a glance over to the doorway. Bonnie had a hankie to her throat.

"Excuse me, I'm so sorry," Bonnie muttered, fanning herself.

Johan jumped to his feet. "It's not what you think, Bonnie," he said, holding his hands out in front of him in surrender. "We just agreed to be married. Emily is going to be my wife."

"Your wife? But--"

"I know," Johan looked back to Emily. "We understand the timing is wrong but the agreement is right." He grinned at Bonnie. "We love each other. We will marry soon, I hope."

Gus stepped up behind Bonnie, his face red. "There's only one week until Christmas, why not then?"

Bonnie slapped him. "That's too soon."

"Why?" Johan and Gus chimed in together. Emily sat on the couch, silent.

"I think it's appropriate to wait a little longer." Bonnie ventured, "Don't you think so, Emily?"

Just then, Seth woke with a piercing cry. He wailed at the top of his lungs as he never had before. All eyes in the room were on him instantly.

"See?" Gus said, taking Bonnie's arm. "You've upset him. He doesn't want to wait either."

Bonnie chuckled. "Now, don't you go manipulating that sweet baby's cry to fit your wants."

"No," Emily said, quietly. "It's right. Why should we wait? There's nothing wrong with being married sooner rather than later. Johan is going to be Seth's father. We need to become a family. Ronald would understand. My parents won't, though."

Johan leaned over and took Seth in his arms. The baby quieted right away, nestled into Johan's right arm. "We'll handle that challenge when it comes. Right now we have to convince Bonnie to make our wedding cake." He grinned.

Gus thrust out his belly. "Well, I'll make the salmon!"

Emily's face turned green and they all laughed.

CHAPTER THIRTY-SEVEN

"Come, neighbor, sit down.
You shall get a taste first of my wife's Christmas glogg."
Beer Bowl inscription, 1818

Christmas Day, 1853

The plate of cinnamon rolls was wiped clean and the carafe of coffee was drained dry. The evergreen tree in the parlor lay cluttered with the strings and brown paper of the Christmas gifts. Uncle Frans snored on the horse hair couch. Bonnie and Sikkus were milling about in the kitchen, making Christmas dinner. Gus, Spurgeon and Luther took to their beds for a much-needed nap.

Johan quietly opened the front door. He, Emily and Seth slipped outside. He took her hand and they strolled down the boardwalk. The crisp, salty air greeted them from the ocean. The sky was a blanket of thick, cotton clouds. Johan looked around. "It won't rain today. We should be fine." He grinned at Emily who had Seth strapped to her front like a native woman. "Come on," he said, tugging her up the hill onto Eighth Street.

"Where are you taking me?" Emily giggled. Her cheeks were flushed and she locked her fingers between his.

"You'll see," Johan said, bringing her hand to his lips and kissing it. "I want to show you something." Their strides matched climbing the hill. "Are you alright holding the baby?"

Emily drew in a deep breath. Mist hung in the air when she exhaled. "I'm fine. Besides being tired all the time, I feel well."

"He still wakes you up at night?" Johan asked.

"Yes," Emily said, smiling. "I'm sure this will be my lot in life for a few more years."

Johan stopped in his tracks and leaned over. "It will be *our* lot," he corrected, smiling and giving her a soft kiss. Two sailors came down the hill toward them with some painted ladies between them and a bottle of whiskey. Johan pulled away and hurried past them. Their laughter filled the quiet afternoon air.

"Oh look at the baby, Daphne," the blond woman crooned. "I want a baby someday!"

"Not me," the brunette said, pulling her sailor closer. "I wouldn't want to be tied down to someone else. I like my freedom."

The sailor planted a kiss on the blond's cheek. "Come on, Rose. You don't mean it."

The young woman named Rose watched Emily and Johan pass by. Her eyes were fixed on the baby. She gave them a weak smile of greeting which Emily returned.

"Rose LeFleur," her sailor said, seductively. "How did you get a name like that?"

"My real name is Rose," she said, passing by Emily and Johan now. "LeFleur just means 'flower.'" The girl never took her eyes off of Seth. The sailor made a crude comment which made the young woman's face blush.

Johan and Emily chose to ignore them and kept walking briskly up the hill. Emily glanced back down the hill when they reached Irving Street. To her surprise, the young woman was looking back up at her. Emily gave a little wave of her hand which the young woman returned.

"That girl," she muttered.

"What about her?" Johan asked, putting his hand on Emily's waist.

"They don't belong in the bawdry houses. They want what we have, Johan," Emily said quietly. "They don't have hope."

"They don't have someone who cares about them enough to rescue them," Johan said, frowning. "Maybe we can help her someday."

Emily looked up to him and nodded. "I think we will, Johan. I really do."

They turned onto Irving and walked east, enjoying the slight descent.

"This place is overrun with hills...like San Francisco," Emily said. "Did you go to shore when you sailed past there?"

"We weren't allowed to leave the ship," Johan said, grimly, not wanting to remember the *Hai*. He looked down at Emily. Her nose was red from the cold. He tucked her arm tighter against him. "I remember the fog."

"Yes!" Emily laughed. "It could be the most beautiful day one moment and then that thick fog would roll in and ruin it!"

"I remember the docks," Johan said, looking downhill at the docks along the river. "They were so busy with people from every nation, it seemed. Chinamen, Finns, Irish..."

"Astoria is diverse in its own ways," Emily said, smiling up at him. "There are Finns...and those who are not." She giggled.

"We'll have to make sure there are plenty more Finns to come," he teased.

Emily's face grew red. "Where are you taking me anyway?"

"You'll see," Johan said, keeping his eyes ahead of them. "It's worth the effort to get there." He grinned at her. "I might end up carrying you and Seth back down the hill, though."

Seth rested his head on his mother's chest. She had a protective hand behind his head so he stayed tight against her, protecting him from the cold. Johan smiled at the pair of them, his new family to be. It was more than his heart could hold.

Emily seemed to be sharing his thoughts. "You spoke with your pastor? About marrying us next Sunday?"

"Yes," Johan said, grinning. "We didn't give him much time to prepare a message but he was pleased to marry us."

"Reverend Malcolm is in Portland until the New Year," Emily said, quietly. "He has been so gracious since Ronald..."

"I know," Johan said, keeping his eyes ahead of them. "He's a good man. I can't blame him for trying to win you."

"He will find someone better suited for him in time," Emily said, looking at the ground as they walked. "I don't see myself as one of the society women in Astoria. There's so much more to life than tea parties."

"There is?" Johan teased. "I can't imagine what else one could possibly want to do than serve tea to one's friends."

Emily smirked and adjusted Seth's blanket to cover his ears. "I can't wait to have a garden this spring. I want to dig in the dirt and work hard and use all the knowledge Bonnie has given me this last year. I want to can and dry out meat and berries. Sikkus showed me how to make a dried berry cake with oatmeal and nuts. They're delicious, you'll love them--"

Johan laughed and pulled Emily tight against him. "I love *you*."

Emily looked up to him in surprise. "What brought that on?"

"I'm so impressed with how you've grown this year," he said, the pride in his voice shone through. "You've worked hard, sold property...you can cook!"

"That's all you care about, isn't it?" Emily laughed, punching him in the arm.

He caught her fist and pulled her to him. "You are all I care about. You and Seth," he leaned over and kissed Seth on the top of his head. Then he glanced and looked into the woods to their right. "I believe this is where we want to hike in."

"Hike in?" Emily gasped. "Johan Nevala, where are you taking me? I'm carrying a baby here, remember?"

"It's not far," he said, pulling her into the woods behind him. Then he stopped. "Do you want me to carry Seth for you? I don't mind."

Emily looked down at the baby and back up at Johan. "Are we scaling the side of a mountain or just walking?"

"Just walking a bit further," Johan said, looking over his shoulder into the thick forest of evergreens. "We can rest in a few minutes. You'll love what I have to show you."

"Promise?"

"I do." Johan's neck grew red with the heat rising in him. It was best to keep moving. Emily would get tired, the baby would need to eat soon and he didn't want to miss this time because of delays. "Come on," he said, grinning.

A thin, worn path stretched up into the woods. Ferns lined the way with roots criss-crossing over the path.

"Watch your step. Be careful," Johan warned, leading Emily. "Take a deep breath."

Emily drew in the sweet smell of the evergreens all around them. The firs and hemlocks and redwoods towered over their heads, permeating the cold air with their scent.

Johan turned and helped Emily step up onto a set of roots, covered in mud. "Good, you're doing great." He lifted a low branch and held it as Emily passed by him. He let her lead up the path, her hem dragged in the mud behind her. Her new leather boots sank into the muddy patches in the middle of the path.

"Here step on the side of the path," Johan said, touching her waist and pushing her to the right to avoid a mud puddle.

"I'm so silly," Emily chuckled. "My feet would be soaked by the time we get there if it was up to me."

"We've got to teach you how to hike like this," he said. "We'll need to walk our property often. Three hundred twenty acres is a lot to manage."

"Can you get more acreage when we are married?" Emily asked, over her shoulder.

"Possibly," Johan said, thoughtfully. "But the river gives us more than what we need. My native friends live close by. I don't want to take more of the land they use for hunting and farming. What do you think?"

Emily smiled. "I think I agree with you. Why take more than what we need?" She turned toward him and stopped. "Thank you for asking me, though."

"Your opinion matters to me, Em," he said. "Wait til you see your house."

"My house?" Emily spun around again. "You mean your house, don't you?"

"*Your* house, Em." Johan put his hands on her waist. "I built the house you described. A large bedroom for us, two bedrooms for our children. A kitchen, a fireplace and mantle. There's a cleared field beside the house for your vegetable and flower gardens. Just like you said."

"Johan," Emily whispered. "You built that house for me before you even asked me to marry you. How did you know that I would say yes?"

"I knew."

"What about Ronald? When he came back…"

"I wanted to die. The land, the home, the farm – it doesn't mean anything if you are not with me."

"Would you have left Astoria?"

"Probably."

"Where would you go? Back to Finland?"

"Definitely not. This is my home now."

"Well, I am with you. I will be your wife. That will be my home, too."

Johan leaned in to kiss Emily but she clapped her hands and giggled. "I can't wait to see my new home!" She turned on the path and hiked up the hill with new vigor. Johan had to walk briskly to keep up with her.

"We're almost there," he called to her. "Turn left at the Y in the path."

Emily took off to the left, lifting her skirt to get over a fallen tree.

"There," Johan called. "Look to your right, Em."

Emily stopped midstep and gasped. "It's beautiful. Absolutely gorgeous, Johan." She put her fists on her hips and took in a deep breath. Spreading before her were the massive roots of two trees intertwined. The base of the tree had a huge opening that she could almost walk under. The roots spread out like lace, weaving in and out of each other. Emily put her hand on the trunk of the right side of the tree and climbed inside it.

"I wish Seth was older so he could remember this," Emily whispered. "You knew this was here?"

Johan nodded, leaning against the other side of the tree. "Chief Wah-tut-kum brought Uncle Frans and I here last summer. He calls the tree by a different name in his language but people around here call it the Cathedral Tree. Makes you feel insignificant doesn't it?"

"On the contrary," Emily whispered. "It makes me feel valuable."

Johan stepped closer to her and leaned his hand on the tree above her head. He stood tall over the little woman and child while the tree towered over them both. "Why do you say that?"

"God made this for *us*," Emily said, looking up into the branches. Soft winter sunlight drifted through the barren branches, scattering light over them. "I love this place, Johan. Thank you for bringing me here."

"Look how the two trees connect here," Johan put his hand above his head. "They would be weaker apart. The tree is stronger because the two stand together rather than separate."

Emily put her hands on the front of Johan's overcoat. Their breath made fog hang in the air around them. "Let nothing ever separate us then," she whispered, leaning in to kiss him. Seth's little head bumped against Johan's chest. The baby whimpered and began to cry.

Johan laughed. "He looks hungry. Come sit down here." He patted his hand on a soft seat of moss over a fallen log.

Emily gratefully sat down and turned away from Johan.

He sighed with contentment. "I couldn't ask for a better Christmas present than to spend today with you," Johan said, quietly.

Emily turned her head sideways and smiled. "I want to see my new home. Does it need to be cleaned already?"

Johan feigned offense. "I take my boots off at the door. The floors are still pristine. Not a speck of dirt on them."

"That will come in handy with a baby crawling around soon," Emily sighed. "Seth changes so much everyday. You haven't been able to see him much since he was born. I think you'll enjoy watching him grow."

"I know I will," Johan said, reaching inside his coat. He pulled out small piece of paper. "Back home in Finland, we have a tradition to gather as a village around this time on Christmas Day." He straightened out the small paper and read its contents. "In the city of Turku, in southern Finland, the people gather just before noon."

Emily turned to focus on Johan better.

Johan looked up into the sky, remembering. "After the Turku Cathedral Bell strikes twelve, the Declaration of Christmas Peace is read. Everyone from the local village is there to listen. When I was very young, my parents took me there. I remember holding their hands as the local magistrate read the declaration. I'd like to see that tradition started here among the Finns of Astoria." Johan glanced over at Emily to see her reaction.

"What does the declaration say?"

"I wrote down all I could remember," he began. "Today, God willing, is the graceful celebration of the birth of our Lord and Savior; and thus is declared a peaceful Christmas time to all, by advising devotion and to behave otherwise quietly and peacefully, because he who breaks this peace and violates the peace of Christmas by any illegal or improper behavior shall under aggravating circumstances be guilty and punished according to what the law and statutes prescribe for each and every offence separately."

Emily giggled. "Everyone on Taylor Street would be arrested every Christmas Day! I think it's a great idea!"

Johan laughed out loud. "It's meant to show a reverence for the birth of Christ. Maybe it would clean up the streets as well." Johan looked down at the ground and kicked at a clump of near frozen ferns. "Since we don't have the Cathedral bell of Turku, I guess the Cathedral tree of Astoria will have to do."

"It's a wonderful idea, Johan. We need to have traditions of our own. How thoughtful of you to begin one today for our family." Emily turned away from him again. "Would you hold him for a moment, please?" she asked, trying to hold the baby and fix her dress.

Johan stepped behind Emily, reaching over her to pick up Seth. He wrapped Seth's soft, wool blanket tight around him and slipped him into the warmth of his coat. Seth cooed and reached for Johan's face. With no beard to grab onto, the baby just slapped at his chin.

Emily buttoned her coat up and stepped back over the log to Johan. The Cathedral Tree rose up behind them. She smiled at the picture before her. "So if I'm half and you're half of this tree. Which branch is Seth?"

Johan spun around. "The low one right there, see? The next one above it will be our daughter, Aina. See that one there, the next one? That will be our son, Ismo."

"Ismo? Is that right?" Emily giggled.

"Above Ismo, there will be Juhani."

"Is that a boy or a girl?"

"Boy. Can't you tell? Come on, Em, you've got to keep up here."

"Sorry."

"Next will be Henriika. She's going to be a handful."

"How do you know?"

"Because her name means 'home ruler'." Johan grinned.

Emily laughed. "Maybe we could just name her Sarah instead. That means 'princess'. Oh wait! That's just as bad, isn't it? Alright, carry on. Please state the gender of the child so I can keep up."

"Above Henriika will be Kivi...a boy. He'll live by the river."

"How do you know?"

"His name means 'dweller by the stone.'"

"Do I get to name any of these babies?"

"Yes, you can name a few. We still have to name those branches over there. Are you sure you want this many children?"

"You tell me! You're the one with all the weird names!" Emily giggled, slugging Johan on the arm.

He caught her behind the neck and drew her in slowly. "I don't care how many children we have..." he said, whispering. "Just as long as they're all Finnish names." Just as Emily was about to protest, Johan stopped her mouth with a kiss. She feigned fighting him off and then melted into him. He deepened their kiss but Seth cried out in protest.

Johan leaned his forehead against Emily's. "Next Sunday can't come soon enough." Emily laid her head on his chest and wrapped her arms around him under his coat. Through his dress shirt, she could feel the tender scars of the flogging. His shirt had come untucked and her hand rested on his skin.

Johan shuddered at her touch.

"Do your scars still hurt?" she asked, running one of her fingers along a scar as gently as she could.

"Scars heal with time," Johan said. "If you let them maim you, they can. If you find the *sisu* to forgive, they are just a reminder of another victory the Lord has brought you through."

Emily slid her hands around his waist. "*Sisu*? Another Finnish name, I presume?"

"You have it, too, you know," Johan said, his eyes on her lips.

"I do? How did I get it?"

"You've always had it. You just didn't know it until the shipwreck when you met me."

CHAPTER THIRTY-EIGHT

"Nature spread a carpet in patterns of clover, grass and fern under the shade of trees with wide-spreading branches..."

New Year's Day, 1854

Johan and Emily emerged from the simple, white Lutheran church to a shower of rice thrown by the Emersons, Veiths, Sikkus and the Kuntas family. It caught in Emily's myrtle wreath and lace veil which hung over her black, fitted wool skirt and jacket. Johan wore his black Sunday suit. His face was clean shaven in spite of the brisk, winter weather. A wedding was reason enough to keep his beard shaved.

"On to the wedding feast," Gus bellowed, patting his belly.

Bonnie swatted his arm and laughed, snuggling Seth in the crook of her other arm.

Luther slapped Johan on the back. "Momma's been cooking up a storm for you two."

Johan grimaced, ready for pain from his flogging. To his surprise, it didn't hurt. He helped Emily up into the wagon seat. Bonnie placed Seth in her arms.

Arriving at the Emersons, evergreen wreaths hung on every window and on the front door. They stepped inside to a lovely red cloth garland hanging across the entry way to the dining room. Their long table was lined with extra chairs from Kuntas' boardinghouse to accommodate all the wedding guests. Two tables were pushed together and it stretched into parlor.

Emily clapped her hands. "Oh, Bonnie, it's lovely." Small yuletide logs with candles in them lined the middle of the table. "It smells wonderful!"

Bonnie pulled off her cap and held the door open for her guests. "Johan, you and Emily must sit at the head of the table today." She glanced over at Gus who smiled in agreement. They were seated with the Lutheran pastor beside them with places for Gus and Bonnie on the other side. All the guests filed in and took seats around them.

Bonnie and Sikkus hustled into the kitchen to fetch the first course of the meal. They came back in toting huge trays of cold cuts, pickled onions, braided bread, and hard cheeses.

"We're going to need some coffee," Gus piped up. "And maybe something to celebrate with." He grinned. Bonnie nodded and returned with a tin coffee pot and four bottles of wine.

Uncle Frans stood to his feet and held up his wine glass. "Finnish passion is best compared with sacrifice." Everyone snickered and murmured their agreement. "Emily, when Johan built that house for you, I knew that you were the one for him. That's what Finnish men do for the people they love, they sacrifice. All his work, care, and love went into making that home what you would like. You may not hear him say the words 'I love you' everyday. But you'll see that he loves you with the work he puts in. To your happiness – cheers!"

"Hear, hear!" Everyone cheered.

Bonnie stood to her feet and tapped the edge of her wine glass to quiet the crowd. "To Johan and Emily, may the Lord bless you and keep you. May He cause His face to shine upon you and give you peace."

"Hear, hear!" Everyone cried again.

"I'm not done yet," Bonnie said, flustered by the chuckling. "May the Lord give you back tenfold what you've left behind in family and in homelands. May He give you the desires of your hearts."

"Hear, hear!"

"I'm not done yet," Bonnie said, adjusting her waistband. "May the Lord give you a house full of children of your own." Johan and Emily blushed and grinned at each other. "May He--"

Gus stood to his feet and kissed Bonnie soundly on the mouth to quiet her. He cried, "May He bless this food. Amen," He pulled Bonnie down to her seat.

"Well, Mr. Emerson," Bonnie said, wafting her face to cool herself down. "You still have it, my dear!"

The table erupted with laughter and the food disappeared from the trays.

The second and third courses of dinner came with salmon, potatoes, squash and turnips and more coffee.

Finally, Sikkus came in from the kitchen carrying a wedding cake. She set it on the table in front of Johan and Emily. "You cut," she ordered Johan. "Give piece to wife."

Johan cut a thin slice and fed it to Emily, his face warm from the attention on him.

Emily took the knife and wiped the corner of her mouth with her napkin. "It's delicious, Bonnie and Sikkus," she said, her eyes dancing with joy.

"Hurry up and feed him so I can have a piece," Gus said, licking his lips.

"Oh you!" Bonnie said, swatting him.

Emily took a small piece of cake and fed it to Johan, meeting his eyes. He winked at her and took the bite. "I think Seth needs some," he said, his mouth full.

"Oh no, he doesn't," Emily warned. But Johan stood to go retrieve him from Emily's bedroom. Emily stood to follow Johan in protest. At that instant, Mr. Kuntas pulled out his violin and started playing a lively waltz.

"Time to dance!" Mr. Kuntas cried.

Johan spun Emily around the table into the parlor. The floor was clear in the middle of the room. They spun around and around, laughing.

"I'm going to be sick," Emily cried. "I'm so full."

Johan spun her around again. "Nonsense, we're just getting started."

Gus stood to his feet and grabbed Bonnie's hand. "Come on, Mrs. Emerson. It's not everyday you can get me to dance. But I reckon, this is one of them."

Bonnie dragged him around the table, "Come on then!"

Spurgeon and Luther pulled the long tables against one wall of the dining room to make more room. Spurgeon asked Mrs. Kuntas to dance and Luther kept the beat by clapping near Mr. Kuntas. Sikkus stood beside them, grinning from ear to ear, and clapping off beat.

Gus, Luther and Spurgeon took turns dancing with Emily while Johan danced with Bonnie. The final notes of the waltz played out and everyone clapped. Seth's cry rose above the celebration and Emily put her hands on her hips and drew in a deep breath. She pulled her myrtle wreath and veil off her head and placed it on Bonnie's head, kissing her cheek.

"I'll be back in a few minutes," she said. She hurried down the hallway to Seth. Johan followed her with his eyes and before she closed the door she caught him watching her. She smiled and slowly closed the door behind her.

Emily leaned her head back against the door. She was a married woman again. She held her hand up and played with the new silver ring on her finger. Her whole life opened up in front of her and she liked what she saw.

Seth cooed from the bed, watching her and biting on his fist. "Oh Seth," she whispered, scooping him up in her arms. "I'm so happy. Nothing could ruin this day."

CHAPTER THIRTY-NINE

"Let us hope that we are all preceded in this world by a love story..."– Don J. Snyder

The door to Johan and Emily's room creaked open, waking Emily. The soft, winter sunlight poured through the leaded glass windows in their bedroom. Johan padded across the floor with his long underwear hanging from his trim waist. Against his bare chest, he snuggled Seth. The baby still slept peacefully with his thumb in his mouth. Johan's large hand held Seth's head against him and he walked over to the window to take in the new day.

A sigh of contentment escaped his lips and he hummed his childhood Finnish lullaby to his new son.

Emily sat up in bed, pulling the sheet around herself. Her long braid hung over her shoulder. The picture of her new husband and son was priceless.

"*Hyvää huomenta, aviomies,*" Emily whispered, stifling a giggle when Johan turned suddenly in surprise.

"When did you learn to say that?" he whispered back, careful to not wake the baby.

"Your uncle taught me yesterday at the wedding," Emily said, smiling. "I wanted to know how to say 'good morning, husband' in Finnish."

Johan came over and planted a kiss on her lips and whispered, "*Hyvää huomenta, vaimo.*" He kissed her again. "Good morning, wife." He handed Emily the baby and turned to stoke the fire in their room. The scars criss-crossed his back and Emily's eyes teared up at the sight of them. She laid Seth in the middle of the bed and wrapped herself in a quilt. She tiptoed over to Johan and embraced him from behind. He straightened and took her hands in his own. Emily laid her cheek against his scars and held him tight.

Johan kissed Emily's fingers, enjoying the warmth of the fire before them. "You know, wife. It's customary for a Finnish husband to give his new wife a gift on their first morning together."

"It is?" Emily whispered back, kissing his scars. "What could you possibly give me that you haven't already?"

Johan turned to his new bride, brushing her braid off of her bare shoulder. He placed his hands on her arms to ward off the morning chill. "Well, usually she gets a new dress," he began, his eyes followed the line of the quilt wrapped around her. "But it seems you prefer to keep things simple."

"Yes, a quilt is fine for me, thank you," Emily said, with a crooked smile.

"Fine with me, too," Johan teased. "Or sometimes, the groom will give her some money." Johan watched her eyes.

"I'm an independent woman of means," Emily said, meeting his gaze. "Money means nothing to me."

Johan leaned in and nibbled on Emily's ear, making her giggle. "Perhaps you'd like the traditional gift of a sheep or goat?"

"Now you're starting to interest me," Emily said, seriously. She clutched Johan's arm. "Could we get a few sheep, Johan? They would keep my garden clear of weeds for me."

"They would also *eat* your whole garden," Johan said, smiling. "We'll see, though."

"So what do you have for me?" Emily asked, now curious. Suddenly she grinned.

"What's so funny?" Johan asked, surprised.

"I just realized that I'm standing here, in a quilt, talking about sheep and gardens and weeds," Emily said, giggling. "I never thought I'd live in a log cabin, out in the middle of nowhere, with a husband who runs around in his long underwear."

Johan grinned and put his hands on his waist. "This wasn't your idea of spring fashion for 1854?"

Emily clasped her blanket more tightly around herself. "I'm still waiting…"

"For what?" Johan asked, playing with the edge of her quilt.

"For my gift," Emily said, her cheeks flushed.

Johan looked down at the floor before proceeding. "Do you want to see your family this spring?"

"Well, I'll see Aaron in February, most likely," Emily said, confused.

"Do you want me to take you back east to see your parents?" Johan glanced over at Seth sleeping soundly on their bed. "They haven't met Seth. They don't know that we are married. I feel it's only right to meet them."

"If I know my parents, they will be with Aaron on the next boat here," Emily said, resolutely. "My home is *here* now. There's no need to go anywhere." She leaned into Johan's embrace. "By the way, I sent a letter before we got married telling them all about you."

Johan pulled back, shocked. "You didn't tell me that."

"I'm just full of surprises," Emily said, running a finger down Johan's side. "I bet you didn't know that I have something special in me called *sisu*…it will get us through anything…even meeting my parents." Emily giggled and Johan stopped her mouth with a passionate kiss and lifted her up into his arms.

"You're going to need it being married to me," Johan teased. "I can't promise you that we will ever be rich like your parents, but we will always have an adventure."

EPILOGUE

"What can we ever hope to do with the Western coast, the coast of three thousand miles, rockbound, cheerless, and uninviting and not a harbor on it? What use can we have for such a country? Mr. President, I will never vote one cent from the public treasury to place the Pacific coast one inch nearer to Boston than it is now."
1844, Daniel Webster quote

Valentine's Day, 1854

"Button, button, who's got the button?" Emily cried, giggling. She glanced around the Emerson's parlor from one face to the next. "Gus? Is it you?"

He grinned, growing red all over. "Nope, it ain't me."

"Isn't," Bonnie interjected.

"Spurgeon?" Emily said, grinning. "Is it you?"

"No, ma'am," Spurgeon said, laughing. "You know it ain't me cuz I can't lie for nuthin'."

"Isn't and 'because'," Bonnie chided, slapping Spurgeon's arm. "Just because we live in the sticks...

"...doesn't mean we have to sound like it," Luther finished for her.

"Luther, is it you?" Emily said, grinning.

"No, ma'am, it sho' ain't!" Luther cried, slapping his knee and jumping aside just in time to avoid his mother's swat.

"Lord, help me," Bonnie mumbled, exasperated.

"Bonnie," Emily said, her hands on her hips. She pointed to Bonnie and grinned. "It's you! You've got the button, don't you?"

Bonnie's face flushed crimson and she giggled. "Me? Goodness, no!"

Everyone burst into laughter.

"She's lying!"

"Momma's got it! I know it!"

Emily pursed her lips and held out her hand. "Give it up. You don't lie any better than Spurgeon does!"

Bonnie handed over the button to a room full of laughter. Just then, a soft knock sounded at the door. "I'll get it," Bonnie said, fanning herself from her laughter. She waddled over to the door, and lifted her candle from the table nearby as it was getting late.

Bonnie opened the door to see a wide-eyed young woman in a bright red, silk dress standing before her. "Can I help you, Miss?" Bonnie asked, putting her hand to her chest. She looked out into the street behind the young woman to make sure there wasn't any danger.

"I'm so sorry to disturb you, ma'am," the young woman stammered. "I've seen you around town and you seemed to be a good Christian woman."

"I hope so," Bonnie said, bewildered.

"I'm in trouble and need some help," the girl looked behind her and shuddered. "I didn't know where else to turn."

"Come in, honey. Come on in." Bonnie opened her door wide and ushered the young woman into the entryway. All laughter from the parlor ceased when everyone saw the prostitute.

"What's your name, honey?" Bonnie asked, wrapping the girl in a warm blanket.

"Rose," the girl answered. "My name is Rose Le--"

Emily stood to her feet and crossed over to the young woman with her hand extended. She smiled warmly. "I thought we would meet again. Do you remember me?"

Rose smiled briefly, revealing perfect, white teeth and a beautiful smile. "You are the lady I saw on Eighth Street that one day. You have a baby, right?" Rose's smile faded. She absentmindedly put her hand to her stomach and glanced around the room. She met with stares from the Emerson men, Johan, and the Veiths. Her face turned bright red and she turned to leave. "I'm so sorry, I didn't realize you had company. I should go."

"You should not," Bonnie said, firmly, taking the girl's hand. "Come here, honey. Come sit at the table and have some food and hot coffee."

The young woman's face softened and her eyes filled with tears. "I'd love some coffee...and some food. Thank you." She allowed Emily to lead her to a chair at the table and be seated.

Spurgeon, Luther and Heinrich followed Emily into the dining room.

Luther put his hand out to Rose. "Rose, is it? I'm Luther, nice to meet you."

Rose tentatively took Luther's hand and gave it a weak shake.

"No, girl," Luther said, grinning. "You gotta shake it like this." He shook her hand firmly. "Like you mean it."

Spurgeon pushed his brother aside. "Howdy, ma'am. I'm Spurgeon." He took her hand and shook it politely. Rose met Spurgeon's gaze shyly and smiled.

"Nice to meet you, Spurgeon and..." Rose scrunched her nose, trying to remember.

"Luther, it was Luther," Luther said, glaring at Spurgeon.

"I'm Heinrich," the Veith's son said, pushing the other two boys aside. Rose gave him her hand and he took it in both of his. "Glad to meet you, Rose. That's my mother's favorite flower."

Rose smiled sadly. "My momma's favorite, too. Lord rest her soul." Her southern accent slipped off her lips like honey. The boys were mesmerized.

Emily had to do something. "Alright, gentlemen, time to give this young lady some space to eat. Back in the parlor with you!" They obeyed begrudgingly, casting backwards glances at the blond beauty sitting at the table.

Despite Rose's upset hairdo with tendrils falling all over her bare shoulders, Rose was a lovely girl. A smudge of dirt on her cheek with some faint bruising caused Emily some alarm.

"Are you in danger, dear?" Emily asked, putting her hand over Rose's.

Rose shot a quick glance over to the parlor to make sure no one was listening. Then leaned forward to whisper, "I'm gonna have a baby." She put her hand over her mouth.

Emily clasped the young woman's hand tightly in her own. "Don't be afraid, dear. I knew that we would help you somehow and here you are. It's Providence."

"Providence, what's that?" Rose asked, wide-eyed, her stomach grumbling.

"Well," Emily whispered. "It's like needing something really bad and at just the right time, a knock comes to the door and it's just what you need." Emily smiled, trying to reassure the young woman.

A sharp knock sounded at the Emerson's door and Emily gasped in alarm. She glanced over her shoulder to Johan in the parlor and caught his eye. She nodded her head to the door and mouthed, "Be careful."

Johan strode nonchalantly over to the front door while the others continued their game. He opened it just a crack to see who was there. Muffled voices poured through the front door. Emily could only hear bits and pieces of the conversation. But the voices sounded strangely familiar.

Emily rose to her feet, letting go of Rose's hand. "Mother? Daddy?" She gave a confused glance to Rose who sat white as a ghost at the table. Emily took a step or two toward the door and clasped her hands in front of her.

Johan stepped to the side and Emily's younger brother, Aaron, burst into the entryway in the candlelight. Emily gasped and clamped her hand over her mouth to suppress her tears.

"Aaron!" she cried, jumping into his embrace.

"Em!" he said, laughing. "You look great, sis! Congratulations!" He turned back to Johan. "This is your new husband, am I right?"

Emily smiled and nodded, wiping the tears from her eyes.

A regal, middle-aged woman in black silk with a large feather coming out of her bonnet stepped in next.

"Mother," Emily said, stepping forward to take her hands and lead her into the home. "How did you find us here tonight?"

"Well," her mother said, slowly, surveying the room. "It was quite an interesting story to say the least." She touched her finger to her nose at the strong smell of coffee lingering in the air.

Bonnie pushed through the kitchen door with a plate of chicken and dumplings and a cup of coffee for Rose. "Oh my!" Bonnie cried, astonished. "Who have we here?" She set the food down before Rose and wiped her hands on her apron.

"Mother, this is Bonnie Emerson," Emily said, proudly. "Bonnie, this is my mother and my brother, Aaron."

"Pleased to make your acquaintance finally," Emily's mother said, extending her hand limply toward Bonnie.

Bonnie shook it with just the ends of her fingers, not sure how to react.

Aaron stepped forward and pulled Bonnie into a warm embrace. "Thank you, Bonnie, for taking such good care of my sis," he said, firmly. "We are ever in your debt." He pulled away from Bonnie and noticed the young woman sitting alone at the table.

Rose's cheeks flushed with embarrassment and she started to rise to leave. Bonnie quickly reached over and pushed her back down to her seat. "Eat dear," she ordered. "You are our guest here tonight. You might as well get comfortable." Bonnie smiled sweetly at the young woman disarming any excuses she tried to come up with.

"I'm Aaron," Aaron said, extending his hand to Rose. "I'm new in town." He grinned. He was a handsome young man with Emily's blue eyes and dark brown hair. His ready grin and sharp features showed his good breeding. He stood a whole head taller than Emily, matching Johan's height and strong build. But his tailored suit and fine, leather boots were a marked difference.

Rose took his hand politely but looked to Bonnie for assistance.

Emily's father engaged Johan in conversation at the front door. His wool cape and top hat covered his expensive suit. His distinguished expression and twinkling eyes made him an inviting individual in spite of his obvious wealth. Emily glanced over to her father as he pulled Johan into a tight embrace and clapped him hard on the shoulder.

"You're a fine son-in-law," he beamed. "I couldn't be more proud. Now where's my girl?" He looked up in time to see Emily. Holding out his arms, she ran into them.

"Hello daddy," she cried. "What a surprise this is! We didn't expect you for another week at least."

"It seems we arrived to a house full of company already," her father said, looking around at the full parlor and dining room. "Fortunately, we have rooms reserved at the Boelling's hotel."

"Yes, of course," Emily said, pleased. "Mr. Boelling will take good care of you. He has looked out for me since my arrival."

"So we've heard," her father said. "I'd love to meet everyone but first things first. Where's that grandson of mine? I must see him!" He laughed in spite of himself.

Emily turned to go retrieve Seth from her old bedroom which would surely become Rose's new bedroom. Her eyes met Johan's and she held his gaze to see how he fared with the surprise. He winked at her to reassure her and nodded once. Emily grinned. To her shock, Aaron and her mother were seated at the dining room table, drinking coffee with Rose LeFleur. Aaron was obviously enjoying the young woman's company. Emily's mother was so out of place, she just seemed relieved to have a warm drink in her hands.

"My mother hasn't drunk a cup of coffee in her whole life," Emily muttered, "and never with a woman of ill repute!" She turned to walk down the hallway. "Wonders will never cease to amaze me here in this crazy town of Astoria!"

52155889R00176

Made in the USA
San Bernardino, CA
13 August 2017